PTERANODON

A Powers Beyond Their Steam Story

by
Tom M. Franklin

Pocket Moon
PMP
Press

www.tommfranklin.com
PowersBeyondTheirSteam.com

Pocket Moon Press
www.pocketmoonpress.com

Cover design by Robert Thibeault
www.teabowstudios.com

Interior design and composition by Rebecca Evans

Paper ISBN: 978-1-952834-01-1
Cloth ISBN: 978-1-952834-02-8

Printed in the United States of America

First Edition

For Tony, Tigger, Haley, Maggie, Ani;
Xander, Soren, Mika, Maxx, Jacques,
and Sigrid

With a Grateful Tip o' the Hat to
Ethel Bing and Birdie Law

And My Appreciation to sunsets, the ocean,
music, baklava, and lilies

CONTENTS

ACKNOWLEDGEMENTS

I could not have written this book on my own.

Actually, I did write this book on my own. The first draft, that is. The version you have in your hands now is a far better book, a far better story, with far better characters, all thanks to the help of a great many people.

My thanks first needs to go out to Steve DePalma, a friend since the second grade who suffered through each major revision of this manuscript. That's what you get for encouraging me to write for all these years, Steve.

Thanks also goes out to:

All the early readers of this story whose comments and suggestions helped to transform that first draft into a much better story, especially Scott Murdock.

Joan Slattery for making me believe in the potential of the initial story.

Caryn Wiseman for believing in me and the story enough to try finding it a home.

Bob Thibeault for his great cover illustration.

Rebecca Evans for her typesetting and book design.

Andrew Cooksy for his character of Smentley (a not-so distant relative of Bentley) and his scientific expertise in determining that the Leyden Jar experiment *could* actually work as described.

Anne Runyon for her first sketches of Sophie, which brought her more fully to life for me. (And her husband Rick, who really should write a book on Seeking Joy.)

Vance Briceland for early guidance, support, and tolerance.

The members of The Writer's Loft in Sherborn, MA, especially Josh Funk and Anna Staniszewski, for their support and feedback.

The members of the now defunct Nathan Bransford's forums for their help in crafting my query to agents.

Joanna Ruth, Tom, and Harris Marsland, genuine friends of Ib if ever there were such a family.

All of my former students for teaching me far more than I ever taught you.

Natalie Perkins for having me read to so many of her classes and getting me back into classrooms to read to kids again.

Chuck Bernstein, who hired me to work at The Kite Site straight out of high school, for providing me with some great life lessons and a place where I could write letters to friends at college where I began developing my voice as a writer.

My parents, who raised me to be a reader, for their love and support throughout the years.

My brother, his wife and family and their fine backyard fire pit.

The members of The Pocket Moon Press community for their support in the lead-up to the Kickstarter campaign.

Heather Kelly for her determination in getting me to publish this book and her annoyingly insistent "We Can Do This!" attitude.

Our cats for helping me to keep my ego in check on a daily basis.

And Sigrid Van Horn for everything else.

T·H·E
PTERRIBLE
PTERANODON

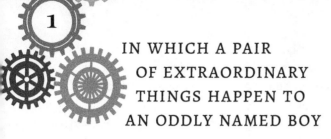

1

IN WHICH A PAIR OF EXTRAORDINARY THINGS HAPPEN TO AN ODDLY NAMED BOY

A rough hand pushed Ib's head down into the darkness. The boy pressed his arms and legs against the slick black sides of the chimney, trying to keep his balance.

"And don't come back up sayin' there's nothing worth stealing down there," Mr. Bertram growled. "I've had enough of that story. A house this big must gots lots of things worth a handful o'shillings."

He prodded Ib with the blunt end of a pole covered with an assortment of gears and cloth. Ib took hold of his former chimney-sweeping machine and hesitated.

"Well?" the big man said.

"I hate daylight jobs," Ib said finally.

"Which is why you gots to be quick about it, innit?" he hissed. "It ain't my fault them dice was against me last night. Besides, I've been keeping an eye on this place. It don't look like no one's ever home."

When Ib hesitated again, Mr. Bertram pushed him further into the chimney.

"Move it," the man said through clenched teeth. "Brooker wants his money by this afternoon and you just sittin' here ain't helping with that, now are ye? Now get down there and fill this weird sack o' yer's up!"

Ib took a deep breath and began inching his way downward.

From the first day Mr. Bertram had bought him for a few coins from the orphanage, Ib had been forced to make the terrifying descent into slick, cramped blackness, cleaning brickwork chimneys with only a meager broom. After months of scrounging parts, Ib had managed to put together a special sweeper. He had taken pride in making something that would allow him to do his job more safely and not get so dirty; Mr. Bertram, however, had just seen it as a way for Ib to clean twice as many chimneys each day.

The extra work had given Mr. Bertram money to gamble with. Soon enough, his losses exceeded an honest day's wages. That was when he decided to add some unscheduled, after-hours work to their days — or, more properly, their nights. He told Ib to start searching the houses they cleaned during the day so they could return when everyone was asleep. To Mr. Bertram's mind, Ib's upside-down umbrella could collect valuables as easily as it could soot.

At first the boy had said no to becoming a thief. Risking his life as a chimney sweep had been bad enough. However, Mr. Bertram's fists had been very convincing.

Ib double-checked the knot in the rope tied around his chest. The rope was supposed to catch him if he slipped. That is, if Mr. Bertram was actually holding on to the other end of the rope. He had never wanted to take that chance.

After many minutes of inching down the slick chimney walls, the rectangle of light above him was small enough to cover with his hand. Ib paused. He knew he was getting close to the main floor.

That was when the first extraordinary thing occurred.

As he looked up, he saw an odd flash of light through the narrow blackness above him. He scanned the dark walls for some inkling of what the light might have been.

A second glint flickered, this one closer than the first. Then it was gone.

The shape of a small bird appeared to the side of his upside-down umbrella. As it fluttered inches from his face, the thought came to him that something wasn't quite right. Before he could work it out, the bird tilted its head and appeared to be glaring at him.

Despite the circumstances, Ib could somehow tell that the bird was becoming impatient with him.

Keeping himself pressed against the chimney walls, he raised a tentative hand. It might have been a trick of what little light there was, but for a moment he thought that the bird had nodded at him before it landed on his finger.

He brought the bird closer to his face. Deep flashes of red reflected off of the creature's eyes. Looking at the bird's body, he was certain there were no feathers. Instead, he saw a warm, brownish metal along

the surface of the body and what looked like thin material stretched across the wings.

A machine? he thought.

Without realizing it, Ib rubbed his thumb across the fingertips of his free hand.

His fingertips started to itch whenever he felt the urge to take learn how something worked. He wished he had his collection of cobbled-together tools so he could try to learn more about this strange creature.

A metal half-dome of an eyelid covered one of the bird's jewel-red eyes and rose up again.

He was only half-aware that the bird had folded its fabric-covered wings against its metal body and had raised its head towards the top of the chimney. Instead, quite understandably, he was struggling with the idea that a mechanical bird had just winked at him.

Then the bird swung its head down, striking Ib's finger with its metal beak.

"Owwww!" Ib cried. He jerked his hand to the side, smacking his elbow into the bricks beside him.

The bird leapt into the air, hovered for a moment, then landed on the top of Ib's sooty-black head.

He felt the tiny metal claws dig into his scalp. "Hey," he cried, trying to swat at the bird with his hand.

That was when his legs first lost their foothold on the slippery chimney walls.

Instinctively, he threw his arms against either side of the brickwork and scrambled to get his feet wedged against the chimney wall. Holding his breath, he tried to will himself into place.

The rope tied around his chest dug into his armpits. Maybe Mr. Bertram had been paying attention after all.

When he was certain he wasn't falling, he gasped, sucking in a lungful of air. He managed a brief sigh of relief.

"Quit yer playin' around, ye miserable brat," Mr. Bertram hissed down the chimney. "Just get in and out quick-like."

Ib felt the rope yank tight and then slacken again, like a dog being told to behave.

The bird jumped off his head and landed on the back of his hand.

It looked toward the light above them again. He tensed, ready for another painful peck, but the bird simply looked back at him.

Then it blinked at him and lowered its eyes. For a reason Ib could not explain, he felt the bird wanted him to pet its shiny metal head. When he hesitated, the bird looked up at him and nodded.

He pushed even harder against the chimney wall with his legs and cautiously pulled his arm away from the chimney. With his now-freed hand, he wedged the handle of the umbrella between his knees and the sooty wall in front of him.

The bird's eyes followed his trembling finger as it approached its head. Before he could touch it, however, another extraordinary thing happened.

The bird blinked, then spattered and snapped about. Its wings and head seemed to knock about as they somehow disappeared into its body.

When the spluttering stopped the bird was gone. In its place, he saw a smooth brass egg falling onto his chest.

Ib stared at the egg. An impossible mechanical bird had turned into an even more impossible egg. He opened his mouth, but no words came.

The egg, for its part, responded as any egg would. It began rolling off of Ib's chest.

Forgetting everything else, Ib grabbed at the egg. For a moment he had it trapped against his ribs. Then the egg popped up and over his hand and tumbled towards the darkness below.

He lunged for the egg. Just as he felt his fingers get a firm hold on the smooth, oval surface, he felt his legs slip away from the wall in front of him.

And that was when Ib fell.

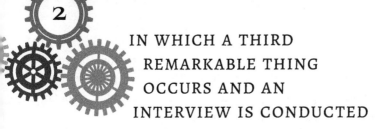

2

IN WHICH A THIRD REMARKABLE THING OCCURS AND AN INTERVIEW IS CONDUCTED

In his nightmares, he seemed to fall forever. His would shake uncontrollably, anticipating the impact with a stone chimney floor. That he only ever fell, never hitting the ground, only made the dreams worse.

Now, however, he found himself landing amid a great deal of clattering and soot atop a pile of wood and a metal fireplace grate.

He lay still for a moment, wondering why his leg hurt so much. It took him several moments to realize a most extraordinary thing: he was still alive. He had feared dying in a chimney fall for so long that he had never considered the possibility of living through one.

He pushed aside the broken and torn pieces of his umbrella. When he saw he was still clutching the brass egg, he gave a short, nervous laugh—which he regretted immediately. His ribs hurt. He rubbed his side and felt several new rips in the side of his vest and shirt. Well, at least he wasn't bleeding.

He took in an uneasy breath.

Steeling himself, he took a quick look around. Two large chairs sat on either side of the fireplace and crowded bookcases lined the walls in front of him. He nodded. That usually meant small trinkets and curios that could be easily pocketed.

When he looked more closely, he saw that the same glint of warm light he had seen in the bird was reflected throughout the room. From all of the bookshelves, side tables and desks, bits of shimmering metal surrounded him.

A collection of glass domes sat on a table next to an easy chair. Inside, lights flickered a dizzy, golden dancing sheen. Ignoring his reason for being in the room and choosing not to hear the grumbled curses echoing down the chimney, Ib tilted his head wondering how the objects in the domes reflected so much light.

He had never seen anything so dazzling, so mesmerizing. He took a step, hardly noticing the pain in his leg, drawn toward the table and the sparkling lights inside the glass domes. There were whirling rings of copper, brass, silver, and gold. They appeared to be inside and outside of one another, each spinning at different angles.

How do they do that? he asked himself, rubbing his thumb over his fingertips again.

"Ah, ha!" exclaimed a voice from the other side of the room. "Curiosity!"

Ib jumped.

Across the room stood the oddest man he had ever seen. Tall and thin, he had a shock of white hair that stood straight up on end. As the man approached, Ib could see the man's bushy white eyebrows spilling over the top of his round eyeglasses. His long canvas coat was stained with such a variety of splotches that it was hard to tell what color it had originally been.

Ib was about to stammer out a well-rehearsed excuse when he noticed the strangest thing of all: the man was smiling at him.

Growing up in the orphanage, he had not seen many adults smile at him. Those who did often had the bad habit of lying to him all the same. Ib knew for a smile to be real it had to reach into a person's eyes and then go somewhere deeper. Then, of course, there was the voice. A truly happy voice was very difficult to fake.

Ib had learned to listen more to how something was being said than to the words themselves. However, the man across the room left him feeling disoriented. Not only did this man's smile reach well past his eyes, it practically radiated all about him. And his voice sounded interested, not angry.

He felt the hairs on the back of his neck prickle. He was not used to adults being happy to see him. Certainly not an adult who he had been about to rob.

"Curiosity is the light behind intelligence!" continued the man, snapping shut the book he held in his hand. He turned and opened the curtains more fully.

Ib took a breath, eager to tell the man he had been chosen to receive a free chimney cleaning—but stopped. There was something in the man's twinkling eyes that made the lie unnecessary.

The man walked over to him and pointed to one of the shiny, many-ringed objects with his book.

"I created these simple amusements, but tell me: what do think you they are?"

The boy screwed up his face. He had no idea what they were supposed to be, nor how the rings could be spinning the way they were spinning. He also had no idea why the man was so interested in what he thought. No grown-up had ever done that before, either.

Ib started to shrug his shoulders, thinking it better to not say anything. Just then, the man reached over and adjusted two small dials at the base of the glass dome. The rings started spinning in unison, going around and, somehow, through one another.

Ib stopped in mid-shrug and stared, his mouth open. His fingertips tingled. Looking at the spinning rings, he could feel his mind starting to whirl along with the circles of reflected light.

"What do they remind you of?" the man asked, eyes wide and smiling.

Gleaming flashes sparked off the spinning surfaces. Ib flinched when a flare appeared to leap out of the dome and shoot right at him. In that instant, he relived a day that had occurred the previous year. He had been stranded on a high roof in a tempest of wind and rain that people still referred to as the worst storm of 1848. The sting of windblown water on his face hurt all over again while gales of wind threatened to blow him off the roof. He ran his tongue against his upper teeth, trying to chase away the charged taste the air had taken on as lightning sizzled and split through the skies all around him.

"A storm," he whispered, without realizing he had said anything.

"A storm!" the man exclaimed, slapping Ib on the back and knocking him forwards. Ib staggered, suddenly back in the room again. He bumped his bruised knee into a chair and felt his ankle trying to twist under his weight.

"Complex, abstract thinking!" the man continued. "A surge of thought processes blazing across what is clearly an amazing brain!" He shot his hands towards Ib's forehead, causing Ib to duck. "Then forming a simple phrase that grounds the thought to everyday life."

The boy looked back at the strange man. He was smiling and shaking his head in wonder as he gazed at Ib.

"Intelligent boy," the man said, sounding pleased.

Ib doubted that. No adult had ever called him anything nicer than stupid before.

Maybe the man wasn't dangerous, he hoped. Perhaps he was just a bit odd. He knew that, when it was necessary, it was much easier to get away from someone who was a bit odd.

He followed the man's gaze to the broken mess that had been his chimney-cleaning machine. Before he could say anything, the man's eyes widened, and his tall frame swooped over the tangled parts and bits of cloth.

"I do hope this didn't inconvenience you. You must have defended yourself most bravely against this unfortunate creature!" the man said, still eyeing the scattered bits of metal.

Ib looked up to find himself nose-to-nose with the strange man. He staggered backwards, bumping into the chair again.

Then, as if a new thought has struck him, the man arched a bushy eyebrow. Turning back to the broken remnants he added, "Wait a moment. This isn't one of mine, is it?"

"N-no, sir," Ib managed. "It's mine, sir." He looked back at the badly damaged machine. "Or was," he added, quietly.

The man picked up a piece of torn fabric that still had a bent metal arm attached.

"Not exactly a wing," he said tapping his chin with his finger. "Perhaps more of a . . ."

"It was my chimney-cleaning machine, sir," Ib said, leaving out the part about how it also carried away stolen goods.

"Yours?" the man asked, obviously impressed. "Are you the inventor?"

Ib had no idea what an inventor was. It sounded like something you needed a license for, or at least a proper education.

"Well, sir," he said, hoping his answer would at least allow him salvage what was left of the machine, "I made it."

"Remarkable!" the man said. "Tell me, how does it work?"

He looked down at the broken pieces, unsure he could make his explanation clear enough.

"Well, sir, when I get to the bottom of a chimney, I would open what used to be an upside-down umbrella." He pointed to the tattered bit of

8

cloth the Professor had mistaken for a wing. "Then I would turn this crank handle and it would move these gears above the umbrella."

"What about these?" the man asked, pointing to the bristled ends of several bent rods.

"Brushes, sir," Ib said. The gears would move the brushes up and down the inside of the chimney."

"Allowing the inverted umbrella to catch the falling soot, thereby making less of a mess!" the Professor finished, nodding with another genuine grin on his face. "A very fine solution to a particular problem. That's all the interview I need!"

Ib wasn't sure what an 'interview' was, but he did know he had been in the man's house for far too long. Before he could move back towards the chimney, though, he felt something vibrate in his hand. Looking down, he was surprised to find that he was still holding on to the inexplicable egg that was now shaking in his hand.

Not knowing quite what else to do, he murmured, "Please, sir."

He held out the brass egg. He could never give Mr. Bertram something so full of mystery.

"Ah!" the man said, once again full of curiosity. "Would you be so kind as to tell me where you found it?"

"I didn't steal it," he said, looking at the floor.

"A good dose of self-respect and an indignity towards injustice!"

He looked up to see if the man was making fun of him. Instead, he appeared to be dancing a little jig.

Definitely odd, Ib thought.

He took a slow step backwards towards the chimney.

"Hmmmm?" the man said at Ib's movement. "Oh, yes, of course! Sit *sitsitsitsitsitsitsit!*" He pointed to a nearby chair.

Ib knew he needed to leave, not sit down. Besides, he was definitely not accustomed to being asked to sit in comfortable chairs like the one the man was pointing to. Still, he wasn't going to find a way out if the man continued to be so excited. Looking down at the filthy rags he was wearing, he decided to compromise. He sat at the hearth of the fireplace.

Taking a chair himself, the man nodded, "Pray, continue. Where did you find it?"

Ib thought that should have been obvious. He pointed a finger behind him, toward the fireplace opening.

The man's eyes widened with amazement. He smiled so broadly that he raised himself out of the chair.

The man stepped around him, looked up into the black of the chimney and then back at the boy, shaking his head.

"And you found it there?" he asked.

Ib nodded and held out the metallic egg once again. Maybe if the man got the egg back, he would calm down and he could find a way out of the house.

Instead, the man swooped down to within an inch of the egg and examined it top to bottom, side to side. Opening up his coat, he pulled out the small hammer again and tapped it lightly on the shell.

"More important is the fact that it likely did not look like this when you found it," the man said with a knowing look. "Did it?"

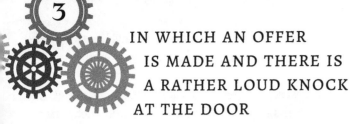

Ib's curiosity silenced him. He looked back at the egg. *How did he know?*

The man smiled another broad, genuine smile. When he hesitated, the man nodded and Ib felt obliged to answer.

"No," he said softly, looking back at the egg. Had he really seen what he thought he saw? It was really all too impossible, wasn't it?

Not knowing what else to say, he added, "I didn't mean to break it."

"Break it? *Break it?*" the man repeated. "Why don't be foolish! Taking personal responsibility for your actions is all well and good, but you haven't broken a thing!"

He looked back up at the man's eyes, and saw that whatever the man was saying, he certainly believed Ib was innocent.

"But . . ." he started, then stopped. He had to admit he wasn't sure what it had done.

"Tell me," the man insisted again. "What was it when you found it?"

Ib looked at the cold, metallic egg in his hand. It was going to sound crazy, and he felt certain the man wouldn't believe him. He searched his mind for the right way to phrase it. Finally, he gave up.

"A bird," he answered.

The man grinned, raising his bushy eyebrows even higher.

"And what did you do to turn it into this egg?" he asked.

He shrugged his shoulders. The last thing he remembered doing was trying to scratch the bird's head.

Slowly, he raised a grubby finger to touch the egg where the bird's head had been.

The man swooped down to inspect Ib's finger, suspended in mid-air, over the brass egg. Ib felt his face grow red as the man stared at his finger, tilting his head to the side. After a moment, the man moved his own finger over the egg and studied both fingers as they imitated scratching an invisible bird's head.

Suddenly, he grabbed Ib's finger. "Why, you're filthy!" he exclaimed.

Ib tried to scramble backwards. The man's grip was surprisingly strong.

"No no *nonononono*," the man said, calmly shaking his head. He turned Ib's wrist so Ib's finger and his own finger were inches from Ib's eyes.

"Don't you see?" the man continued to explain. "You're filthy! She simply didn't want to get dirty! Machines of all kinds need to be kept clean. Dirty gears don't move as well as clean ones will."

He stopped struggling. Not only did that make some strange sort of sense, but there was something the man had said that confused him.

"She, sir?" he asked.

"Well, yes," the man said. "By the time I was finished making her I rather thought she was a she. Don't you agree?"

The odd thing was that he did agree. He couldn't say why, exactly, but there was something about the bird in the chimney that had made him think it was a girl and not a boy.

"But, sir," he said with a boldness he didn't recognize. "That wasn't a real bird. It didn't have feathers. It was metal."

"Ah," said the man, nodding his head again. "That may be true. But tell me this: When I made this little diversion in my laboratory, I only designed it to walk. How then did it fly away on its own and then roost inside the chimney?"

The boy shook his head. That sounded impossible, but then again, so had the entire conversation.

"Oh, I can assure you," the man said, nodding. "She's been missing for days. I've searched high and low for her. No idea where she went to at all."

He gestured to Ib's hand with a look that made Ib feel as if he was holding a trophy instead of a brass egg.

"Until now, of course," he added. "Incredible Boy!"

Then, nodding to himself again, the man looked Ib full in the face. "So, will you take the job?" he asked.

Ib squinted at the man. *What was he was talking about?*

"The job, the *job!*" the man repeated.

From another part of the house came the sound of someone pounding on a door.

The boy winced.

"Of course, it doesn't pay much—only a pound per week," the man said, waving his hand before him. "But you will get your own workspace down in the laboratory. Oh, I can't wait to see what things you will create there!"

Ib shook his head slightly. A pound a week was a fortune! The man must be either crazy or playing him for a fool.

"You don't know anything about me," he protested. Then, more quietly, he added, "I've done bad things."

The man appeared to not be listening. Instead, he squinted his eyes and appeared to be reading from an invisible list somewhere across the room. "Hmmm, what else? Oh, yes, a proper room of your own. A good, soft bed. Food. Clothes. All that sort of thing."

Ib's questions failed at the thought of these things. He allowed himself to forget his life and be carried off by this dream for a moment. His current bed was a small bit of wooden floor in a locked shed behind Bertram's shack. It was uncomfortable, cold, and smelled of sewage. And even though it came with Mr. Bertram, he reminded himself at least Mr. Bertram was just mean. The man in the long, messy coat pacing wildly in front of him was odder than odd.

Mr. Bertram.

He looked at the rope that hung loosely from his chest to the floor.

Angry pounding erupted again from somewhere in the house. Ib jumped, knowing Mr. Bertram was expecting the house to be empty and for Ib to open the door.

The man looked up, mildly curious. "Whoever can that be? We aren't expecting visitors."

Ib pointed to the rope in his hand. He had to go. Didn't this daft man understand that Mr. Bertram was not going to like having to come to the door to get him?

Instead, the man looked at the rope with profound respect.

"He brings his own rope! You know, one can do so many ingenious things with rope. *Incredible* boy!"

The pounding on the door became more insistent, causing tiny glass baubles on the candle chandelier overhead to tinkle against each other.

Ib began to shake. Even the thought of Mr. Bertram's rage made him feel sick to his stomach.

"Ah, a beautiful sound," the man said, pointing to the chandelier. "Reminds me of glass chimes at the seaside. You've been, haven't you? Most fascinating things can be done with the winds there using large kites."

More pounding caused dust to fall from somewhere overhead. The man held out his hand, looking about distractedly, as if to see if it was snowing.

Ib heard voices on the other side of the house. One voice was calm; the other was loud and very, very angry.

"Whoever is that?" the man asked, quite taken aback. Opening the Library door, he called out into the hallway, "Bentley, whatever that ruffian is selling, we don't want any!"

"Sir—"

The man closed the door behind him and looked down. "Don't worry, my new lab assistant, Bentley will take care of this minor distraction. We should be getting down to the laboratory and setting up your new workspace!"

Ib shook his head. "You don't understand, sir," he said, trying to keep his voice from trembling. "That will be Mr. Bertram of Bertram's Chimney Sweeping Service. He closed his eyes, trying to recite the lie Mr. Bertram had worked out in case they were ever caught like this. "Congratulations, sir. You have been chosen..."

Confused, the man looked over at the chimney.

"But we don't need our chimney swept," he said, gesturing towards the fireplace and the small explosion of soot spread out over the floor. "We could use a fireplace sweeper, though."

The man swung the door open. "Bentley, ask him if he is a fireplace sweeper!" he called before slamming the door closed again.

"But, sir," Ib pleaded, hearing Mr. Bertram roar on the other side of the door. He knew that meant he likely wouldn't be eating for days and have to endure weeks of blows to the back of his head and the smack of Mr. Bertram's belt whenever the mood struck the thief.

"Mr. Bertram is the man I work for," he explained, not wanting to feel the sadness weighing on his shoulders.

He closed his eyes for a moment and continued reciting. "Congratulations, sir. You have been chosen to receive a free, introductory chimney cleaning by the Bertram Chimney Sweeping Service."

He took another look around the room. As peculiar as the man was, he had to admire the man for being able to imagine and create such wonders. He took a long look about him, wanting to commit everything around him to memory: the swirling spheres, the furniture, the books, everything.

"That's all well and good," the man responded. "However, I just hired you as my first ever lab assistant at the princely sum of one pound per week. We don't have time for chimney sweeping now!"

Before he could respond, the stomping sounds of a rumbling, furious Mr. Bertram came down a hallway towards them, followed by the protests of a cultured and highly indignant man.

"Where is that miserable brat?" yelled Mr. Bertram's gruff voice. "If he isn't dead already, I'll kill him meself!"

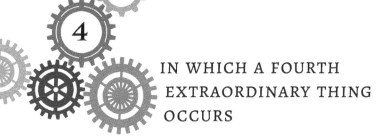

The man with the white hair gave the lock to the door a sharp twist.

"You do want to stay, don't you?" he asked the boy.

Stay? Ib asked himself. All of his life, he had been told that he was nothing more than a worthless orphan or a grimy chimney thief. That's all he was and all he ever would be. Wasn't it?

His breath caught in his chest. "I—" he started, but he wasn't sure what should follow that. Instead, he said, "You can't be serious," before adding a cautious, "can you, sir?" He wasn't sure which answer he wanted to hear.

The man pulled his head back, a confused look streaking across his face. "I can assure you," he said, "we men of science are always serious when it comes to such things."

Ib jumped at the pounding of heavy feet in the hallway outside the door.

"B-but what does a lab assistant do?" he asked.

"Assist!" the man said. "And labs. And creates! Oh, don't bother yourself with silly details. You're perfect for the job!"

Ib looked at the broken remains of his sweeping machine. He didn't know what 'labbing' was, but he had created his sweeper. Did that mean it wasn't foolish to think he might become something better?

He felt the egg in his hand start to vibrate again. Looking down, his mouth opened in astonishment as the egg cracked open. The small brass bird's head popped out, piecing itself together from bits of the shell. It angled its eyes at the boy, winked again, then sputtered, shook and snapped all around.

"Fine, fine," the man added. "I'd rather not give out promotions before you've even started, but how's this: I'll make you my lab assistant *extraordinaire!*"

Ib tried to not think how quickly the argument was coming down the hallway towards them.

He rubbed his thumb over the perfectly smooth surface of the egg where the bird had appeared and shook his head.

How could something so simple be so complex?

He felt the egg shaking again, helping to settle a decision deep inside of him.

Ib met the man's gaze. "Yes."

"Excellent!" the man cried. "You drive a shrewd bargain, but I respect that in a lab assistant *extraordinaire!*"

A heavy pounding on the door cut short his resolve.

"Open up!" a voice bellowed.

Ib gulped with the enormity of what he had agreed to do. He tried to plead with the man before him for help, but no words would come.

"Yes, well," the man whispered. "I think it would be best if you were to lie in the fireplace in a broken, dead sort of way."

"What?" Ib mouthed. His heart was beating far too hard in his chest to ever pretend it had stopped.

The man waved the boy towards the fireplace.

"Go. Fireplace. You. Dead. We shall handle the rest."

He was about to ask the man how this would ever work, but he was waved off again. Holding his head, Ib turned and crept back to the fireplace. How exactly should he look dead?

"Oh," the man said in a loud whisper. "Remember: don't breathe!"

Ib shook his head, wondering how long he could possibly hold his breath. He tried to cover himself with a handful of broken rods and torn cloth from his umbrella. Then he lay down over the firewood and the metal grate as awkwardly as he could. He tried swallowing his fear before taking a deep breath and closing his eyes.

"Excellent!" he heard the man's voice move away from him. Through the floor he felt steps crossing the floor. "And now . . ."

The gentleman unlatched the lock and swung the door open.

"Bentley, what is that awful racket?" he called out.

"Sir," intoned a voice from the doorway. "You have a most insistent visitor. He requests to see you concerning something of his that he claims has fallen down the chimney during an apparent introductory offer."

"Down the chimney?" the man asked.

"Indeed, sir," the other voice stated. "The gentleman claims to be a chimney sweep."

"Well, what good timing," the man said, "considering things have started falling down through it!"

With a roar of frustration that Ib recognized all too well, came the sound of people being pushed aside and a table bumping against a wall. Something large and heavy stomped into the room, shaking the floor around him.

Ib fought very hard against the urge to get up and run.

"Where is that miserable brat?" Mr. Bertram stormed. "He's my boy and I wants him back. We gots, um, *work* to do today."

"Hmmmm?" asked the man with the white hair. "Oh, where are my manners? I'm afraid we haven't been properly introduced. Bentley, when you're finished straightening the table that rudely forced itself into our visitor's way, I'm sure you'll present me with this gentleman's card. In the meantime, sir, allow me to introduce myself. I am Professor Humboldt Ignatz Delby, Scientist, Inventor, and Seeker of Knowledge. And you are . . . ?"

"What?" growled the oafish man. "Ye the customer what owns this house?"

"That I am, sir." Professor Delby replied. "Professor Humboldt Ignatz Delby, Scientist, Inventor, Seeker of Knowledge and, please forgive the omission, owner of this humble home. Now, I believe there was some mention of an introductory offer?"

"Oh, right. The offer." Mr. Bertram cleared his throat. "Congratulations, sir. You have been chosen as today's lucky winner. May I interest you in a free, introductory chimney cleaning?"

"No, I don't believe so, my good man," the Professor replied. "Despite the sincerity of your generous offer, I fear what we need most is a fireplace cleaner."

"A what?" Mr. Bertram said in slow way Ib recognized as the thief trying to decide if he had been insulted. "Fine, then. I just wants me, um, apprentice, anyways," he snapped. "He's around here somewheres."

"Apprentice?" asked the Professor. "Bentley, do we have any apprentices lying about?"

"No, sir," Bentley said. "However, perhaps our guest is referring to the assortment of soiled rags in the fireplace."

Ib felt the stomping of heavy feet coming towards him from across the room.

"Bloody 'ell," Mr. Bertram spat. "I didn't think he fell that far."

"Hmmmm?" Professor Delby said. "Oh, that. Yes. Quite disconcerting. Fell with a great deal of crashing and cracking and cranking and credulity and . . . *whatnot*."

Ib heard the Professor being roughly pushed aside before he smelled a familiar combination of stale ale, tobacco, and sweat. *Hold still, hold still, hold still,* he told himself.

As if in answer, his nose began to itch. Badly.

"Ye sure he's dead?" Mr. Bertram asked. "When they falls theys usually gots bits of bones sticking out and blood somewheres."

"Dead? *Dead?*" Professor Delby exclaimed. The boy heard the Professor's voice move closer to him and then move off to the side. "Why, of course it's dead! I am a scientist! I know the difference between the living and the dead. I am most sorry to say this heap of rags is most certainly of the dead variety!"

Ib heard Mr. Bertram's foot prod at the broken pieces of the umbrella's gears. "I suppose this is dead, too, eh?" Mr. Bertram said with something like genuine regret in his voice.

"Most assuredly," Professor Delby stated. "No doubt the poor lad died as a result of an epic battle against this bizarre creature."

"Wha—?" Mr. Bertram asked. "Hey, what about all o' them?" From the sound of the man's voice the boy could tell Mr. Bertram had stepped back into the room. "Who made these footprints 'round here?"

"Footprints?" Professor Delby asked. The boy felt Professor Delby's long lab coat sweep past him towards the center of the room. "Why, mine of course! It's not every day a dead pile of clothes comes down your chimney, you know. Had I not investigated, my scientisting license might have been revoked."

"Them looks awfully small to be your feet," Mr. Bertram said, suspiciously. Ib could hear Mr. Bertram's thick hand scraping against the stubble on his chin. The thought made Ib's nose itch even worse.

"I know," Professor Delby said. "Tiny feet. It's been a long-held shame

in the Delby family now for centuries. I do hope you'll keep this our little secret."

Knowing their attention was not on him, Ib gave in to his bursting lungs. He breathed out and in as silently as he could.

"What was that?" Mr. Bertram snapped.

Ib tensed. Every bit of his body tingled. He did not understand why everyone in the room couldn't hear his heart beating as loudly as he could.

"That?" Professor Delby asked. "Just a touch of indigestion. Please forgive me."

Ib felt Mr. Bertram kick at his sore leg. It took all his concentration not to grimace in pain.

"Blast," the large man muttered. "Now I'll have to find me some other way to, ah, meet me afternoon appointments. Say, did his nose just twitch?"

He hadn't meant to move, but itches can be downright stubborn things, neither listening to pleas nor willing to make deals if they hold off a bit longer. In an instant, Ib's nostrils had flared in spite of his efforts.

"Ahh," Professor Delby said quickly. "I didn't see anything. Did you see anything, Bentley? Of course, you didn't! No, my good man, I fear that was merely your deep, unexpressed grief. As any compassionate soul might do, you are profoundly wishing to see life in one so young where, sadly, there is none. Don't you agree, Bentley?"

There was a loud, heavy stomping on the floor somewhere in the outer hallway, near the entrance to the room.

"Oh, listen, sir," Bentley said, his voice re-entering the room. "It must be the police at the rear entrance. What a good thing you thought to send for them when you did, Professor Delby."

"The police!" Mr. Bertram stammered. "Here? Now?"

Professor Delby chuckled slightly. "Well, of course, my good man. Heaps of dead rags and mechanical monsters falling into one's fireplace must not only be investigated by scientists but by the local police, as well!"

"Um . . ." Mr. Bertram said. The boy recognized the panic in the larger man's voice. During their chimney sweeping days, Mr. Bertram was well known to the police for his drinking and fighting. Now that they were full-time thieves, Mr. Bertram tried his best to avoid them.

Another series of stomps came from outside the room.

"My goodness, sir," Bentley said, his voice coming back to the doorway again. "It would appear the police are most eager to begin their painfully thorough investigation. Perhaps we should all sit comfortably and await their lengthy and probing questions about the unfortunate lad, not to mention whether we have any knowledge of the many daring robberies of the nearby houses that have seen evidence of the thief entering the home through the chimney."

After the briefest of pauses he added, "Unless, of course, one would care to go back down the entryway and exit through the front door while I see to our guests at the rear door."

Ib heard the pounding of heavy boots through the room and down the hallway, followed by the slamming of a door.

"Well played, Bentley!" cried Professor Delby. "Your foot stomping in the hallway was an excellent imitation of pounding on the rear door."

It took several moments for Ib to realize what had just happened. Mr. Bertram was gone! He sat up, taking in a huge gulp of air, and rubbed wildly at this nose with the palm of his hand. He felt like laughing.

"Oh, look, sir," Bentley said. "It's alive."

"Not only alive, Bentley," the Professor said, walking over to Ib and helping him up. "Meet my first-ever laboratory assistant *extraordinaire!*"

"I say, sir," Bentley said. "What a proud moment this must be for all of mankind."

"Exactly!" Professor Delby said, shaking his head and breathing a deep sigh. "Ah, what it must be like to be like us."

"Yes, sir," Bentley said. "What indeed."

Ib's smile faded at the man standing next to Professor Delby. The butler was tall and thin and looked as if he could have been carved of wood. Not a hair was out of place. His formal suit and tie looked as if he had only put it on moments ago. Most striking of all, where Professor Delby's face was alive and expressive, the only part of Bentley's face that moved was his mouth and that was only when Bentley was speaking. He was quite used to stern and severe adults, but the blank look on Bentley's face made him feel even more uncomfortable.

"Tell me, sir, does this apparently not-so-dead pile of befouled rags of a new laboratory assistant have—"

"Laboratory assistant *extraordinaire*, Bentley," the Professor interjected.

Bentley paused. "Yes, sir," he said with a slight nod. "Does your new laboratory assistant *extraordinaire* have a name?"

Ib stiffened at the man's tone. Was Bentley mocking him for being nothing more than a dirty chimney thief? The expressionless way Bentley looked at him made him nervous.

"An excellent question, Bentley," Professor Delby said. Looking at Ib he asked, "Well?"

The boy frowned and shook his head. "I'm sorry, sir. What did you ask?"

"Your name, my lab apprentice *extraordinaire*," Professor Delby repeated. "What is your name?"

"At the orphanage they called me Ib, sir" he said finally. "I think it might have been short for something, but no one could ever tell me what." He shrugged. "Mr. Bertram only called me Miserable Brat."

"Miserable Brat? *Miserable Brat?*" the Professor asked. "Oh, no! That simply will not do. You're not a miserable brat. Why, you're a remarkable lad! An amazing assistant. An incredible boy!"

He was about to correct the professor. He wasn't an incredible boy at all. He was just another nobody. Then he looked at Bentley and the hard, cold look on the butler's face made believe that Bentley was already thinking that. Why should Ib say anything, then? This was his one chance at something better in life and he wasn't going to make it easy for anyone to get rid of him.

Professor Delby paced for a moment. "You need a name that stands out like the exceptional chap you are. Something distinctive, something bold," he muttered, tapping his chin with his fingers.

"Yes, an Incredible Boy," he repeated with a curt nod. "And with an original and inventive name befitting an such incredible boy. We shall call you Ib!"

The boy pursed his lips. "Sorry, sir?" he asked.

"Ib!" exclaimed Delby. "I. B. Incredible Boy. Don't you see?"

Actually, he didn't see.

"Not Ib, sir?" asked Bentley.

"Indeed, Bentley, Ib it is!" Professor Delby said with an air of finality.

"It's short, it's profound, and it even rolls off the tongue quite well, if I say so myself."

Ib shrugged his shoulders. It wouldn't take any getting used to, and it was certainly better than Miserable Brat.

"Now then, Ib," Professor Delby said with determination. "The first thing we need do is introduce you to the laboratory and get your workbench set up with all of the things we scientists, inventors and seekers of knowledge require for our, um, scientisting, inventing and general seeking of knowledge. Then, of course, I'll introduce you to my latest invention. It's a mere prehistoric apparatus, but one I hope you might find rather diverting."

"If I may, sir," Bentley said. "Might I suggest an alternate first step might be to prepare a bath for Master Ib along with procuring him a more suitable attire and, perhaps, a meal."

Ib had no idea what either of them had said, but he did know he was hungry.

"Hmmmm," the Professor thought aloud. "What do you say, Ib? Laboratory or lavatory?"

"I like the one with food, sir," he replied, his stomach grumbling in agreement.

"Lavatory it is!" Professor Delby exclaimed, giving Ib another congenial slap on the back. Ib was propelled a few feet forward towards the door. "Off you go, then!"

He started to accompany Bentley out of the Library. Stepping forward, his right leg buckled. His leg and ankle still hurt from the fall down the chimney. Catching himself on the arm of a chair, he found he could walk but only if he went slowly and didn't put much weight on his ankle.

Trying not to look weak in front of Bentley, he took his time following the manservant down the hallway and into the foyer. He allowed himself plenty of time to take in his new surroundings. The walls were of dark wood and the thick carpet had a pattern of flowery vines running along the borders.

Ib had so many questions. Questions about the house, questions about the Professor, questions about how he was supposed to live now. He needed to ask someone, but he didn't think the Professor would give him a clear answer. He wasn't sure he could trust Bentley, but what other choice did he have? Surely the butler wouldn't begrudge him a few questions.

Bentley was halfway up the flight of stairs by the time Ib reached the first step. When he reached the mid-floor landing, he saw that Bentley was waiting for him. The composed look in Bentley's eyes told Ib nothing about whether the butler was being impatient with him or, well, anything.

Ib shook his head, trying to collect his thoughts. "What just happened?" he asked.

"If I am not mistaken, Master Ib, I believe you have left one life behind and have begun another."

That sounded right to Ib, but it was still hard to believe.

"I do hope this meets with your approval," Bentley added, gesturing to the front entrance. "If not, you should know the doors are rarely locked and you are free to leave at any time."

Ib clenched his teeth. The butler had not exactly told him to leave, but he felt Bentley might as well have done so.

He shook his head, wanting to try a different question, one that kept him in the house. He managed to ask, "Who is the Professor?"

"Professor Humboldt Ignatz Delby is, as you undoubtedly heard, Master Ib, a scientist and inventor. He comes from a long line of men of science, practitioners of medicine, and philosophers. If the legends are to be believed, there are also more than a few successful alchemists in his lineage as well."

Bentley gestured to the dark red wallpapered walls of the stairway. He turned and continued climbing the stairs.

Ib climbed after him, favoring his good ankle. He looked at the stairway walls and saw the painted eyes of men who all bore some resemblance to Professor Delby staring back at him. In some of the paintings the men stood next to bookshelves or desks with balanced scales, in others the men were surrounded by beakers and test tubes filled with colorful chemicals. He noticed many of the faces had a familiar, slightly wild look in their eyes. He nodded, guessing these must represent all of the strange professions Bentley had mentioned.

Something shook in his hand. Looking down at the brass egg, he showed it to Bentley hoping to impress the butler.

Bentley stopped and raised an eyebrow a fraction of an inch. "Ah," he said. After a moment, he called out, "Sophie."

The egg cracked open once again and a small brass head began stretching its way out of the egg. As more of the bird appeared, more of the egg disappeared. With a final little hop the eggless bird jumped and shook out its metal and leather wings.

"Sophie?" Ib asked Bentley.

"Yes, Sophie. The Professor is rather fond of naming things, as you may have noticed, Master Ib." As if to answer, Sophie nodded. Bentley gently scratched the top of the metal bird's head with a finger. Sophie twittered approvingly. She leapt from Ib's hand and flew up the staircase.

Ib noticed that not even Sophie could make Bentley change his impassive expression.

"He said when he made her, she was only supposed to walk," he said.

"Indeed, he did," Bentley replied. "However, with the Professor you will also likely come to learn that the general laws of science frequently become mere suggestions."

Ib nodded, acting as if he understood this as well.

Sophie landed on the railing at the top of the flight of stairs and chirped down to them.

"It was quite clever of her to find you," Bentley said.

"What do you mean she found me?" Ib asked. "I was the one who found her in the chimney."

Bentley turned and continued walking up the carpeted stairs.

"And you're quite certain of that, are you, Master Ib?"

Ib's first impression of the main bathroom was one of complete bewilderment. Bright white towels hung from hooks on radiant white walls. Under his bare feet lay cool, white tiles that practically gleamed in the daylight. He squinted as he followed two shining brass pipes from the ceiling to a pair of odd handles at the end of a polished steel tub. He had no idea anywhere could ever be so clean.

When he was finished with his bath, he left behind water that was more mud than bathwater and towels that were more black than white.

Then Bentley walked him down the hallway.

"Your room, Master Ib."

Ib looked into the room. It was the size of Mr. Bertram's entire shack.

"I have laid out a change of clothing for you, Master Ib. I do apologize for the ill fit of your wardrobe. Had we anticipated your arrival we would have been certain to procure you more suitable attire. I shall, of course, speak to Professor Delby about scheduling you an appointment with the Professor's tailor on the morrow."

Ib continued to stare into the room, uncertain as to what to do.

There were two large, comfy chairs situated by the windows along the left wall. A handsome dresser stood opposite them. Along the far wall, however, was the thing that had stopped Ib from entering the room.

There stood the largest bed he had ever seen. At the far end sat pillows half as large as Ib himself, while a hand-stitched comforter was spread across the top. It looked soft and inviting. If Ib had ever known such beds existed, he would have dreamt them.

"Who else sleeps here?" he asked, stepping in the room. At the orphanage they would have stuffed at least a dozen boys onto a bed that size, if not more. When Bentley did not answer, Ib turned to look at him. He thought he saw the faint arch of an eyebrow.

"In the past this room was held for guests, Master Ib. However, once again, this room is now yours and yours alone." Bentley paused before adding, "I shall come back to collect you shortly."

Ib scowled as the door closed. "I know you can't understand what I'm saying," he said quietly, trying to sound like the manservant, "but what can we expect from a common chimney thief?"

He put on the clothes Bentley had laid out for him. They were all too large, but there was something about the size that he liked

As he struggled with all of the small buttons, he realized that his arm no longer hurt. Come to think of it, he hadn't limped on his way from the bath to this room, either. He shrugged, thinking he must not have been that hurt in the fall after all.

Then something startled him. From the corner of his eye, he saw a posh boy in the room with him.

It took him several moments to realize he was looking at his own reflection in a looking glass.

His longish dark hair was still unruly but, remarkably, there wasn't a trace of soot on his face and hands. His clothes were without rips or tears and made from whole pieces of cloth, not crudely stitched together patches of rags. The shirt, though big, had been recently pressed. A pair of suspenders held up black trousers that, despite having been hastily hemmed, were still far too long for his legs.

His reflection looked so unlike how he thought of himself that he raised his arm to make sure that the stranger in the mirror lifted his arm, too.

He stared at himself, his new self, and saw with surprise that his eyes were green. He'd never known that about himself before.

Then came another thought. The clean, green-eyed boy in the mirror wasn't the kind of person who was going to die in a chimney. Instead, this new boy looked like one of the young gentlemen he had seen from the rooftops. A young gentleman with a future.

As can happen, such a large thought made the room feel smaller. In light of this, Ib did what many young lads have done in similar situations for centuries: he tried to stop thinking about it.

And what better way to forget about something than to do a bit of exploring?

Ib opened the door to the room and poked his head out into the

hallway. It was empty, save for a narrow table against the wall beside him and several portraits on the wall opposite the stairs.

He stepped lightly on the hallway carpet. He ran a finger over the highly polished hall table, tracing over the wavy patterns of the wood grain. With a mix of genuine curiosity and old habits, he looked to both sides and slid open the table drawer. Inside he found only paper, pencils, and wax candles. With a frown he closed the drawer again.

There were two other doors on the floor. He tried the one closest to him, down the hall from his own room, but found it was locked. When he peeked through the keyhole, he saw only shadows and darkness.

The other door was closer to the stairway that led back down to the main floor. It was a lone door for the entire length of the wall. Ib turned the knob clockwise with well-practiced ease until he felt the latch click silently into place. As all the best doors do, this one opened without a sound.

The room was a mad collection of books, papers, pens, sketches, machinery and tools. Many of the surfaces were coated with pools of wax that had dripped down from the numerous candelabrums hanging from the ceiling. A painting of an English countryside hung on the wall next to several elongated, carved, wooden masks. A collection of glass cases lined another wall, the light from the windows igniting the brilliantly colored, fragile wings of insects Ib had never seen before.

Several chairs sat before an empty fireplace, their seats sharing the support for a long plank of wood. On top of the board sat a shiny metal casing with a series of wheels on the outer edges, all connected by thin belts. A tiny smokestack stood above the other parts.

His fingers itched. He wished he had some of his tools to see how it all worked.

Amidst the wonderful confusion of the room, he saw one item that seemed very out of place. In contrast to the rest of the room, a four-poster bed in the far corner was freshly made. The sheets were even folded at crisp angles.

"Professor Delby insists that the staff may only arrange his bedding," Bentley said from the doorway behind him.

Ib jumped.

"The remainder of the room, as I'm sure you'll understand, Master Ib, is to be left undisturbed."

The boy slowly turned to face Bentley. He knew this did not look good.

"And I do apologize that the hallway desk drawer contains only the barest of utilitarian necessities. I can speak to the Professor about storing items of greater interest there should you wish."

"I was only looking," Ib blurted, his heart pounding.

Once again, he tried to judge what might be behind the manservant's lack of expression. Why didn't Bentley simply accuse him of trying to find things to steal?

"Of course, Master Ib," Bentley said finally, his facial expressions remaining unchanged.

After a moment, when it was clear Bentley had said all he was going to say, Ib swallowed. "I was curious to know what all was here. That's all."

"An admirable quality to possess, given your new role as lab assistant *extraordinaire*, Master Ib."

Ib looked away from the man he could swear was making fun of him.

"I would be pleased to provide you with a tour of the Delby Manor, if you so wish, Master Ib." Bentley stepped aside, gesturing to the hallway outside the Professor's room.

Ib could feel his face grow red at Bentley's new name for him. He blurted, "Why do you call me 'Master Ib?'"

He immediately regretted it. From his days in the orphanage, he knew he shouldn't let a bully get to him like that. Trying to soften his tone, Ib added, "It's not like I'm some sort of fancy lord, Mister Bentley."

Bentley held up a finger.

"If I may, Master Ib," Bentley said. "Proper decorum states that the Professor be referred to either as The Professor or Professor Delby. In charge of the kitchen, we have Mrs. Hudson. I, however, am simply Bentley. No 'Mister' is required."

"But why do you call me 'Master Ib?'"

"You are Professor Delby's scientific aide-de-camp," Bentley explained. "As such, you are not a member of the household staff."

Ib looked blankly at Bentley.

"You are now the Professor Delby's professional colleague. Therefore, you should be addressed accordingly."

"I see," he said slowly. It was true that the Professor called the man-servant Bentley, but Ib wasn't sure if that was because Professor Delby was an adult. He looked at the sleeves of his new shirt and remembered that so many rules were different now. Which ones applied to him and which ones were only for the Professor?

"Thank you," he said. He paused then added, "Mister Bentley."

"I assure you, Master Ib, that the Mister is an unnecessary appellation with regards to my position within the Delby household."

Ib wasn't sure what that meant, but he thought he saw a hint of annoyance in the butler's expression. He tried very hard not to smile.

"Now, if it meets with your approval, we may begin our tour, Master Ib," Bentley continued. "As you are already acquainted with yours and the Professor's chambers, I suggest we begin with the servant's quarters on the floor above us."

"What about the room next to mine?" he asked.

Bentley paused. "Ah, yes. That is a room Professor Delby graciously keeps reserved for his sister, Master Ib. Thankfully, it has not been used in the past decade or more. Now, if you will follow me upstairs?"

When Ib hesitated going into each of the rooms first, Bentley took the lead, escorting the boy into each bedroom. He was more than a little confused to discover that his room was larger than all of them. Each of the rooms was sparse, only a bed, a dresser, a wardrobe, and a single framed painting on the wall.

As they walked back down the stairs, Sophie came fluttering towards them. She landed on Ib's head and then hopped down to his shoulder. She twittered at him, looking down at his clothes from her new perch.

"I believe Sophie approves of your new attire, Master Ib," Bentley observed.

Ib couldn't help but smile. Sophie seemed as magical as she did mechanical. He didn't understand her, but her apparent pleasure at seeing him made him feel good.

"I believe we shall next visit the kitchens and pay a visit to Mrs. Hudson. This shall also allow us to see about the aforementioned meal you had requested. After that, the Professor shall undoubtedly wish to continue your tour of the house with the basement laboratory."

Bentley stopped. He turned his head slightly towards the staircase.

"Unless . . ." Bentley said, raising a finger.

"Unless, what?" Ib asked, his eyes narrowing.

"Unless the Professor calls up the stairs with characteristic Delby urgency, Master Ib."

"Why would he —"

"**BENTLEY!**" the Professor shouted from the base of the stairs several floors below. "**BENTLEY!**"

At the sound of Professor Delby's voice, Sophie leapt from Ib's shoulder and flew off.

Ib stared at Bentley with disbelief. "How did you know —?"

"**BENTLEY!**"

"The key to proper service, Master Ib, is to anticipate needs before they arise," the manservant replied, gesturing down the steps. "If you will follow me, we shall see what pressing matter has attracted our employer's attention."

6

IN WHICH PROFESSOR DELBY RE-MEETS HIS LAB ASSISTANT EXTRAORDINAIRE

At the bottom of the stairs, they found Professor Delby pacing between the entryway and the library door, staring down at the carpet.

"You bellowed, sir?" Bentley asked, coming to a stop behind the Professor.

Professor Delby jumped.

"Bentley!" he exclaimed. "I do wish you'd stop coming up from behind me like that. You scared me half to death!"

"Perish the thought, sir," Bentley said.

The Professor opened his mouth to reply when he caught sight of Ib still standing on the steps. The Professor held out his hand.

"Good day to you, young sir. I don't believe we've met. I am Professor Humboldt Ignatz Delby: Scientist, Inventor and Seeker of Knowledge." He shook Ib's hand with great fervor.

"But I'm Ib, Professor. Don't you remember me?" Ib asked, his heart racing again.

"Ib?" the Professor said thoughtfully. "Unusual name. An old family name, perhaps?"

Ib met the Professor's eyes.

"It's been in my family for more than an hour, Professor," Ib said.

"You know, you almost remind me of a poor, dead urchin we found in the fireplace this morning," Professor Delby said. "He was short like you. Only he was considerably more dirty and far more dead."

Ib felt his stomach suddenly become hollow.

"Yes," he said, "um, well, that was me, Professor. I did fall down the fireplace, but I didn't die. You told me to pretend to be dead to get rid of Mr. Bertram, the, um, chimney sweep."

Professor Delby tapped his chin, a smile slowly spreading across his face.

"Did I? That was rather clever of me, wasn't it?" he asked. "And you are certain you're not dead?"

"Yes, Professor."

"Well then, I believe that would make you my new laboratory assistant!"

"Laboratory assistant *extraordinaire*," Bentley said.

"Really?" Professor Delby asked. "How remarkable."

"As was the suggestion for Master Ib to bathe, sir," Bentley said.

"Wonderfully restorative healing powers," the Professor nodded. "Baths, I mean. Especially those taken in the Delby waters."

Ib nodded, forcing a smile. He wondered, yet again, if Professor Delby might be odd, peculiar or just plain mad.

"I feel like a new person," he said, although it came out sounding more like a question. He poked his hand out of the too-long sleeves to try and calm his worried stomach.

"I say, young Ib, you didn't by chance shrink in that bath, did you?" Professor Delby asked.

Ib followed the Professor's gaze to his own hand and sleeve. He tried to hide a nervous smile.

"No, sir," Bentley spoke up. "We must pay a call to Mr. Marlow, the tailor, in the morning to have your lab assistant *extraordinaire* measured and fitted with proper attire."

"Capital!" Professor Delby exclaimed, rubbing his hands together. "Capital! Now, Bentley, where were we?"

"You bellowed, sir," Bentley responded.

"Ah, yes, so I did," the Professor said.

Bentley waited. Ib waited.

Professor Delby smiled.

"Perhaps Sir would care to share with us the reason for his thunderous summons?"

The Professor tapped his chin for a moment and then shook his head. "Sorry. No idea. I was rather hoping you could tell me."

Ib raised a concerned eyebrow.

"Did sir have something of great importance that he wished to discuss?"

Professor Delby tapped at his chin. He narrowed his eyes, as if peering for the answer, then shook his head.

"Another, life-affirming revelation of scientific significance to impart?" Bentley suggested.

Professor Delby considered this and then shook his head again.

"Perhaps Sir had completed a new component to his latest project in the laboratory?"

Ib watched Professor Delby tap at his chin again. This time the Professor began bobbing his head slightly while muttering something. Then he stopped and opened his eyes wide.

"Why, that's exactly it, Bentley! Well done." The Professor looked at his two empty hands and furrowed his brow. "I seem to have misplaced them. I don't suppose you've seen them, have you?"

"Were they, perchance, a collection of small glass spheres, sir?"

"No, I don't believe they were."

"Then, alas, sir. No."

"What about you, my poor dead laboratory assistant extraordinaire?

Ib shot Bentley a quick look, but the butler's expression remained forever passive.

"I really am alive, Professor," he said. "Remember?" When the Professor didn't seem concerned, Ib added, "No, Professor Delby. Your hands were empty when we came down the stairs."

The Professor took a step backwards and looked at the floor.

"Perhaps if Sir were to retrace his steps before arriving in the foyer to bellow, Sir might locate his missing parts."

Professor Delby brightened. "An excellent suggestion as always, Bentley! I shall begin in the laboratory and return shortly." He clasped his hands behind his back and looked side to side with each step, scanning each surface before him.

When the Professor was out of sight, Ib shook his head. He reminded himself that, peculiar or not, Professor Delby had created the swirling objects in the Library and Sophie. He must be some sort of mad genius, that was all. This was—well, he wasn't sure exactly what this was at all. How could someone go from forgetting he wasn't dead to remembering and back to forgetting again, all in the span of a few minutes?

Trusting Bentley with this question wasn't something he was keen to do. However, the manservant seemed undisturbed by their employer's unconventional thinking patterns.

"Mister Bentley," Ib said. "Professor Delby thinks I am dead."

Bentley nodded.

"I said, the Professor thinks I'm dead, Mister Bentley!"

"Your acute attention to detail and ability to accurately report upon observations shall serve you well in your new position as laboratory assistant *extraordinaire*, Master Ib."

Ib clenched his jaw. He knew he wasn't extraordinary.

"How can Professor Delby think I'm dead?" he asked.

"Ah," Bentley said with a slight nod. "That is a far more difficult question to answer, Master Ib. Far greater minds than ours have attempted to discern the reasoning behind the minds of the Delbys and to no avail."

Ib felt his face grow red. Why couldn't the manservant simply speak plain English?

"At the same time, Master Ib," Bentley continued, "you are still recognized as our employer's laboratory assistant, regardless of your corporeal status."

"What?" he asked, anger creeping into his voice before he could stop himself.

"My apologies, Master Ib. I merely meant to suggest that your position within the household appears to be confirmed, regardless as to whether you are dead or not."

He thought about this for a moment.

"So, you're saying it doesn't matter if Professor Delby thinks I'm alive or dead?" Ib asked.

"Precisely, Master Ib."

"How could he forget me so quickly?" he asked. "He didn't even know who I was when we came down the stairs."

"I dare say, Master Ib, that you likely would not have recognized yourself between removing that layer of calcified filth from your skin and dressing in more appropriate clothes."

Ib narrowed his eyes more than he meant to. *How did he know?*

"However, should the Professor's memory fail him again, Master Ib,

I suggest you remind him of your name and position. It has been my experience that regardless of the circumstances, Professor Delby always recognizes the truth when it is presented to him."

A loud, "Ah ha!" burst through from the Library and was followed moments later by several pieces of machinery in the Professor's outstretched hand. This, in turn, was followed by the Professor himself. He stopped in front of Ib and held the items in his hand up to the boy's face like a bouquet of flowers.

"Well, what do you think?" Professor Delby asked in a voice tinged with pride.

Ib tried to think of something to say about the collection of rods with the series of gears attached to the ends closest to him. He had no idea what they were, or what they could possibly be used for. He looked behind the Professor to Bentley, but the butler's face was inexpressive as ever.

"They are . . ." he started, searching desperately for the sort of word he thought a laboratory assistant would use. "Quite something." He added what he hoped was a confident nod.

"Ha!" Professor Delby exclaimed. "Did you hear that Bentley?" The Professor turned his head from side to side. "Bentley?"

Ib watched the manservant take a half step forward and stand immediately behind the Professor.

"Yes, sir?"

Professor Delby jumped yet again, this time dropping his handful of rods and gears.

"Will you please stop that!" the Professor exclaimed. "Honestly, a man should not have his own servants sneak up on him in his own house!"

"I do beg your pardon, sir. Perhaps Sir would prefer that I should adorn myself with bells that would signal my every movement?"

Ib walked down the remaining stairs to the main floor. He bent down and picked up the rods, hoping to hide the amused look on his face at the thought of Bentley wearing a suit of jingling bells.

"That sounds a bit festive for this time of the year, Bentley," Professor Delby finally replied. "Perhaps we should revisit this tintinnabulation wardrobe option of yours sometime closer to the winter festivities."

"Very good, sir."

Ib stood, holding the rods in his hands as he had seen the Professor do. "Excuse me, Professor Delby," he said.

Professor Delby spun around, still looking at eye-level to Bentley, a height that was several feet too tall for him to see Ib. The Professor jerked his head down and pulled his head back in surprise. Reaching out, he picked a single gear-ended rod from the handful Ib was holding and brought it close to his eyes. Ib raised an eyebrow as the Professor inspected it. To Ib, it looked as if the Professor regarded it as if it was a flower and not part of a machine.

Satisfied, Professor Delby sighed and gave him the proudest smile the boy had ever received in his life.

"Why, look at this, Bentley!" Professor Delby exclaimed. "This incredible boy has been with us for mere days now and already he has precisely the parts in hand that I need!"

"Remarkable, sir."

"I dare say, Bentley, but it's high time we go down to the lab, get these parts installed and then put some fire in his belly! What do you say?"

"I would say, sir, that this sounds like the perfect task to perform with a new laboratory assistant *extraordinaire*."

The Professor started to tap his chin. "A fine idea, Bentley, but not altogether practical. Where, for instance, would I find a laboratory assistant, much less a laboratory assistant *extraordinaire*, on such short notice?"

Ib took a chance and stepped forward. "That would be me, Professor."

Professor Delby stepped back, regarding the boy, his eyebrows raised. "You?" he asked. "I thought you were the unfortunate dead lad from the library."

"And your new laboratory assistant *extraordinaire*," Bentley added.

"Why, that's right, isn't it?" Professor Delby asked. "What a remarkable stroke of luck!"

Ib looked at the Professor and smiled. *All-out barking mad*, he thought.

Professor Delby put a hand on his shoulder and smiled. The warmth in the Professor's eyes and the confidence in the Professor's grip on his shoulder made him wonder if his judgments weren't being too harsh. Ib felt himself leaning more towards merely eccentric.

"Tell me," the Professor asked as he guided Ib down the narrow hallway. "What do you know about dinosaurs?"

7

IN WHICH WE
MEET PTERRENCE

"Dinosaurs?" Ib asked.

"Yes, dinosaurs," Professor Delby said. "Specifically, the flying variety."

Ib slowed his pace, furrowing his brow. He had never heard the word before. Was a dinosaur a machine? Something you ate? A type of rock? Taking a deep breath, he decided it was best to be honest, even if it meant failing his first test of laboratory assistantship.

"Professor," he said, swallowing hard, "I'm afraid that's not—"

"No, no. You're quite right," the Professor said, stopping in the middle of the hallway. "Strictly speaking, dinosaurs were land-based creatures. Pterosaurs were the flying creatures of the day. You obviously have a highly developed mind and a deep appreciation for accuracy. I shall have to be more careful than to generalize with an assistant like you around!"

"But Professor—" Ib started.

"Picture it, Ib," the Professor continued. "Millions of years ago, long before there was a London, or even a Londinium for that matter, our world was inhabited by huge, monstrous reptiles." He turned sideways as he walked so he could stretch his arms wide without hitting the walls.

"Fascinating creatures," the Professor continued as he reached the rear stairs. "Bigger than a house. Some had teeth as long as broadswords! Which genus is your favorite?"

He followed the Professor down the steps and off to the side, away from the kitchens to a landing where the smells from the kitchen made his mouth water. His stomach growled as he walked down a second set of stairs until Professor Delby opened a large wooden door.

"My favorite happens to be the Pteranodon, a Cretaceous period, tailless Pterosaur. Content to spend his days soaring in the pre-civilized skies. Huge wingspans. We know they were huge because we've found bones," the Professor continued. "A colleague of mine at the University is making a plaster replica of the bones for public display. Plaster! Can you imagine?"

Stepping into the room, Ib heard the crackles of discharged static electricity and smelled hints of grease. He stood still, trying to take in everything around him in the huge laboratory.

If the lavatory had stunned him with its immaculate cleanliness, the laboratory practically left Ib flabbergasted with its epic confusion.

Looking around him, he saw the scattered, imaginative workings of Professor Delby's mind. Along the walls and on the tables were collections of machinery. Boxes, jugs, and brightly colored bottles filled the shelves. Hanging on the wall to his left, Ib saw a pair of badly singed human-sized wings made of wooden frames and thin leather. Next to them hung an assortment of bug-eyed masks with wide tubing that led from the mouth to strange brass objects the size and shape of a lady's muffler.

His fingers had never itched so much in his life.

"I mean, honestly, what can plaster do?" Professor Delby asked incredulously. "Plaster merely sits there collecting dust."

High widows, slightly above ground level, provided light by day. For the evening, six wrought-iron chandeliers, fitted with gas jets, hung from the ceiling over the main section of the room.

Above the chandeliers, Ib saw objects suspended from the ceiling that looked like a series of paddle wheels connected by thick belts. To one corner of the ceiling, an assortment of chairs sat around a table, somehow suspended upside down as if waiting for someone to come walking on the ceiling, looking to play a nice game of cards.

He had no idea what the Professor was talking about. Rubbing his fingers over his thumb, though, he wasn't so sure he cared. The library and the Professor's room had been filled with amazing things, but they seemed like toys compared to the incredible possibilities he saw around him. If being a lab assistant meant working with whatever all of this was, then he wanted to start right away.

He shook his head. The Professor had been speaking the entire time, but he hadn't heard a word he was saying. Now he realized Professor Delby was asking him a question.

"I—I'm sorry, Professor," he stammered. "I was distracted by . . ." Ib motioned all around him once again, unable to find words.

"Hmmm?" the Professor asked, looking about him. "Distracted by what?"

He looked back at the Professor, trying to put what he saw into words. "Everything," he said finally.

Professor Delby re-surveyed the laboratory.

"Yes, well, there is quite a lot of that about, isn't there?" he agreed.

"Did you make all of this, Professor?" Ib asked.

"Well, not the walls," the Professor conceded. "They were here long before me. The ceiling and the floor as well, for that part. Mind you, the gaslights and the ventilation system attached to the ceiling are my work."

"But all of this . . ." Ib tried to find a word for all of the things around him. Not coming up with anything, he took a guess at, "Science."

"Oh, that? Yes, that's my work," the Professor acknowledged. "Soon to be *our* work!"

Ib rubbed his fingers over his thumb and smiled. He decided he could live with a bit of all-out barking madness if this was what came along with it.

They walked between workbenches filled with glass beakers of varying shapes connected by tubing suspended by metal braces. Along one part of the wall, brass sheets were organized by size into a great many shelves.

He followed as the Professor turned a corner and stopped in front of a large workbench on that side of the room.

"I said to myself, 'Why make something that merely sits there when you can make something that moves!'" The Professor shrugged his shoulders, looking quite pleased with himself. "It was a simple process of taking the basic structure of the skeleton and substituting rods and gears for the bones and joints."

Looking past the Professor, Ib saw something that made him catch his breath. His eyes grew wide. Very wide.

"So, tell me, what do you know about steam?" Professor Delby asked.

Ib's mouth formed an elongated 'O' shape.

"I agree. Steam is fascinating," the Professor said, nodding in appreciation. "Can you think of anything else in nature that is so simple and yet so elegant? Take water, apply heat and you get steam. And with it comes an abundance of such wonderful pressure! Harness that pressure and you can do all sorts of things, from powering the railway all across England, to making huge ships sail across the sea."

Ib lifted a shaking hand to the huge mechanical monster with a great many pointy bits looming behind the Professor. The beast looked ready to spring off the table and grab them both with its tremendous claws.

"Th—that..." he said, gasping for breath. "That's steam?"

"Exactly!" the Professor said, leaning forward and slapping Ib on the back. Ib was thrust forward, only barely stopping himself in front of the bench. When he looked up, he saw two large eyes staring down at him. He tried to remember to breathe.

"Well, not exactly, of course," the Professor acknowledged. "Pterrence isn't exactly steam itself, of course. He is, however, a perfect example of a steam-driven device. Once again, your insistence upon accuracy serves us well!"

Ib turned back to the Professor and swallowed. "T—Terrence?" he managed.

"Pterrence," Professor Delby said with a smile. "The 'P' is silent."

Ib shook his head, not understanding.

"Pterrence?" he asked, trying to sound as if he was making a non-existent letter be silent.

"Pterrence," the Professor agreed. "I considered Pterry, but it seemed too informal for such a large device. Besides, Mrs. Hudson has a nephew named Terry who has a rather long nose. I didn't want to risk her thinking I was being offensive."

Ib turned back to the ominous, mechanical beast. Madness was one thing, but vicious-looking machines were something else entirely. He gripped the edge of the workbench. Then, walking slowly around the table, he confirmed that the huge monster was, indeed, not moving. He began telling himself this was only a machine with large, folded wings, very sharp claws and a pointed beak and not a sleeping monster with large, folded wings, very sharp claws and a pointed beak.

The Pteranodon stood more than six feet tall on the tabletop. Its brass head was a honey brown with long oval eyes that narrowed partway down its beak. The body was decorated with overlapping, swirling designs. Pterrence's arms were bent close to his body, his thin leather wings draped in folds like a huge cape around him. At the end of each brass rod arm were a series of hooked claws.

"He doesn't eat people, does he?" Ib asked once safely behind the creature.

"Eat?" Professor Delby asked, clearly confused.

The Professor gathered screwdrivers and wrenches from another workbench and brought them to the table where Pterrence was perched. "Well, we'll be feeding him some water and coal in a short while. Until then, give me a hand with these, will you?"

Professor Delby pointed to the rods and gears he had laid out on the workbench. "Hand me those sprockets and axles, will you Ib?" The Professor pulled a chair over for Ib to use as a step to climb onto the workbench. Despite the brass sheeting and rods that made up the bulk of the Pteranodon's body, he still gave the machine a long look before moving.

Gritting his teeth, he climbed onto the table.

Ib stared into the Pteranodon's eyes, trying to think of something reassuring to say just in case Pterrence was alive and hungry.

Then he told himself that was silly. Still, after checking to see that the Professor wasn't looking, he gave the silent Pteranodon a tap on the chest. He heard a muffled *clang* from inside the metallic torso. When Pterrence made no other response, he let out his breath.

"We have ten of these rods and gears to fit into place, my lab assistant *extraordinaire*," the Professor said. "The two largest need to be inserted in either shoulder, by the wing joints. Take this screwdriver and open the covers, won't you?"

He watched the Professor unscrew the first of the tiny screws that held a brass plate in place on the left side of the Pteranodon. His fingers gave a nervous itch.

It took Ib a moment to get a proper grip on this real screwdriver. His hands were used to holding his crude versions of tools. This screwdriver was slim and refined and took some getting used to. Working to get a comfortable grip, Ib tried fitting the thin, flat end into the slotted head of a screw.

He twisted the screws out of their slots with ease. His hands liked the way a real tool felt.

The Professor showed Ib how to insert the axle into the opening, how to align the gears with those already in Pterrence's shoulder. His explanation and actions were quite thoughtful, showing no signs of the crazed madness Ib had come to expect.

Ib bent down and picked up one of the sets of gears and held it close to his eyes. He ran a finger over the sharp-toothed gears and the ends of the rod. He nodded.

His smaller fingers meant that he was able to reach into the Pteranodon's internal gearwork much more easily than Professor Delby. He finished inserting the axle and gears into the shoulder and moved on to the second panel.

He felt better seeing the Pteranodon's gears. Ib was able to see it more as a machine. And machines were nothing to be frightened by.

"Professor," he asked, "how, exactly, does Pterrence work?"

Professor Delby pulled at a ringed latch at the side of the brass torso. Inside was what looked to be a small coal stove.

"The fire in Pterrence's belly will be provided by a coal fire in this stove," the Professor said, tapping the cold inside of what would be Pterrence's stomach. "This furnace in his chest holds the water. The fire heats the water, the water produces steam, and the steam provides the pressure to move the rods in his head, arms and legs."

Ib looked inside and saw rods and pistons going in all directions.

"But how do the rods move?" he asked.

"With this!" Professor Delby said. He handed Ib a large box with a great many levers and toggles on the top. "These will move the head, these will stretch and retract the arms, and these are for the legs."

He pointed to two levers that ran perpendicular to the others. "What about these, Professor?"

"Those cause the arms to move up and down, causing the wings to flap."

"Flap? Do you mean it will fly?" he asked, fighting the urge to step down from the table again.

"Oh, no," the Professor said with several shakes of his head. "No, no.

Heavens no. *Nonononononononono.* The flapping is for demonstration purposes only." He chuckled to himself. "I may have strived for authenticity in how the wing joints work, but that was merely what science requires."

He was replacing the last of the brass panel screws onto the Pteranodon's body when there was a knock on the laboratory door. Bentley entered carrying a tray of sandwiches and lemonade.

"Ah, Bentley!" the Professor said, wiping a touch of moisture from his brow. "You've missed all the fun. My new lab assistant *extraordinaire* and I have already finished installing all of the retooled parts."

"I shall do my best to hide my bitter disappointment, sir," Bentley said. The manservant cleared a space on a nearby workbench for the tray.

Professor Delby began moving each of the Pteranodon's joints manually, listening carefully to the linkages.

"Ib, I think it is time to see how well Pterrence's new joints are working!" he said. "Why don't you bring up that bucket of water and pour it down our Pterrence's beak?"

Ib, who had been staring at the sandwiches Bentley had set down, shook his attention back to the Professor.

"Um, certainly, Professor."

Bentley picked up the large coal bucket and several water jugs and set them on the table next to Ib. Professor Delby lifted a chair from beside the workbench onto the table.

Ib dutifully hefted a jug and climbed up onto the chair. Cautiously, he tilted Pterrence's head back and opened his beak. Water sloshed around him until Ib got the hang of pouring it in a thin stream down the brass Pteranodon's gullet.

"Perhaps, sir, I might persuade you both to take some refreshment while the fire begins heating the water," Bentley said.

The Professor turned to him.

"Food?" Professor Delby asked. "Bentley, who would think of food at a time like this? We are about to mark another milestone in the annals of science and you're suggesting we pause to consider *food?*"

Ib's stomach rumbled. More water spilled around him.

"I do beg your pardon, sir. It is only that you promised Master Ib a

meal shortly after you hired him. One would hate to have him think a Delby was not true to his word."

"Wasn't that days ago?" the Professor asked.

"No, sir," Bentley said. "Merely earlier this morning."

"Really? Well, then there is only one thing to be done about it: Bentley, sandwiches on the double!"

"Yes, sir."

Bentley stood motionless, not looking at the tray by his side.

Then, after an additional moment, he gestured to the sandwiches and said, "Lunch is served, sir."

The Professor looked over at the tray, his eyes wide.

"Amazing!" he said. Turning to Ib, the Professor added, "You can see why Bentley is an indispensable part of the household."

Ib tried to hide a smile. "I'll finish with the water and get the coal, Professor." He thought it sounded very laboratory assistant-ish of him to forgo food for another few minutes. "Please start without me."

Two more buckets of water and a pair of buckets of coal later, he accepted a set of matches from Professor Delby. He struck the match and took care in setting the coal alight. As the conclusion to his first official job as a lab assistant *extraordinaire*, he wanted to make certain everything was perfect.

While waiting for the fire to catch, he took a rag and rubbed it against the sides of Pterrence's stomach. There was something pleasing about making the brass shine a bit more.

Satisfied that the fire was burning, Ib climbed down from the chair and the workbench. After wiping his hands on a rag, he turned his attention to the modest slices of bread on the tray. He resisted the urge to grab handfuls of them. Instead, he followed the Professor's lead and took a single sandwich and took a small bite.

A moist crunch and the taste of delicate green filled in his mouth. This sandwich was nothing like the thin gruel he had been forced to eat at the orphanage or the scraps he scavenged from Mr. Bertram. He looked in wonder at the slices of bread in his hand. *What is this?* he asked himself.

"Cucumber and watercress, Master Ib," Bentley said from the far side of the workbench.

He looked over at the manservant, wondering, once again, how Bentley had known what he was thinking.

As he continued to eat, the Professor set about connecting a series of wires from the back of the Pteranodon into the multi-levered gearbox. After checking on the fire and the water temperature, Professor Delby wiped his hands on the rag and sat down next to his lab assistant.

"How do you turn it on, Professor?" Ib asked through a mouthful of his sixth sandwich.

"The steam will take care of that," the Professor said, motioning towards the Pteranodon with another sandwich of his own. "Steam does such wonderful things!"

"Then, how do you turn it off, Professor?" he asked.

"Ib, Ib, Ib," the Professor said, through his own mouthful of sandwich. "Why would we need to turn it off? It's not as if Pterrence is going anywhere!"

Bentley cleared his throat.

"Now, Bentley," Professor Delby said, patting the gearbox by his side, "I have full faith and confidence in this controller. I spent almost as much time designing it as I did in designing our friend Pterrence here!"

"As you say, sir."

Ib tilted his head, looking at the Professor.

Professor Delby shook his head dismissively. "Bentley is referring to some previous, unfortunate events. Pay him no mind, Ib."

Ib looked up at the Pteranodon and jerked backwards, knocking against the tray of sandwiches.

A long, foreboding snort of steam was hissing from two vent holes at the end of Pterrence's long beak.

"Steady on, Ib!" the Professor said with a reassuring wave of his hand. "That's only a bit of excess steam indicating that our friend here is ready. Think of it as nothing more than a kettle that's ready for tea!"

Ib wasn't sure about having tea. He was even less sure about a smoldering Pteranodon.

Professor Delby moved the controller and all of the attached cables to a position directly in front of the gearwork Pteranodon. He flexed his fingers, as if preparing to play an instrument.

"Sir, might I suggest—"

"Thank you, Bentley."

"It is simply that I would be remiss, sir, were I not to point out—"

"Thank you, Bentley," the Professor said in a dismissive, singsong voice, "but I don't think that will be necessary."

"You don't think *what* will be necessary, Professor?" Ib asked. From the Professor's attempt at appearing unconcerned, Ib was certain he was missing something very important.

"Again, nothing to concern yourself with, Ib," Professor Delby said with a quick wave of his hand. "Bentley can be something of a worrywart sometimes."

The Professor moved the controller slightly to the side and placed a hand on one of the levers.

From the corner of his eye, Ib saw Bentley move towards the far side of the room.

"Where are you going, Bentley?" the Professor called out.

"I simply wished to better see the full majesty of your gearwork replica in motion, sir."

"Perspective is everything, isn't it, Bentley?"

"Indeed, sir."

Ib hesitated for a moment and then decided to follow Bentley's lead. Trying to act nonchalant, Ib moved away from Pterrence and the Professor as well.

Professor Delby moved a lever, crying out, "Observe!"

An extended snort of steam hissed from the pointed beak. It stopped. For a moment, nothing happened.

Then a long, brass arm bent outward from the shoulder and the elbow. The leather wing stretched out.

Another shot of steam was followed by the other arm extending outward.

Ib's mouth fell open.

It was incredible. He guessed that each arm stretched out over twelve feet long. As Professor Delby moved another set of levers, the arms began to move up and down at the shoulders. Ib felt air billowing from the gearwork Pteranodon's flapping wings. He squinted his eyes against the dust that was starting to swirl around him.

With the push of another lever, the Pteranodon's head swiveled at its neck. The head moved from side to side. Ib tried to follow the levers and cables back to the huge brass machine to understand how they worked.

A shiver ran down his spine. Looking up, he saw the two dull orbs of Pterrence's eyes staring down at him.

A glint of red flickered deep within the eyes.

Ib's mouth became very dry.

From deep behind the eyes, he saw a second spark. It was followed by a third and then a fourth.

And then the faint light changed to a deep, glowing ruby red.

"Professor?" he asked, not quite sure what he was seeing.

"I know! Quite the triumph, isn't it?" Professor Delby said, beaming. "Won't the lads at the University be wild about it?"

The Pteranodon's head turned again, this time facing the Professor. Only, Ib hadn't seen the Professor move any of the levers.

"That's odd," the Professor said. "There must be a loose fitting around Pterrence's neck. I should check that."

Professor Delby reset the levers back to their original position. The wings stopped beating and the arms folded back against the brass body.

Ib worried about the eyes that were somehow still glowing red.

"Professor, the eyes—" Ib started.

"It's only a minor adjustment, I'm sure," Professor Delby said, waving his hand behind him towards Ib. "Won't take but a moment." He set the controller down and climbed back on top of the workbench.

Ib watched the Professor push the brass head down and tighten several screws around the base of the neck. The Professor lifted the Pteranodon's head and released it. The head stayed in place for a moment, then it turned towards the Professor.

Professor Delby seemed to notice the red light behind the eyes at last and frowned.

"Now, Pterrence," he said, sternly. "I want you to stay right here."

Ib's eyes widened even further.

Was the Professor really talking to—?

Pterrence dropped his head long enough for Professor Delby to stop shaking his finger at him. Looking almost like a dragon that had been caught being naughty, the Pteranodon breathed out a whiff of smoke from its nostrils.

Then, with a swift jerk, the Pteranodon swung its brass head and hit the Professor full in the chest with its beak. Professor Delby flew off the workbench, knocking over several boxes of gears and sprockets, before sprawling onto the floor.

Ib was about to go and help the Professor up when he saw Professor Delby leap to his feet and shake a finger at the gearwork Pteranodon.

"Now, Pterrence, that was most uncalled for!"

Pterrence looked at the controller at his feet. Reaching down with his long beak, he picked up the control box and shook it back and forth. Once all the wires had been disconnected, Pterrence threw the box against the laboratory wall.

Pterrence looked around him, his red eyes pulsating. Seeing Ib, he tilted his head to the side and uttered a faint, *"Kawrr?"* Ib tried to move to the bench behind him but stopped when Pterrence jumped to the workbench in front of him. Tools, glass beakers and machinery bounced off the bench and scattered to the floor with a tremendous crashing. He could have sworn he felt the stone floor jolt beneath him.

The Pteranodon reached out a long, winged arm and poked Ib in the stomach. Despite his racing heart, a part of him thought Pterrence's poke had seemed playful.

"*Kawrr!*" Pterrence said.

His feet felt too heavy with panic to move. He hoped Pterrence wasn't hungry.

"N-nice Pteranodon?" he managed.

Pterrence spread his wings and sprung off the workbench, leaping at his head. Ib ducked, holding his arms over his head. When the brass Pteranodon claws failed to sink into his body, he ventured a glance around him. To his complete amazement, the gearwork Pteranodon had leaped over his head and begun beating his wings. Pterrence was flying in a tight circle around the vast laboratory.

It seemed that anything not nailed down in the laboratory was blown about by the force of the air from Pterrence's wings. Boxes were upended, tools and metal all clattered to the floor, and glass shattered all about him.

In the midst of this chaos, Ib stood still, watching as the Pteranodon flew around the room.

It was the most amazing thing he had ever seen in his life.

"Sir, might I suggest—" Bentley shouted over the beating of the leather wings and the sounds of crashing scientific materials.

"No need!" Professor Delby shouted back. "I have the situation well under control, Bentley!"

Pterrence landed on a tall ladder at the far side of the laboratory. Using his clawed feet and beak, he climbed to the top of the ladder and looked below him. Then, with easy, fluid movements, he began pecking at the wooden boards that made up the ceiling.

More curious than fearful now, Ib ran as close to the ladder as he dared. Looking up, he saw streaks of light coming through the boards Pterrence was attacking. He realized the boards weren't part of the ceiling but were a pair of hatchway doors that led outside.

"Sir, it would appear—"

"Thank you, Bentley. I am in *complete* control of the situation!"

Professor Delby rushed past Ib and stood at the bottom of the ladder.

"Pterrence, I insist you come down from there this instant!"

The Pteranodon banged at the wooden doors with the top of his head.

"Pterrence, this behavior is really most unbecoming of a scientific device!"

Pterrence stopped and looked down the ladder. To Ib's amazement, Pterrence hopped down several rungs of the ladder.

"Well, that's more like it!" Professor Delby said. "See, Bentley? As I said, I have the situation is well in—"

Pterrence looked up at the wooden doors again. Clutching the ladder with his claws, he opened his beak wide. A burst of flame shot out of his mouth and burned through the dry wooden doors.

Pterrence flapped his huge leather wings, causing more smoke and dust to swirl around the laboratory, knocking Ib off his feet. Above him, he heard a metallic *"Kawrr!"* moments before the storm inside the laboratory subsided.

And then all was quiet.

At the sound of the Professor coughing somewhere in the other side of the room, Ib opened his eyes. Not able to see Professor Delby, he reluctantly looked above him. The smoldering remains of the hatchway doors hung loosely from their hinges.

"Sir?" Bentley called from across the room.

"Yes, yes. Just fine, thank you," the Professor called out from the midst of the murkiness.

"I say, Ib," the Professor added after another coughing fit. "Would you mind seeing where Pterrence has gone off to?"

"Yes, Professor," he said, trying to sound eager. He climbed the ladder and scrambled onto the ground at the top of the ladder. He took a deep breath of fresh air and looked upward.

In the sky above him, he saw Pterrence, his brass and leather wings beating in long, powerful strokes. As Pterrence flew higher and higher, Ib thought he could almost believe he was seeing nothing more than a bird.

He shook his head, trying to clear his thoughts. He now lived in a world where a steam-driven model could tear away its controls and burn its way out of a laboratory before flying off into the evening sky.

How could things possibly become any stranger?

"Oh, bother," Professor Delby said, coming up the ladder. "Don't tell me I've lost another one."

9

IN WHICH THE
AIR IS CLEARED

Ib climbed back down the ladder after Professor Delby. Once in the laboratory again, Ib coughed as he tried to see through the dust and disarray Pterrence had stirred up.

The Professor seemed to not be affected by the dust storm and mess at all. He stood, hands on his hips, surveying the laboratory and alternately nodding and shaking his head.

"Alas, Bentley," he said, shaking his head one last time. "I must say, I'm rather shocked by the mess Pterrence has left behind. I fear he has created an afternoon's worth of work for us."

"As much as I should enjoy complying with your request, sir," Bentley said, "I feel, again, that this is another instance in which your new lab assistant *extraordinaire* should share in the enjoyment of the task."

"By gum, you're right again, aren't you!" the Professor said. "Where did he go? Bentley, perhaps you should check the library fireplace again."

"I'm right here, Professor," Ib said, not thinking he was that invisible.

"Ah, so you are!" Professor Delby turned and gestured about him. "Tell me, which part of the laboratory would you like to start with? Personally, I prefer to start with my own workbench in instances such as these."

"But, Professor," he asked, "shouldn't we go looking for Pterrence?"

"Why? I'm sure he knows where he is by now," the Professor replied.

Ib shook his head. "No, Professor. It's not that. Don't you think people might be afraid of seeing a giant Pteranodon flying in the skies?"

"Whyever would they do that? I should think they would marvel at his beauty and the intricacies of his movements!"

"But Professor," he pleaded, trying to find a reason Professor Delby might listen to, "he is our responsibility, isn't he?"

Professor Delby stopped and though a moment.

"Ib, Ib," he said. "I fear you worry far too much. I'm sure once our Pterrence has had a nice fly-around he will either become tired or lonely or hungry and choose to come back to the roost, as it were, all on his own."

Ib raised a doubtful eyebrow.

"Bentley?" the Professor asked. "Your thoughts?"

"I believe Master Ib's concerns may well be justified, sir. However, if you feel confident that a single evening's escapades should prove sufficient to force Pterrence's attention back to the laboratory—"

"Which I do," Professor Delby interjected.

"Then perhaps a compromise of some sort can be reached?" Bentley concluded.

"Fine," Professor Delby conceded, glancing at the ceiling. "If Pterrence isn't back by tomorrow's breakfast we shall go off in search of him. Will that make the two of you happy?"

"Immeasurably, sir." Bentley answered.

"Wonderful," the Professor said. "Now, where were we?"

"Cleaning the laboratory after Pterrence's shocking and fully unanticipated departure, sir."

"Ah, yes! So, we were. Ib, where would you like to start?"

Ib hesitated, then admitted, "I don't know where anything belongs, Professor."

"Nonsense!" Professor Delby replied. "All of this belongs in the laboratory! That's why it's here."

"No, Professor, I mean, I don't know where anything belongs here in the laboratory."

Professor Delby pulled his head back slightly. "Really? I would have hoped in the weeks since you've been with me you would have taken some notice."

Ib furrowed his brow. This was almost as confusing as the Professor not remembering who he was. "I've only been here since this morning, Professor," Ib said, hoping he sounded more helpful than concerned.

"Have you, indeed?" Professor Delby tapped at his chin. "Bentley? Is this true?"

"I am pleased to confirm the veracity of your new lab assistant's words, sir. In fact, Master Ib has yet to utter a single false statement since entering into your employment."

"Good show, Ib! If there's one thing a scientist needs in a laboratory assistant *extraordinaire* it is the strength of character to speak the truth regardless of the circumstances or outcomes!"

Ib wondered at Bentley's choice of words. What was he trying to tell Professor Delby? Looking back at the Professor he saw his new employer still beaming at him.

"Thank you, Professor," he said.

He watched as Bentley went into a back section of the laboratory. Soon the large paddle wheels attached to the ceiling bicycles began to turn.

"I have activated the ventilation system, sir," Bentley announced upon his return. "You should notice an appreciable improvement in the air momentarily."

"Excellent, Bentley," Professor Delby said. "You know, Ib, a good mix-up does the imagination a world of good. It swirls items into close proximity with one another in ways that might never happen otherwise. I think it's imperative to make the best of such situations."

Ib kept his eyes on the spinning paddle wheels. The wheels were each hung at different distances from the ceiling. Some turned clockwise and others counter-clockwise, as if they couldn't make up their mind what direction they should be going. Even more interesting to Ib was the fact that they really were pushing the dust up towards the open-slatted windows near the ceiling.

"A ventilation system of the Professor's own design, Master Ib."

Ib jumped at the sound of Bentley's voice. The manservant had appeared beside him so silently that he had thought Bentley must still be across the room.

Looking back at the ceiling, a thought struck him. He hated being dependent on Bentley for answers, but what choice did he have?

"You know this works because you have had to use it before, haven't you, Mister Bentley?"

Bentley responded with a placid nod.

"Does that mean this happens a lot?" he asked.

"If by 'this' you mean to ask 'Do Pteranodon replicas often fly throughout the laboratory creating such chaos,' the answer would be no, Master Ib. If, however, your question was meant more broadly, as in, 'Do unexpected events occur in Professor Delby's laboratory which

then necessitate a clearing of the air and a cleaning of the surfaces,' then, Master Ib, I would answer with a conditional affirmative."

Ib wanted to ask Bentley to repeat that, but he wasn't sure he would understand it any better a second time. Instead, he tried another question.

"Are you telling me strange things often happen in Professor Delby's laboratory?"

Bentley thought for a moment.

"I fear the word 'strange' carries with it a connotation of unnatural suspicion, Master Ib. Certainly Professor Delby would not use the word. My own preference is for either 'unexpected' or 'curious.'"

Ib raised an eyebrow.

"Pterrence came to life, Mister Bentley," Ib stated.

Bentley raised a finger.

"Life is a very strong term, Master Ib. At best it might be said that the Professor's experiments have acquired powers beyond their steam." Looking about them Bentley added, "I believe the visibility has improved sufficiently for you to begin assisting Professor Delby, Master Ib. Perhaps you can locate a suitable section of the laboratory to reorganize. I fear I am needed upstairs."

After Bentley left, his thoughts returned to Pterrence. Professor Delby might see Pterrence as merely a machine, but Ib was certain anyone else who saw Pterrence would see him as something more and be scared.

Images of Pterrence burning his way out of the laboratory came to his mind. Would Pterrence burn down buildings? Surely seeing Pterrence breathing fire in the nighttime skies would be enough to cause a citywide panic.

He thought about talking to the Professor about this but decided against it. Bentley seemed satisfied with Professor Delby's willingness to search for Pterrence if the creature wasn't back by morning. Maybe he was being worried for nothing.

Ib found a broom and began sweeping up broken glass from the floor and the workbenches. It did not take long, however, before he was sifting through overturned boxes of tiny rods, gears, and oddly shaped brass fittings.

Running his fingers over the edges and ridges of so many bits and pieces, he tried to learn as much as he could about them by himself.

Soon he was fitting together some of those bits and pieces. He could not describe what he was building, but with the addition of each new component, he felt he was coming that much closer to understanding. It was as if the jumble of items around him were all parts to a puzzle and, by not thinking too hard about them, he was able to see how the pieces all fit together.

For Ib, the experience became all-consuming. Never before had the lad been given the opportunity, the tools, or the luxury of time to give the mechanical patterns in his imagination the chance to run wild.

It felt that only a few minutes had passed since he had given up on sweeping the laboratory floor. Instead, when he looked around him, he was surprised to find himself working at a table near the Professor's bench surrounded by gears, rods, and tools.

Even more surprising was that the chandelier gaslights were all alight and that the sun had long set over the London skies.

Ib shook his head. He had never lost an afternoon before.

"Ho, ho!" Professor Delby exclaimed. "I see a workbench has chosen you!"

He looked up at the Professor, wondering how he could explain all this.

"And look! Your first invention here in the lab! Tell me, Ib, what does it do?"

Ib looked at the collection of gears and rods and brass flaps. He turned a handle and watched as dozens of toothed wheels turned in concert with one another, small wheels turning bigger wheels that caused rods to rise and fall inside the brass box.

"I have no idea, Professor," he admitted.

Professor Delby beamed.

"Isn't that one of the most dependable, most satisfying things about science?" he asked.

Ib looked around him and saw the laboratory was no cleaner than when Pterrence had flown off.

"I-I'm sorry, Professor Delby," he said, suddenly fearing for his job. "I know I'm your assistant and should have been cleaning! Don't worry, I'll get it straightened even if I have to stay up all night."

Professor Delby pulled his head back and looked from side to side. "Whatever are you talking about? Oh, that. There are always plenty of

things in need of cleaning, Ib, and so little time for science. When in doubt, science should always prevail."

Professor Delby paused and cocked an ear towards the door to the laboratory. "As it is, we should be hearing the gong telling us it is time to prepare ourselves for dinner any minute now."

At the mention of food, Ib's stomach let out a low rumble.

"And just in time, too!" Professor Delby added.

Ib thought for a moment. "What is a gong, Professor?"

"If you took a very large bell and smashed it flat from the top, you would have a good approximation of a gong," Professor Delby replied. "They each serve a similar purpose as well. They signal the formal start of an announcement." He looked up at the ceiling and shook his head. "It is my one concession to Bentley's insistence on etiquette, I'm afraid. We must be properly dressed for dinner."

Ib looked down at the dirty cuffs and sleeves of the oversized shirt he had been given to wear.

"Do not concern yourself with the current state of your wardrobe. If I know Bentley, he will already have something suitable laid out for you to wear."

"He must take this very seriously," Ib said, hoping he was wrong.

Professor Delby shook his head once again.

"Impossibly so," he lamented.

When the gong sounded, the reverberations transformed into a mechanical chirping sound. Ib looked around him and saw Sophie fluttering down on top of his head again. She landed and then tapped at his head before jumping onto the workbench. Taking a few cautious steps, she surveyed the table with a slow shake of her head.

Using her beak, Sophie flicked several sprockets and curled metal shavings from around a clean rag. She settled herself onto the cloth as the gong rang a second time.

"I believe, my lab assistant *extraordinaire*, that Sophie has decided to claim not only a part of your workbench, but you as well."

With several quick flicks of her wing, Sophie waved them both off before snapping and sputtering back into her egg-shape.

Professor Delby nodded his head slightly.

"And that we have both been dismissed."

10

IN WHICH DINNER
IS SERVED

Ib sat in a large chair and frowned at the place setting before him. He tugged at the collar of his freshly starched shirt. Even though the shirt was too big for him, Bentley had seen to it that the bowtie was properly snug around his neck.

He had thought working with science was going to be the hardest part of his new life. Science now looked simple compared to the intimidating array of china plates, crystal glasses, forks, spoons, and glasses fanned out across the table in front of him.

When he was living in the orphanage, his two meals a day had been a thin gruel served in a battered tin bowl with a single spoon. Things were even worse with Mr. Bertram. He had been lucky to get the scraps from the large man's plate after Mr. Bertram went to sleep off that night's ale. Ib had taken to eating with his fingers to keep from making any noise that might awaken the always-irritated thief.

The Delby dining room table looked like it belonged in an exhibition hall. The light from the candles sparkled through facets in the crystal glasses. The detailed design on the china plates looked far too fancy to ever be covered with food. He worried that even touching the polished silverware with his freshly scrubbed hands might smudge them.

Ib was hungry, but the unfamiliar formality kept him still.

Professor Delby sat across from him, his elbow on the table. With a heavy sigh, the Professor sank his cheek into the palm of his hand.

Bentley entered the dining room carrying a large silver platter with an ornate cover.

"Personally," the Professor said, looking off to the side where the tapered candles were burning, "I would prefer to simply eat in the kitchen with the rest of the household."

"Which would then cause considerable discomfort amongst the downstairs staff, sir," Bentley said, lifting the lid from the platter.

Ib's nose tingled with the first of a meal's worth of new, inviting scents. He lacked the words to properly describe the delicate, complex smells and their accompanying tastes—a notion his stomach reminded him was for people who had been well-fed all their lives and were not hungry.

A short, plump woman wearing an apron followed Bentley into the dining room and opened a wooden window in the side wall. From the dumbwaiter she retrieved a tureen and placed it on the table. When she lifted the lid, another smell filled the room.

His stomach convinced him that, despite the maze of plates and forks in front of him, he must try and soldier through.

"Bentley," Professor Delby sighed. "I do not see why you insist on making something so pleasurable as an evening meal such a difficult chore."

"As a university professor, a scientist of note, and the eldest member of a prominent London family who has dined with Royalty, you have a duty to maintain your position in society, sir."

"Yes, yes," the Professor said, waving his hand and then gesturing to his place setting. "But why must my duty and position and society always come with such a confusing array of utensils?"

"To allow the upper classes to distinguish themselves from the lower classes, sir."

Ib shot Bentley a look, but the manservant's attention was given to their employer.

Professor Delby rested the elbow of his dinner jacket on the table, his cheek falling into his open palm again.

"What did I tell you, Ib?" he said, shaking his head. "The man is impossible."

"You are exceedingly welcome, sir. Fish?"

"Yes," the Professor said, sighing. "Thank you, Bentley."

"Hello, dear," said the woman in the apron coming over to Ib. "I'm Mrs. Hudson. Would you care for some soup?"

Ib was torn between the smell of the soup and the smell of the fish. He didn't want to appear greedy, and he couldn't decide between them.

"You can have both, you know," Mrs. Hudson whispered.

Ib smiled. "Yes, please!"

She set a shallow bowl of thin, brown liquid in front of him. He inhaled, closing his eyes. He never knew food could be like this.

"If you insist on laying all of these confusing utensils out at once like a set of surgeon's tools," the Professor continued, "you could, at the very least, color-coordinate them. White for fish, brown for soup, green for vegetables, red for mutton."

"Fish, Master Ib?"

"Yes, please, Mister Bentley," he responded. He looked again at the silverware in front of him. He noticed there was a certain cascading precision to the way they decreased in size. He tilted his head to the side, considering this.

"Professor Delby will undoubtedly inform you at some point as to the proper order of your silver, Master Ib. Until then, allow me to advise you start with those utensils furthermost from your plate and work inward with each remove."

"Remove?" he asked. He groaned silently, imagining Bentley taking away all of the wonderful food before he could eat any of it.

"A remove being the next series of dishes from which you may choose, Master Ib."

"You mean there's more?" he asked before he could stop himself. The soup and fish alone were more food than he could ever remember being allowed to eat at once.

Mrs. Hudson clucked her tongue. She turned back from the dark multi-shelved sideboard that took up the better part of a short wall. "Don't you worry yourself over that, Master Ib," she said. "You'll not be going hungry in this house!"

He smiled, the thought making him feel warmer than any soup could.

Still, with such appetizing soup and fish in front of him, he thought he should at least give the food a sporting chance.

Picking up the spoon farthest from his plate, he picked at a piece of the fish. The white flesh flaked away, taking with it flecks of finely minced red and green. He watched Professor Delby and saw that he was using a fork for his fish. Ib picked up his own fork and tried to imitate the way the Professor was picking up his fish.

He was only partially successful, but the bit of fish that made it to his mouth was worth the work. The herbal scent came with a sweet, buttery taste that ran down the sides of his tongue while the red and green flecks were mildly spicy. He had never tasted anything like it before.

He supposed he could tolerate a stiff collar and the confusion of silverware if this was the reward.

After dinner, Professor Delby sat with a large, wide glass in his hand that contained a small amount of amber liquid.

"Do you know the brightest spot of this entire meal, Ib?" he asked.

He could think of several: the fish, the soup, the roast fowl, the roasted potatoes, the gravy, and the bread pudding.

"It was having such fine company!" the Professor said. "During the roast fowl I wondered what it was that was making this meal more tolerable—enjoyable, really—more so than many others. And there was my answer, sitting across from me. It was clear how deeply you were enjoying Mrs. Hudson's fine cooking. That alone made me appreciate it all the more!"

He felt his face grow red. All he had done was sit and eat the most marvelous meal of his life.

"Thank you, Professor," he managed to say.

"Now then," the Professor said, a single eye narrowing. "Tell me, Ib, do you play chess?"

Ib swallowed hard. What was that?

"N-no, sir."

Professor Delby's eyes relaxed as he leaned back in his chair. "Too much to ask for, really," he sighed. He took a sip of his drink and nearly lost his balance in his chair, struggling to rise up too quickly.

"My lord, Ib!" he said, rushing out of the dining room. Moments later he returned with a long, thin wooden carving. It looked like two boats sitting side by side, only instead of seats, each boat had a row of cups carved into the wood. At each end, there was much wider cup that was full of small, gray and yellow stones.

Ib looked at the wooden base, making out the carved shapes of people and animals. The creatures held the twin boats with either their hands, heads, or paws. Some held a boat up with curved, tapered appendages sticking out from their heads.

"What is this?" he asked, his voice almost a whisper.

"This is either a game masquerading as art, or art masquerading as a game, my lab assistant *extraordinaire*!" Professor Delby said, scooping up the stones from one of the end cups. "As with many things in life, it can be difficult to tell the difference."

"Where did you find it?" he asked.

"Well, strictly speaking, I didn't find this. Rather, it was made for me by a grateful gentleman in one of the islands to the north of South America."

"South America?" Ib asked, looking from the carvings to the Professor. "Where is that?"

Professor Delby finished counting out the number of stones he placed in each cup on the boat closest to himself.

"BENTLEY!"

"Sir?"

The Professor jumped in his seat, sending gray and yellow stones spilling across the dining room table.

"Will you please stop doing that!" Professor Delby exclaimed.

"Cease what, sir?"

"Sneaking up on me like that!" the Professor responded, scooping up the stones in his hand. "Knock or cough or announce yourself when you're entering a room!"

"I shall endeavor to become more obvious, sir."

"Fine," Professor Delby said, shaking his head and taking another sip from his large glass. "In the meantime, would you please bring the globe from the library to us? I feel a brief geography lesson coming on."

Leaning towards the twin boats, the Professor pointed to the two rows of cups carved into the surface. "We start with four nickernuts in each cup," he said.

"Nickernuts?" Ib asked, stifling a laugh.

"Nickernuts," Professor Delby confirmed. "Or sea pearls or gray and yellow stones, if you prefer. Also known as seeds from the warri bush."

Ib nodded, trying to put on a serious face.

"We each take turns picking up the stones from one of our cups and placing one nickernut into each of the cups down the rows going counter-clockwise." Professor Delby swirled his finger above the cups to indicate the direction. "If the last cup you place a nickernut into ends up with either two or three nickernuts, you claim them by moving them into the big cup at your end of the board."

Ib nodded. He had always surprised himself with being good with

simple sums, even though he had never learned to read or write his numbers or letters. He stared at the boats and the stones in each cup.

"It's a game?" he asked.

"Exactly." Professor Delby said. "One of the oldest games still played throughout the world!"

He looked from the boats to the Professor again.

The Professor pushed the board aside and turned to Bentley who was wheeling in a large, colorful ball held in an odd, curved frame.

"Your globe, sir."

"What's a globe?" Ib asked.

"Why, a representation of the earth, my boy! *Terra firma*. Our home planet." Professor Delby pushed the globe sideways and watched it spin for a moment. Then, slowing it down with his index finger, he brought it to a stop on an island in the upper half of the sphere.

"This, Ib, is where we are. The seat of the world's power. Our beloved Queen Victoria's own green and pleasant land. Our England!"

Ib looked at the globe and at the Professor's finger.

"Really?" he asked.

"Well, in a manner of speaking," Professor Delby added hastily. "We aren't actually under my finger, of course. It would be significantly darker outside and my finger would be poking through the roof of the house as I speak. However, as a representation of where we are relative to the rest of the world, yes, this is where we reside."

Ib looked the globe over, top to bottom. He had never seen anything like it before.

"How does it work?" he asked.

"It doesn't so much work as it shows us where things are," the Professor admitted.

Ib looked up, his eyebrows tightened.

"Take us, for example," the Professor continued. "England is this large bit here, and above us is Scotland, and to the west is Ireland. This bit of blue is the English Channel, and on the other side are France, Germany and Italy."

He was familiar with the names, but he had never known where any of these places were, nor how close or far away they were from anywhere else.

"Where did this game come from?" he asked, looking at the large spread of countries on the globe.

"That would be ... here," Professor Delby said, spinning the globe and moving his finger across a wide stretch of ocean until it stopped next to a small spot of land in the midst of the blue.

"England is very big, isn't it, Professor?" he asked.

"Of course!"

"How much bigger is that blue between England and France and where this game came from?"

"All of that blue is water, Ib," the Professor explained. "It was a long voyage between here and there. Over two months, in fact."

Ib's eyes widened. He had never seen the ocean before, and the thought of being on a ship for two full months was beyond his imagination.

"How did you do that?" he asked.

"Oh, I simply booked passage aboard a sailing vessel. That part was quite easy, really." Professor Delby looked at the globe and breathed out through his nostrils.

"I was young, you see. I had just completed my studies at Cambridge and had already decided to devote my life to science." The Professor spun the globe again. "Still, I suppose you could say I had something of a broken heart, and like most young men, I went off seeking adventure to cure it."

"During this time," Bentley interjected, "Professor Delby put into place a new process for digging wells for clean water in several areas of the African continent." Ib's eyes spun with the globe until the manservant pointed to a section of land in the bottom part of the sphere.

"Our employer also put down a rebellion in a Chinese Province." Bentley turned the globe halfway around and pointed to the largest land mass. "He taught the mountain-dwelling natives of Chile how to increase their crop yields." Bentley turned the sphere again as Ib struggled to keep up. "Then cured a rather nasty tropical disease on several islands of the Caribbean."

"Where a grateful village elder presented me with the carved game that you see before you as an offering of his appreciation," the Professor said loudly as he gestured to the elaborate carving. "Now, the first player to move in this game is decided by chance." He took a single nickernut and shook it between his cupped hands. Then, after lowering his hands beneath the table, he presented Ib with two closed fists.

"Choose a hand, Ib."

Ib looked at the two hands before him. In the one hand, he could see a young Humboldt Delby traveling the world doing what he could to improve the lives of those he met. In the other hand he saw the eccentric, barking mad Professor who a built steam and gearwork Pterosaur that somehow came to life. He wondered what had happened during the years in between.

Ib shook his head. Looking from the two fists in front of him to the eager eyes of the Professor, he smiled.

He chose a fist. The Professor opened his hand, revealing a smooth, shiny stone.

"Excellent! You make the first move, then!"

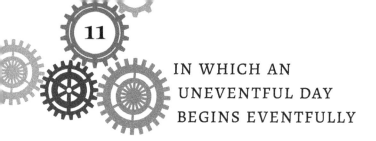

11

IN WHICH AN
UNEVENTFUL DAY
BEGINS EVENTFULLY

With no sign of Pterrence by the time they finished breakfast, Professor Delby and Ib set out to begin what the Professor referred to as "Pterrence Watching."

"It's quite simple really," the Professor explained as he put on his walking coat. "We shall take a leisurely stroll through Hyde Park and keep our eyes to the sky. Bentley's sources assure him Pterrence has already been seen there twice since his determined departure from the laboratory."

Ib arched an eyebrow. Even the best night's sleep of his life hadn't changed his thoughts on how difficult capturing Pterrence would be.

"Shall we be off, oh lab assistant *extraordinaire*?" Professor Delby asked.

"Certainly, Professor," Ib replied with a slight shrug and a smile.

They walked along the wide, semi-circular gravel path that led from the house, past carefully tended garden spaces and ancient trees. The Delby Manor stood alone in the middle of a full city block on the edge of one of the nicer neighborhoods in London. It wasn't until he walked through this part of the grounds that Ib had any idea how large they were.

"I expect we shall find the day rather uneventful," Professor Delby said. "I'm sure finding Pterrence and bringing him back to the laboratory should take little more than an hour at most. After we fetch Pterrence back to the laboratory and have a nice spot of lunch, perhaps we can visit the tailor. Bentley was rather insistent that we should find you some better fitting clothes today."

If this was the Professor's idea of an uneventful day, Ib wasn't sure if he wanted to know what an eventful one was like. Instead of asking, he stretched out his arms, his hands extending slightly past his rolled back shirtsleeves.

"I like my clothes as they are, Professor."

As they approached the main roadway, he saw the wrought-iron fence that marked the boundaries of the Delby property. The sharp spikes atop each point had worried Ib when he had opened the gate for Mr. Bertram's cart the day before. Now they looked as though they were keeping him safe against the outside world.

He stayed behind the Professor as they walked through the gates and his employer pulled them closed. The latch made a solid clicking sound as it locked in place.

Coming up behind the Professor, he heard a gravelly voice that sent a chill so deep down his spine that he felt frozen in place.

"I begs yer pardon, sir, but I comes to see ye about that, er, weird sack me former apprentice had with him in yer chimney yesterday."

Professor Delby stopped and turned to face the man approaching from his left. Ib willed himself to take a small step back and to the side, trying to stay hidden behind Professor Delby.

"Oh, yes," the Professor said. "That poor, unfortunate dead child in the library. Tragic thing, wasn't it?"

"Er, yeah," Mr. Bertram said. "Downright inconvenient."

"You have my deepest sympathies."

"And ye has me bits and bobs collector," Mr. Bertram said. "I wants to, um, see if me next apprentice can make use of it."

Ib had stopped breathing. The thief was standing close enough to Professor Delby that Ib was certain Mr. Bertram would see him if the Professor moved at all.

His heart raced. If he could unlatch the gate and throw it open, he might be able to run back to the house before Mr. Bertram caught him. He knew, though, that Mr. Bertram was not the sort of person who would let a closed front door stand in his way. The boy looked to his right and saw a long, enclosed wagon drawn by a team of two well-groomed horses coming their way. Eight men in dark coats and bowler hats were holding on to the outside of the wagon and standing on runners. Under different circumstances he would have been curious about this, but for the moment all he could think about was whether he could run under the wagon and down the street before anyone could catch him.

He knew he couldn't make it to the wagon in time. Instead, he decided staying hidden behind the Professor was the best of several bad options. That his feet didn't want to move at all made the decision that much easier.

"I say," Professor Delby said cheerfully, "allow me to introduce my new lab assistant *extraordinaire!*"

Ib's eyes popped open wide.

"Yer what?" Mr. Bertram asked.

"My new lab assistant *extraordinaire,*" the Professor said. "Incredible boy. A brain just filled with science. Where did he go? He was here a moment ago."

Professor Delby turned to look back inside the gate. When he did, Ib tried ducking to the side, but it was too late.

"You!" Mr. Bertram demanded.

Ib couldn't help himself. He turned and faced his former boss as the Professor caught sight of him.

Ib's feet unfroze and he bolted to the right.

Where he ran right into a man wearing a black coat and a bowler hat.

"Hey, that's me apprentice!" Mr. Bertram yelled.

"No, no," Ib heard Professor Delby say. "That's my new lab assistant *extraordinaire!*"

The dark-suited man held on to him too tightly for him to escape. The boy turned his head to see behind him. Had the police finally linked them to the nearby nighttime thefts? Or did Bentley inform the police that the criminals would be waiting by the front gates this morning?

Strangely, the two men with Mr. Bertram pushed the thief away from the wagon. The two men with the Professor, meanwhile, hurried him towards the back of the wagon along with himself.

He tried to keep his footing as he was hustled up some steps and pushed into the back of the windowless wagon.

Ib struggled to see what was happening in the darkness around him.

Two other men crowded into the back of the wagon with him. One growled, "Sit and be quiet."

He felt as though he might be sick.

The wagon door opened again. More of the dark-suited men entered the wagon and sat down. He felt his heart pounding all the way to his neck. He wondered if Professor Delby was all right. It seemed easier to worry about someone else than to worry about himself.

"I say, no need for all the rough and tumble, lads," the Professor said as he was pushed into the wagon.

The men were focused on the Professor; no one seemed concerned with him at all. It seemed unlikely that Bentley would have involved Professor Delby in this way with any plan to get rid of him. Maybe this was about something else, then. *But what,* he wondered.

The last man in closed the wagon door, leaving the daylight outside. Slits of light cracked through gaps in the sides of the wagon. He tried to make out the Professor and the men at the other end of the wagon, but he saw only shadows.

"What's happening?" Ib asked.

"Hush it," snapped a man across from him.

Ib heard a driver snap at the reins. He was wedged in so tightly between two of the dark-coated men that he didn't move when the wagon lurched forward into more darkness.

IN WHICH THE QUEEN
IS NOT AMUSED

Half an hour later, the wagon slowed. Outside, heavy iron gates creaked open. The wagon wheels grated over loose gravel before coming to a stop. Ib heard the gates close behind them as handlers took the reins. Two sets of footsteps crunched toward the wagon, followed by a sharp knock against the wooden door.

The man at the door motioned to them. "Not a word from either of you."

"Oh, really," Professor Delby said, almost laughing. "There's no need for such formalities, is there?"

As if to answer, the men made a show of knocking Ib and the Professor about as the two were forced out of the wagon.

Ib blinked at the bright sunlight. He had expected to find himself at a police station or at the entrance to a dark warehouse being faced by a good many more men in black suits. Instead, he was standing on a gravel path lined with enormous trees. He smelled more flowers than he could name. Just past the trees to his right he could see the edge of a beautiful, sculpted garden. Following the line of the trees, he looked behind him and saw what looked like the top of a fairy story castle.

Before he could put his thoughts into words, he felt Professor Delby slap him on the shoulder. He skidded to a stop several feet away on the gravel driveway.

"What a fine day for a visit to Buckingham Palace, eh, Ib?"

Ib spun his head to face the Professor.

"Buck—Buckingham Palace?" he said. "Me? Us? Here?"

A line of men dressed in guard uniforms appeared from around the wagon and formed a circle around them. The lead officer pointed behind Ib. "Move it," he said, barely moving his lips.

Falling in line behind two of the men, Ib could not help but stare openly. As they walked, a sense of wonder trumped his fears.

The Palace Mews was the most elegant building he had ever seen. That it was a horse stable did not diminish the stateliness at all. Further down he walked past an almost blinding array of golden decorations that were being polished on a most ornate coach.

"The Queen's Coach," the Professor said, motioning to the majestic carriage. "She usually brings it out only for special occasions. A bit garish for my tastes, but that's royalty for you."

"Hush it," ordered their escort.

From the Palace Mews they came to a nearby building. It was a small, eight-sided structure with windowed doors in every other wall. One of the men opened a door and motioned for them to enter.

Once inside, Ib heard their footsteps echo faintly off of the walls. The room smelled of wood polish and dust. The chill in the air, however, came from the only things in the room aside from themselves: two men in markedly different uniforms seated behind an old table.

"Well, well, Commissioner!" Professor Delby said, leaning forward and offering his hand to one of the important-looking men behind the desk. The Commissioner stood automatically and shook the Professor's hand. Then, realizing what he was doing, abruptly ended the handshake, muttering something in annoyance as he returned to his seat.

"This must be serious, Ib," Professor Delby said, leaning towards his assistant. "The Commissioner is the head of the Metropolitan Police and does not concern himself with trivial matters."

Then the Professor turned his attention to the second gentleman.

"And, if I am not mistaken, you, sir, would be the head of Her Majesty's Royal Guard?"

Ib held his breath, fearing the worst.

"Do be quiet, Delby," the man snapped.

"Very serious, indeed," Professor Delby said to Ib.

Ib had a very strong desire to become very small. It wasn't helping that the Professor was speaking to him as if the two other men in the room could not hear him.

"Oh! Gentlemen, where are my manners?" the Professor blurted. "Allow me to introduce Ib, my lab assistant *extraordinaire!*" He gestured towards Ib with both hands. "A most amazing lad. Found him dead in the fireplace months ago. He's been indispensable ever since."

Ib went from wishing he were dead to being embarrassed that these two important men might think he was actually dead.

He looked from the Professor to the men behind the desk. Opening his mouth, he started shaking his head to explain. The scowls on the two faces in front of him stopped him from saying anything.

Instead, he offered them a feeble smile and quickly looked down at the floor.

"Delby," the Royal Guardsman said slowly. "Tell us what you know about fire-breathing dragons."

"*Mechanical*, fire-breathing dragons," added the Commissioner of the Metropolitan Police.

"Flying around London," added the Royal Guardsman.

Professor Delby tapped at his chin for a moment.

"Sounds rather dangerous to me," Professor Delby said. "Dashed irresponsible for anyone to build such a thing, much less let it go flying about."

The two grim officials continued to stare blankly at the Professor.

Ib arched both his eyebrows and looked at the Professor. This was not the time to go off barking mad again.

"Professor—" he started.

"In fact," Professor Delby added, "I'd recommend locking up whatever lunatic created it. No reason to terrify Her Majesty's peaceful subjects, is there?"

"Professor—" he tried again.

"Just a moment Ib, this is important," Professor Delby said, holding up his hand for emphasis. "Gentlemen, I believe that if such a creature has been let loose over the skies of our fair Albion, you should bring the entire weight of the monarchy down on the foolish and reckless person who brought such a beast into being!"

"Professor—" he pleaded.

"In fact," the Professor insisted, "I say bring back the hangman's noose or the executioner's axe for such an unprincipled, unsavory individual!"

Ib closed his eyes and sighed.

"Professor," he said, "I think they mean Pterrence."

"Really?" Professor Delby asked. "Well, that's a different matter entirely, isn't it, then?"

The Head of the Queen's Royal Guard slowly raised a neatly trimmed eyebrow.

"Terrance?" he asked.

"Pterrence," Professor Delby corrected. "The 'P' is silent."

The Royal Guardsman's face folded back into a deep scowl.

Ib waited for the Professor to explain how all of this was just a mistake. However, after several awkward moments of silence, he realized Professor Delby's smile meant he had said all he felt was necessary to say.

"Pterrence is a model of a Pteranodon, a type of flying dinosaur," Ib hastily explained, "not a fire-breathing dragon. Although he does breathe fire and he does have giant, leathery wings like a dragon he really isn't a dragon and—" Turning to the Professor, he added, "Come to think of it, Professor, why does Pterrence breathe fire?"

"Oh, I don't know," Professor Delby mused. "Perhaps it's a spot of indigestion. Perhaps it's simply because he can. I know I'd certainly give it a go if I could!"

One of the men behind the table loudly cleared his throat. Ib looked back to see both men glaring daggers at him.

"Well, it was a reasonable question, don't you agree?"

When the men's expressions failed to change Ib quickly added, "This is bad, isn't it?"

"Young man," the Royal Guardsman said, still glowering, "I can assure you it is very bad indeed."

"But it was only meant to move its wings a bit and turn its head, but only when you moved the proper levers on the control box!" he protested.

The two men looked from Ib to the Professor.

"I am happy to report, gentlemen, that my lab assistant extraordinaire speaks the truth. In fact, I have it on good authority that he has not uttered a single falsehood since entering into my employment," Professor Delby said, as if that settled the matter.

The Professor's eyes brightened.

"Why, this fine young lad had the honor of putting the fire in Pterrence's belly and officially activated the machinery," Professor Delby added. "Pterrence would not have moved a muscle—or gear, as it were—if it had not been for my remarkable assistant!"

"I see," said the Head of the Royal Guard. "So, you had a role in this as well, did you, lad?"

"Well . . ." Ib managed.

"Ho ho! And modest, too!" Professor Delby laughed, slapping Ib on the back.

He caught himself with his hands on the front edge of the table and looked up to see two pairs of official-looking eyes glowering at him.

"Why, before lighting the fire in the old boy, Ib and I were putting the last of the gears into place. Ib even gave Pterrence a final polish to help him shine so brightly! He's an indispensable part of my work— I beg your pardon, Ib. *Our* work!"

To Ib, it was as if the unwavering glares from the two officials had a certain, tangible weight to them. He suddenly felt very dizzy.

"Well?" asked the Commissioner.

He managed to keep from shaking long enough to bob his head up and down.

The Commissioner motioned for Ib to step away from the desk.

"Delby," the Commissioner said. "Is this another one of your . . . *mishaps?*"

"Well," the Professor responded with a slight chuckle, "that's the wonderful thing about science, isn't it, gentlemen? Just when you think you understand it, something completely unpredictable happens and—"

"The Queen has seen your dragon, Delby," the Royal Guardsman growled. "It was flying over Buckingham Palace last night, Delby. Her Majesty's children saw your dragon, Delby. Princess Alice and Princess Helena each had nightmares about your dragon chasing and devouring them, Delby. Her Majesty did not sleep last night thanks to your dragon, Delby. This means *we* did not sleep last night, *Delby*."

"The Queen's husband, Prince Albert, recognized the dragon as your work," the Commissioner added. "Her Majesty would have us kill the dragon to show the young Princesses there is nothing to fear. She would also like to put its head on a pike outside the Palace gates alongside your own head. Prince Albert believes this to be a bit old-fashioned and would rather see you capture the beast."

"That's rather sporting of him," Professor Delby said brightly. Leaning

over to Ib he added, "Prince Albert has always been a great admirer of science. He has invited me to give several demonstrations here at Buckingham Palace over the years."

Ib turned to the men behind the table, hoping they had heard this. Their stony expressions suggested if they had, they were not impressed.

"Her Majesty is also quite keen on seeing the dragon's creator thrown into prison for an exceptionally long time," the Royal Guardsman said. Then, scowling at Ib, he added, "Or *creators* as the case may be. I have already ordered my men to clear out a special section in the deepest parts of the Tower of London, just for the occasion. I shall be certain to request an additional section be cleared, however."

"Again, gentlemen," Professor Delby said with the merest hint of a laugh, "this really does not apply to us. You see, we created a Pteranodon, not a dragon—"

"Prince Albert is concerned that armed soldiers firing into the skies might cause a panic as well as unintended injury to Her Majesty's subjects," the Commissioner said through clenched teeth. "After some severe negotiations with Her Majesty, they have agreed to give you forty-eight hours to reclaim your beast."

"After that, Delby, we capture the monster by any means necessary and the two of you . . . disappear," the Head of the Royal Guard said with a flick of his hand.

"That should give you plenty of time to get your affairs in order, Delby. Close up your house, dismiss your staff, revise your will."

"Now, gentlemen!" Professor Delby said.

"You now have forty-seven hours, fifty-nine minutes and fifty-five seconds before I escort you both to your exceedingly private dungeons."

Ib could see Professor Delby was trying to decide how to phrase something.

"Oh, look," the Commissioner said, his eyes never leaving the Professor's face. "Forty-seven hours, fifty-nine minutes and forty seconds."

As they turned to leave, Ib could hear a dark smile in the Commissioner voice as he said, "Oh, and Delby, we'll be sure to pass along your fine suggestions concerning the hangman's noose and the executioner's axe to Her Majesty should the two of you fail."

IN WHICH PTERRENCE DOES NOT RUN OUT OF STEAM

"Professor?"

"Hmmm?"

"Professor," Ib said, working to keep his voice steady, "we have been here for almost two hours."

"Hmmm?" Professor Delby repeated, still scanning the sky. "Oh, yes. Two hours."

The Professor lowered his elaborate binoculars. He looked down, nodded to Ib, and returned his attention to the sky.

"How many hours does that leave us, Professor?"

"Hmmm? Oh, two from forty-eight? Forty-six."

"That leaves us with only forty-six hours, Professor."

Professor Delby nodded, continuing to study the blue and clouds above him.

He realized the Professor had never explained exactly how he intended to "fetch Pterrence back to the laboratory." After the way Pterrence had left, he was doubtful the mechanical Pterosaur was likely to simply follow them home on a leash.

Ib rocked back and forth on his feet. In front of them was an expanse of green lawn and a short, crooked river. Under other circumstances, he might have been able to enjoy the view.

Around him he could see well-dressed, proper members of polite society enjoying a bit of fashionable exercise on the footpaths winding through the lawns. He did not know how they could walk so easily in clothes that were so heavy and constricting.

Maybe it was something you had to be born to, he thought, looking back at the sky.

In the distance he could see familiar flags atop a building.

"Professor, is that Buckingham Palace?"

Professor Delby glanced over his binoculars. "Yes, indeed, Ib. Although it looks significantly smaller from our view only a short while ago."

"How far are we from the Manor?"

"Oh, not so far. Merely a nice walk over in that direction." He gestured with his hand.

"Then why was the ride in the wagon so long?" Ib asked.

Professor Delby looked at the sky through his binoculars again. "The Royal Guard likes to put on a good show, I fear. I generally find such unexpected rides to be quite relaxing."

Ib put his hands in his jacket pocket and stretched his arms inside the too-large sleeves. There was so much to do, although he didn't know quite what any of that might be.

"Are you sure Mister Bentley is right, Professor?" he asked.

"You mean Bentley's sources?" the Professor asked, lowering the binoculars again. "Ib, if there's one thing you can depend upon in this life, it is the accuracy of Bentley's sources. I don't know how he knows what they know, or how they know what they know. I do know, however, if Bentley's sources say that Pterrence is gathering water from The Serpentine River in Hyde Park every four hours or so, then that is exactly what Pterrence is doing."

Ib looked across the crooked body of water called The Serpentine and sighed. He looked back at the empty skies.

He had never spent so long doing nothing. He was used to doing *something*. Something constructive, even if it was dangerous. Standing still, 'Pterrence Watching' was not only not dangerous, but frankly, felt like a waste of precious time.

"Professor," he said at last, "this morning Mr. Bertram found out I'm not dead, we were kidnapped by the Royal Guard, you were told Queen Victoria wants your head on a pike, and we have been given forty-eight hours to bring Pterrence home or be locked away in the Tower."

"Technically, we were brought in for questioning, not kidnapped," Professor Delby clarified. "The Royal Guard is quite clear on that. I've asked into this before." He raised the binoculars once more, adding a satisfied, "Yes, it's been quite the exciting morning, hasn't it?"

"Professor," he insisted, "shouldn't we be trying something — mind you, I don't know exactly what just yet — but *something* to capture Pterrence?"

"Oh, but Ib, we are! One must do sufficient research before one can ever hope to formulate a plan. And research is exactly what we are doing!" He moved his binocular-assisted gaze to another part of the sky.

"Research is looking at the sky?" Ib asked.

"Well, in this case, yes. You see, a great deal of science is a matter of careful planning and patience and persimmons and … *whatnot —*"

Professor Delby drew in a sharp breath.

Ib looked up from the ground to the sky where the Professor's binoculars were pointing.

"Remarkable," the Professor said in a whisper.

Ib saw nothing but blue sky.

Then there was a flash of light, as if a tiny bit of the sun was winking at him.

The flickering light grew larger. Soon, he could see wings rising and falling in languid strokes. As the creature descended, he saw the Pteranodon's long brass beak was pointing at the pond they were standing next to.

Ib watched Pterrence circle slowly overhead, then fly wide of the park by several blocks. Pterrence's path straightened. He swooped down, flying just above the tops of several taller buildings. By the time he entered the park, Pterrence was brushing against the treetops.

The very proper members of polite society, taking their very proper walks in the park, began very properly and politely screaming and running away. Women lifted their skirts and ran while men clutched at their top hats, trying to keep up.

Ib stepped away from the river.

Pterrence lifted his leather wings again, his reddish-orange eyes looking down at the surface of the river. He dipped down, skimming the surface of The Serpentine with his lower beak open. Ib could not tell how much water the gearwork Pteranodon had scooped up, but when Pterrence angled himself upward Ib could have sworn he heard something that sounded remarkably like a mechanical gulp.

"Nothing short of remarkable!" Professor Delby cried as Pterrence flew off into the distance. "Why Ib, I believe we have witnessed a most amazing event. Do you realize what Pterrence is doing?"

The high-pitched sound of a constable's whistle interrupted the Professor. Ib looked to the park entrance and saw one of the London area constables running into the park, frantically blowing into his whistle.

The constable stopped beside Ib and tried to catch his breath.

"Where is it? Where is it!" the constable panted.

"Where is what?" the Professor said, looking all about him.

"The . . . the monster!" the constable said.

"Oh, really, constable," Professor Delby said. "There is no need to incite panic. That will only frighten everyone away!" Looking around him at the empty park, Professor Delby pursed his lips. "Unfortunately, I see you've already done that."

From habit, Ib looked away from the constable, whose red face was becoming even redder.

"Professor," he said, helpfully, "perhaps we should check on the coal yard Mister Bentley mentioned."

"An excellent suggestion, my lab assistant extraordinaire!" Professor Delby said. "Let us be off and leave the constable to his duties."

They had managed to walk only a few steps before the constable spluttered, "Now see here, you!"

Professor Delby stopped. Ib saw a look of annoyed confusion cross the Professor's face as he turned to face the constable.

"Young man," the Professor said, "my understanding is that your job is to keep the peace and to prevent crimes. Your blaring whistle has, in fact, frightened off the citizenry so there is no peace left to keep, nor anyone to commit any crimes. Now, if you will excuse us, we have science to investigate!"

Ib quickened their pace as they walked towards the road.

Within minutes they were in another hansom cab, trotting through the busy streets of London. After so many years of riding in the Mr. Bertram's open-air cart, Ib found it odd to sit in an enclosed cab, riding high above the streets.

From inside the hansom, he could hear the different costermongers calling out in their singsong voices, each trying to make the case for their goods being the finest anywhere. Looking out the window of the cab, he felt odd. Just yesterday he was one of them, a tradesman, one of the dirtiest classes in London. Now, in his clean shirt and jacket, he was the assistant to a man from an old, landed English family. The ill fit of his clothing suited him well, he thought.

They rode past a smaller park. He could see nurses walking in short, clipped steps, pushing babies in perambulators. By a walled pond, he saw older boys playing with wooden boats.

When another hansom crossed in front of them, Ib saw the driver tip his hat. It took him several moments to realize the driver was tipping his hat to him. He quickly waved back, but the driver was already out of sight.

The closer to the coal yard they travelled, the slower their ride became. Ib had expected the constables to arrive ahead of them. What he hadn't expected was the packed crowd of people blocking the wide entrance to the coal yard and standing in the middle of the road. The disturbance had filled the street with shop clerks, tradesmen, and people who happened to be nearby when Pterrence had landed. It was as if each person who had seen Pterrence making his undoubtedly impressive landing went home and then returned with two hundred of their closest friends and neighbors.

Making matters worse, several men were trying to lead a flock of sheep through the middle of the throng.

As the Professor stretched his legs, Ib leaned out the cab's window, hoping to pick individual voices out of the mass of people.

"I 'eard it was some kind of monster what breathed fire," Ib heard a woman say.

"Never," retorted another. "It was probably just some o' them coal boys taking one snootful too many and telling stories!"

"No, my brother saw it," said a young man wearing a pair of thick, round spectacles. "It were a dragon alright. A real dragon. All gold with a great spiked tail!"

Ib sat back in his seat. Maybe he didn't want to hear what the crowd had to say after all.

After a great many minutes of lurching and stopping, he looked out the window again. He could see a stocky man covered in coal dust speaking to one of the constables. The coalman wore a type of hat with

a brim in the back that reached down to his neck that bobbed up and down as the man's head moved up and down.

"Big as a house he was, with great wings and an 'orrible, shiny mouth," the coalman said. "He could've plucked me head clean off me shoulders with one snap o' them jaws! Flew right into the coal yard, he did. Helped himself to a couple o' clawfulls o'coal and flew off again. I heard of him being here, but this was the first time I ever seen him. I hope it's me last time as well!"

"Still haven't seen a word of this in of any the papers," said a man near the hansom. "Just shows you can't trust any of them!"

Ib turned and found the Professor listening at the window next to him.

"Since our route here took considerably longer than the more direct as-the-Pteranodon-flies path Pterrence took we are, of course, too late to witness the second half of Pterrence's midday meal," the Professor said with a thoughtful nod. He tapped on his chin for a moment before giving the driver instructions to turn at the corner to avoid the crowds and settling back in the cab.

After several minutes, the hansom worked its way to the end of the street and turned. Within half a mile, the tenor of the neighborhood had changed from shops and middle-class dwellings to warehouses and then to run-down row houses with the sounds of coarse voices calling out around them.

The driver made another turn and within two blocks the ride became rougher. The hansom bucked over the poorly kept cobblestone street, leaving Ib feeling rattled.

The boy leaned out to look at the neighborhood.

A moment later, his fingernails were digging into the palms of his hands.

Ib saw familiar rows of tall tenement houses. The streets were filled with running children wearing little more than rags chasing after barking dogs and other screaming children. The air smelled of rotting food and sewage. Women aged beyond their years stood in doorways gossiping with one another. Tinkers pushed their carts, eyeing anyone who looked like they might have a shilling to be spared in exchange for one of their scavenged goods.

He pulled away from the opening in the door, self-conscious of his fine clothes and comfortable seat inside the hansom cab.

Then, a minute later, despite himself, he leaned back toward the window. He knew all too well the long, soot-blackened brickwork and the tall gabled windows of the building they were passing: St. Stephen's Home for Wayward Children.

It had been his first home—or at least the first home he could remember. Being a wayward child meant he had no parents to claim him, no one to be special to, and no one to protect him. It had been a crowded, damp place where he had watched the weak grow sick and the mean grow strong.

He had seen only a few children leave St. Stephen's. Some of the older boys, the meanest of the bullies, were sold off to large men with thick necks who, if the rumors were true, taught them to be street toughs. Some of the smarter girls were sent off to train as governesses. Some who were good at repetitive tasks were taken on by Tradesmen to work in factories.

For a wayward child like Ib, whose only noticeable feature was his small size, there wasn't much hope of a good job.

The hansom cantered past the high peaked front doors to the orphanage. He saw one of the doors open slowly.

The day Ib left the orphanage had been a sweltering summer day. He had been one of ten small boys brought to the front hall of the orphanage, an area where visitors were welcomed but the orphans rarely ever saw. The head matron had tried to make the heavyset man and his profession sound exciting. "Which one of you will be lucky enough to be taken on by Mr. Bertram?" she had asked.

He recognized the insincere tone in her voice and had turned away. A thick hand had grabbed him by the tattered collar of his shirt and yanked him back.

Catching his first whiff of sweat and stale ale, he had been forced through the front doors of the orphanage and into the back of Mr. Bertram's wagon. Turning to the doors of St. Stephen's he watched the matron count off a few coins from one hand to the other before walking back inside.

Less than half an hour later, tears streaking his cheeks and in fear for

his life, he had been slung over Mr. Bertram's shoulders and hauled up a rickety ladder to the peak of a steep rooftop. The large man had hastily tied a rope around the chest of his new, trembling apprentice and forced a broom into the boy's hand. Then he had been picked up and shoved into a narrow, black opening and told to be quick about scrubbing the insides of the chimney or he'd find himself stranded with no way out.

Ib had thought that his life couldn't get any worse, but he was wrong. Within six months, knocked about and bruised, Mr. Bertram had forced him to go up on the rooftops late at night, then sneak down chimneys to steal from the homeowners. He was no longer a chimney sweep, but a common thief, one whom his boss was always quick to say would swing from the hangman's noose if they ever got caught.

Ib hated Mr. Bertram, but he also hated himself for what he had been forced to become.

The building passed. The horse and cab turned down another road.

Ib wiped his sleeve against the corner of his eyes and sat back down. He remained silent for the rest of the journey.

As they alighted from the hansom at the gates to the Delby Manor, Professor Delby stopped and looked around him. Ib saw the green of the lawn and the flowers inside the gates and remembered to smile.

"So, my lab assistant *extraordinaire*," the Professor said as he opened the gate, "we have been witness to one half of an incredible process. Do you realize what is happening?"

He looked to the Professor. There was something in Professor Delby's endless enthusiasm that he hoped he would never tire of hearing.

"Pterrence is starting to frighten all of London?" he guessed.

The Professor waved the suggestion away and shook his head.

"From the beginning of time people have feared what they don't understand, Ib," he said, closing the gate. "Think about it for a moment: are you frightened of Pterrence?"

Ib thought about it as they walked towards the manor. But only for a moment.

"Are you asking, Professor, if I am frightened of a brass and gearwork Pteranodon that has somehow come to life and is capable of breathing flames?"

The Professor seemed confused.

"Why, Ib. I'm surprised at you," Professor Delby said, sounding a trifle hurt. "You speak of Pterrence as if he is a marvel of mechanical mayhem! Is that all he is to you?"

He started to answer but stopped. He tried to work out how best to say this.

"Yes."

It was Professor Delby's turn to study the person walking next to him. After a short time, the Professor burst out laughing, reaching over to shake Ib's shoulder playfully.

"I almost forgot what a sophisticated sense of humor you have, Ib! You actually had me believing that for a moment." Professor Delby continued laughing until they neared a flowering bush with yellow blossoms.

"Of course, you know Pterrence better than that," Professor Delby said as he bent over to smell the flowers. "Pterrence is only gears, cables and brass. Why, he is a nothing but a machine, Ib!"

"Mind you," he added, picking one of the blooms and threading the stem through a jacket buttonhole, "not every invention goes flying off in such a dramatic fashion as our Pterrence did." He picked a second flower and threaded it through the buttonhole at Ib's collar. "That is why knowing your inventions is so crucial. You worked on Pterrence just before you put the fire in his belly. You know what a fine and considerate invention he is!"

"The kind that burns his way out of a laboratory right after being set in motion?" he suggested.

Professor Delby shook his head.

"Pterrence was simply a bit confused. Bewildered. Startled by his new surroundings. Don't you see? It is Pterrence who has cause to be frightened, not these easily panicked people in the streets of London."

They approached the front steps.

Finally, Ib asked the question he was afraid he already knew the answer to.

"Professor, why is Pterrence going to Hyde Park and the Bransford Coal Yard?"

Professor Delby's face brightened.

"Why, Ib," he laughed. "Surely you already know the answer to that!"

Ib sighed. With a nod he said, "Pterrence is feeding himself. He's putting the coal in his furnace and drinking to replenish the water in the boiler."

Professor Delby's chest expanded with pride. "And to think, Ib, we are here to see it all!"

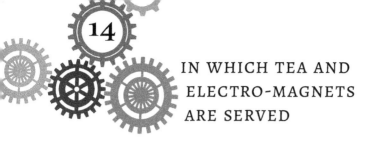

Ib was hanging his coat on a hook in the foyer when the Professor roared, "BENTLEY!"

"Sir?"

Professor Delby jumped, landing clumsily on the entryway wall.

"How do you *do* that?"

"Do what, sir?"

"Appear out of thin air like that?" the Professor demanded.

"I appeared from within the library, sir. While one supposes it might be possible that the library contains air in varying degrees of thickness, I can assure you I was fully in corporeal form when I was there."

Professor Delby narrowed his eyes.

"Bentley," the Professor glowered, "would you please be so kind as to ask the two men who followed us home from our outing today if they would care for some tea?"

"Is Sir referring to the two gentlemen attired in black overcoats and bowler hats who are currently standing outside the manor gates?"

"Indeed, Sir is," Professor Delby said huffily. "And how did you know they were there?"

"I happened to be in one of the second-floor rooms when Sir and Master Ib returned to the manor gates. The two gentlemen in question exhibited little skill in concealing themselves or their motives."

"You mean someone has been following us?" Ib asked, wiping the newfound dampness from his palms.

"Considering they have been following us rather clumsily since we left the Royal Mews this morning, I can only assume they are from the Royal Guard," Professor Delby said. "I'm sure the Guard shall be sending Buckingham Palace regular reports on our progress."

"It would appear that Sir and Master Ib had an eventful morning."

"Just a trifling matter, really," Professor Delby said with a wave of his hand. "Oh, good, Mrs. Hudson," the Professor added as the cook appeared. "Ib and I shall require a strong pot of the Earl of Grey's tea. The oil from the bergamot orange does wonders for the problem-solving faculties. You see, my lab assistant *extraordinaire* and I have a great deal of concerted cogitation to ahead of us this afternoon."

"Pterrence has frightened Queen Victoria's children," Ib explained to her.

"Oh, dear," Mrs. Hudson said. "Not again."

"Only the younger Princesses," Professor Delby insisted, turning to Bentley. "You will likely agree, Bentley, that Prince Albert Edward would have been quite charmed by our Pterrence!"

"We have forty-five hours left to get Pterrence back. Otherwise, the Professor and I disappear forever in a dungeon in the Tower of—"

"Yes, yes," Professor Delby interjected. "Far more details than we need to go into now, Ib."

"And Mr. Bertram knows I'm alive," Ib added.

Mrs. Hudson gave a "tsk-tsk" under her breath.

"That old pot-bellied ruffian?" the Professor said. "He was only asking about a silly sweeper. Bentley, I think that poor dead lad had something with him when he expired in the fireplace. See if you can find it, won't you?"

"Certainly, sir. Shall I begin my search before or after inquiring as to the tea requirements of your less-than-secretive admirers?"

"Oh, after I should think, don't you?" the Professor asked. "Proper decorum would seem to dictate people before things."

"Of course, sir," Bentley said as he turned and left the room.

Ib followed Professor Delby into the library and watched as the white-haired man tapped at his chin. The Professor walked back and forth beside the wall of bookshelves. Looking down at Professor Delby's feet, Ib could see that the path along the rug where the Professor was pacing was much thinner, the carpet's colors more faded.

He tried thinking of a way to capture Pterrence as well, but his thoughts were too much of a jumble. There was too much he didn't understand.

Professor Delby looked to be deep in conversation with himself.

He glanced in the air above him, at times nodding or shaking his head. He looked at various objects in his hands, items that were invisible to Ib, only to shake his hands free of whatever he imagined he was holding in order to pick up a new train of thought.

Ib felt a shaking sensation on his leg. Reaching into his pants pocket, he pulled out a shiny brass egg and held it in his open palm. It snapped and sputtered and gave a final hop as Sophie landed on her feet. She shook her head and thin leather wings, then turned to Ib. She twittered something that did not sound very friendly.

"Oh, now you want to come out?" he quietly chided. "Not when we were getting captured by the Royal Guard or trying to find Pterrence?"

Sophie turned her back on Ib, looking over her shoulder at him. She shook out her wings once more.

He turned again to his employer. Professor Delby was checking what appeared to be an imaginary piece of paper against the equally imaginary items on an invisible shelf in front of him.

"This, Master Ib," Bentley said, causing him to jump, "is one of the methods Professor Delby employs when attempting to solve a particularly complex quandary."

He looked back at Bentley. Why couldn't he speak in words Ib could understand?

"As Sir takes inventory of those items he believes might prove beneficial to a solution, I have found that he responds neither to questions nor interruptions of any kind."

"So, he's thinking?"

"Indeed, Master Ib."

"Has Professor Delby always been like this?"

"Generations of Delbys have each had their own idiosyncrasies. One suspects it might be the price of genius, Master Ib."

Ib nodded. He understood enough of what Bentley had said to get the idea.

"In case your astute mind has begun looking for commonalities and causalities, Master Ib, might I suggest you ruminate upon that most common of liquid refreshments?"

"What?" he asked, turning back to Bentley, only to find the manservant had left the room as silently as he had come in.

He frowned. It was as if the man enjoyed making his life that much more difficult.

A small teacart rattled down the hallway and into the Library, pushed by Mrs. Hudson. The cart held a large, ornate teapot, a plate of scones and biscuits and three small bowls containing the most richly colored jams he had ever seen.

"Tea, Professor," Mrs. Hudson said.

Sophie gave a happy twitter and flew to meet the cart, landing close to the jams. Ib couldn't tell if she was looking at them or trying to sniff them. He wondered if Sophie could smell.

They watched Professor Delby examine two invisible objects, one in each hand. Apparently deciding on the one in his left hand, he reached out his right hand to set that object on the shelf beside him. As he pulled his hand away, he lurched to the side, scrambling to catch the invisible object that had, seemingly, fallen off the shelf.

"Bentley says the Professor is thinking," Ib said quietly.

"That he is, Ib. I've seen the Professor do this sort of thing many times before. Now, how do you take your tea, dear?" Mrs. Hudson asked, the teapot poised over a china teacup.

He looked at the teacup and then back to the housekeeper.

"Milk? Sugar?" she asked.

He felt his face grow warm. Looking back at the teacup, he admitted, "I don't know. I haven't had much tea before."

Mrs. Hudson gave another quiet, "tsk tsk." Ib kept his eyes on the intricate design on the teacup.

"Well, I can assure you that, too, will change," Mrs. Hudson said, pouring the steaming liquid into the cup. "No one under my care goes without a regular cup of tea, especially not a growing boy like yourself."

He ventured a glance up at Mrs. Hudson, but she was busying herself with the creamer.

"When my brothers were your age, they were very partial to both milk and sugar when we had it. I think that's a fine place to start, don't you?"

He nodded with a slight shrug.

"You don't mind if I sit here a minute, do you?" Mrs. Hudson asked. "Only, if I pour the Professor his tea now it might go cold by the time he comes back to us."

Ib smiled. It would be good to have some nice company.

He looked over at the scones, but a sudden worry drove away his hunger.

"Mrs. Hudson," he said, "I don't want to be thrown in a dungeon for the rest of my life."

"Well, I should hope not!" the cook replied, stirring some milk into her own tea.

"But the Police Commissioner and the Royal Guard are going to put us there if we can't get Pterrence back!"

Mrs. Hudson set her teacup and saucer in her lap.

"Ib, I know this may be small comfort right now, but we have seen Professor Delby get himself out of a good many, well, *unusual* situations in the past."

"Did the Queen have people clearing out the bottom of the Tower of London for him before?" he asked.

"Well, no," Mrs. Hudson admitted. "I don't recall anything quite that bad before."

He set his teacup down. He wasn't hungry.

"How many 'unusual situations' have you seen before?"

"Oh, more than I can count, I'm sure," Mrs. Hudson laughed. "Are you sure you won't have a scone? The jams are quite tasty if I say so myself."

He shook his head, trying to smile his appreciation.

They turned their attention back to the Professor who was shaking his head and shoving piles of imaginary items off an equally imaginary surface. He tilted his head to the left and reached forward. Out of the air, Professor Delby picked up a small, invisible something. Holding it carefully between his thumb and forefinger, he stretched out the object. It looked as if the Professor had something long and thin in mind.

The Professor's eyes widened. He quickly began winding it around another small, unseen object. When he was done, he looked at his empty hands and nodded, a satisfied smile upon his lips.

"Tell me, Ib," he said, gesturing to his lab assistant with the still invisible object. "How is your research with electro-magnets coming along?"

"My what?" Ib asked, his heart working to catch up after missing a beat.

"Electro-magnets!" Professor Delby pointed to the figment of science

in his hand in a way that made Ib think he should be able to see it as well. "As I recall, you submitted a paper on your most recent discoveries in electro-magnetism to the Royal Society just the other week."

"Ah, no, Professor," Mrs. Hudson corrected, pouring another cup of tea. "That was your research and your paper."

The Professor jerked his head back, looking from side to side. "I did?" he asked. "Are you certain that was me, Mrs. Hudson?"

"Yes, Professor. Our Ib hasn't been made a Fellow at the Royal Society quite yet. Now take a seat and have some tea."

Professor Delby dutifully sat down. He looked over at his housekeeper as if seeing her for the first time that day.

"Good lord, Mrs. Hudson! Where did you come from?"

"The kitchens, Professor," she said, giving Ib a wink. "Where I was busy making some of your favorite Thinking Tea. I had a feeling you and Ib might have a great deal to discuss today."

"This is simply uncanny, Ib," the Professor said, taking the offered teacup and saucer. "Mrs. Hudson has the most amazing ability to read my mind at times. For instance, before I could even suggest the idea, here she is with precisely the tea we need!"

"She met us at the doorway, Professor," Ib said, looking from Mrs. Hudson to his employer. "Don't you remember?"

"Ah, yes. That." Professor Delby said with a wave of his hand. "But that was days ago. Since then, I've been down in the lab, racking my head over how to resolve our little misunderstanding with Her Majesty." He took a sip of tea and set the cup and saucer down on a table beside him.

"However, it was all for the best, Ib. Why, look at this!" The Professor searched his empty hands. "I had it a moment ago," he said. Reaching into his pockets and finding them to be empty as well, he stood to look on the seat and the floor around his chair.

"Well, no matter," the Professor said. "Tell me, my lab assistant extra-ordinaire, how would you propose we recapture an easily startled steam and gearwork Pteranodon replica using a length of wire?"

A length of wire? Ib tried to think what use a bit of wire might be in helping to catch Pterrence. Was the Professor proposing they go fishing for him? That made no sense at all.

Ib decided the safest thing to do was simply repeat what Professor Delby had said.

"Electro-magnets."

The Professor's jaw dropped. He held up a hand for silence before Ib could even say a word.

"Mrs. Hudson," the Professor said, shaking his head with disbelief. "Did you hear what my new lab assistant said?"

"Professor?" Mrs. Hudson asked.

"My new lab assistant is recommending we recapture our Pterrence with some of the most startling technology our age has to offer. What a stupendous thought!"

The Professor nodded his head. There was a far-off look in his eyes.

Ib wasn't sure if this meant he could start breathing again or not.

"Mrs. Hudson, this is truly one of the most forward-thinking scientists I have ever had the pleasure of working with. One day people will marvel that we knew him when he was only a lad."

"That they will, Professor," Mrs. Hudson said, smiling and nodding to Ib. "Now, Professor, would you care for strawberry, cherry or gooseberry jam on your scone?"

"Oh, gooseberry, I should think!" He sat down and took an enthusiastic bite of his scone.

Ib collapsed back into his chair, his breath escaping in a rush. Sophie flew from the teacart to Ib's shoulder. She pecked at his earlobe. When he turned to look at her, she stroked the tip of his nose with her wing.

"Ib, which jam would you like?" Mrs. Hudson asked.

Ib smiled at the brass bird and passed the smile on to Mrs. Hudson.

He shrugged his shoulders, trying not to jostle Sophie. "Which do you think I would like?" he finally asked.

"I think you'll like them all, dear," Mrs. Hudson said, adding, "although the gooseberry might take some getting used to."

He nodded, his smile widening just a bit.

"My lord," the Professor said, setting down his scone, the plate clinking against the saucer on the side table. "The post! I must send out missives to the other Fellows at the Royal Society immediately!" He shook his head, adding, "What am I saying? We must also contact my other old chums from the London Electrical Society too if we're to

be successful! There is so much that needs to be done in the next few hours to prepare!"

Professor Delby dashed from the room, mumbling about parchment, pens, postage, persimmons, and ... *whatnots*.

Sophie jumped from Ib's shoulder, chirping excitedly, before settling down on the teacart again, this time looking at an empty saucer. She tweeted and tapped at the china plate with her brass beak before looking back at Mrs. Hudson.

"Are you quite certain, Sophie, dear?" Mrs. Hudson asked.

Sophie nodded, twittering.

Mrs. Hudson poured a small amount of tea onto the saucer. Sophie jumped onto the edge of the plate and reached over towards the liquid. She scooped up a tiny bit, and then angled her head back, making a faint metallic gulping sound.

"I suppose I'm spoiling her," Mrs. Hudson said. "But she does get so thirsty at times."

Ib sat still in his chair for several moments. It wasn't until Mrs. Hudson began to pour herself a cup of tea that he felt the courage to speak again.

"Mrs. Hudson," he said, "I ..." But then Ib couldn't think of what to say. Instead, he raised his open palms upward, then dropped them onto his legs.

"Yes, dear, I know," Mrs. Hudson said, stirring her tea. "And so is the Professor."

He looked at his own, untouched cup of tea. Taking a sip, along with the milk and sugar, there was a faint taste of bitter orange. He decided he liked it.

"Mrs. Hudson," he said, trying again, "What does the Professor think I was suggesting?"

"I haven't the faintest idea, dear," she replied. "But I shouldn't let that worry you. Life with Professor Delby is exciting enough without having to know all the whyfors and the *whatnots*."

He took another long sip of tea. It made his mind feel clearer and more focused.

"What is the Royal Society?" he asked.

"It has a long, fancy name," Mrs. Hudson said. "The Royal Society of

London for Improving Natural Knowledge or some such thing. Professor Delby was quite pleased to be made a member some years ago."

"And the London Electrical Society?"

"Oh, my," she said with a laugh. "Now that was an enthusiastic bunch! All sorts of gentlemen working with that strange electrici-thingy. They haven't met since the Professor caused a lightning storm inside that nice Mr. Gassiot's house."

"What is electricity?" he asked, shifting in the chair. "Does it have something to do with magnets?"

"That is one of the many things I have chosen not to bother myself with," Mrs. Hudson said, pursing her lips as she sipped at her tea. "Not since the day I brought some lunch down to the laboratory and found the Professor standing over one of his electrici-thingy devices. Sparks were shooting about all around him, singeing his clothes and papers. And there the Professor stood, his white hair straight up on end!"

Ib stared at her, his mouth open.

"That is exactly how I reacted, dear!" she replied.

Minutes later Professor Delby rushed back into the library, waving several folded pieces of paper in his hand.

"Ib, quickly!" he said. "Your coat and hat. We must get these off to the Royal Mail right away if we're to receive the supplies and assistance we need in time!"

"Which supplies and in time for what, Professor?" he asked.

"Why, the Leyden jars to generate the electricity we need to set your electro-magnetic trap in time for Pterrence's next appearance at the Bransford Coal Yard, of course!"

15

IN WHICH IT TAKES A FORMER ELECRICAL SOCIETY TO BUILD THE WORLD'S FIRST PTERANODON PTRAP

In the Bransford Coal Yard, Ib stared at a collection of the oddest glass containers he had ever seen.

Each Leyden jar was encased in a thin layer of shiny metal that came halfway up the sides. Inside the containers, another thin layer of the same metal went almost to the top. A wooden lid sat atop each jar with a brass rod sticking out. Inside the jars, the brass rods were attached to a chain that reached to the bottom of each jar. Outside the jars, the rods were each topped with an ominous-looking brass ball.

"Twelve," Professor Delby said.

"Twelve?" Ib asked.

"Yes. Twelve should be sufficient, don't you agree, Ib?"

He took a deep breath. Twelve was certainly a number, that much he knew. But, twelve of what? And for what? There were far more than twelve of the strange glass jars in front of him.

He took another breath.

After a careful moment's consideration, he decided on what he thought would be the safest answer. Hoping his voice conveyed just enough of a question to make it sound as if he was still considering the possibilities, he said:

"Twelve?"

Professor Delby stepped back, tapping at his chin.

"You are correct, my lab assistant *extraordinaire*," he acknowledged, shaking his head and laughing at himself. "After all, this is your experiment! I must respect your insights in such matters. A mind as highly developed in scientific reasoning as yours is one that should be trusted implicitly. Obviously, you are taking into account the importance of our success today. Why take a chance with only twelve Leyden jars when we have the opportunity to use so many more?"

"An excellent observation, sir," Bentley said, raising his voice slightly to be heard over the coal cart lumbering past them. "One born of fine scientific reasoning. Perhaps we should begin establishing the experimental site presently. I believe we have less than thirty minutes before we can expect Pterrence to return."

Bentley's tone was a bland as always, but Ib's jaw still clenched at his words.

"A sound suggestion, indeed," Professor Delby said. "Would you help orchestrate the placement and charging of the jars around the iron platform?"

"Certainly, sir. I already have the barrel of water Sir brought with us from the Manor in position to fill the incoming Leyden jars."

At the entryway gates Ib saw two men in long, dark coats and bowler hats staring at the Professor. He recognized them as the men he had seen outside the Delby Manor gates. Despite the Professor's lack of concern about them, he would have preferred they not be there at all.

Another bewhiskered gentleman stepped in from the side, blocking his view of the Royal Guardsmen. The gentleman smiled and held out his hand to Professor Delby.

"Quite the reunion you've orchestrated here, Delby," the man said. "I can't wait to see what you have planned this afternoon!"

As much as he wanted to avoid Bentley, Ib was still drawn to the curious iron bar at the far end of the courtyard. Long and narrow, it sat raised on two wooden boxes. He moved closer, hoping to see what all the Leyden jars had to do with it.

"I say," Ib heard a voice behind him say, "lovely day for a bit of science, eh Cosgrove?"

Ib turned to see two leisurely men of science behind him. He turned back towards the iron platform, not wanting to be noticed.

"Science?" the man named Cosgrove scoffed. "Science is supposed to be verifiable and repeatable, Hancock. Neither applies to any experiments our friend conducts."

"Now, Cosgrove, I will admit I'm not sure if Delby is a scientist who

masquerades as a magician or a magician who confounds with science. I do know, though, that whenever Delby puts on an experiment like this, we are sure to be entertained!"

Cosgrove harrumphed.

"And that, I suspect, is precisely the reason you're here today, isn't it? I know it's why I am."

"You there, boy," the stuffy Cosgrove said. Ib felt the man's walking stick poke him from behind. "You must be Delby's new assistant, eh?"

Ib rubbed the back of his arm before saying, "Yes, sir."

"Tell me then," the man huffed, "what is this experiment all about then?"

Ib looked Cosgrove in the eye.

Mustering his most confident voice, Ib said, "Electro-magnets."

"That much is obvious, boy," Cosgrove said, making no pretense to hide his annoyance. "You have an iron bar with wires coiled around each end that are to be connected to a supply of Leyden jars. What else could it be?"

"Ah, but Cosgrove," Hancock interjected. "I think you may be missing the point. Our young colleague is not simply creating any electro-magnet. He is creating the largest electro-magnet London has ever seen!"

"And, therefore, the strongest electro-magnet as well," added a third gentleman. "Dr. Weekes, young man," he said, extending his hand to Ib. "It is a pleasure to meet such an engaging young scientist."

Ib recognized an unexpected kindness in the man's eyes and shook his hand.

"Yes, yes, Weekes," Cosgrove grumbled. "I'm trying to find out the purpose of such a thing. There must be some reason to go to all this trouble other than to say it has been done."

"Precisely my question!" said another gentleman who approached with a friend. "Bigger and stronger is all well and good, but to what purpose?"

All of the men looked expectantly at Ib.

Ib swallowed.

"Oh, yes, yes indeed," he said, nodding, hoping the right words would come to him. "Of course, there is a purpose to all this. A very important one. Her Majesty is quite insistent upon this succeeding."

"A Royal decree!" Dr. Weekes said. "And for your first public experiment. Well done, lad!"

"Yes, but what about the details?" one of the men complained. "What could you possibly be trying to hold down with such an electro-magnet?"

"You don't suppose it's another one of Delby's *mishaps*, do you?" another man said, joining the group.

"You mean like his electric kites?" asked Hancock.

"Or the unsinkable underwater boat?" asked another.

"Or a giant gearwork flying Pteranodon?" Ib asked.

"Oh, do be sensible, boy," Cosgrove scoffed. "We are men of science here. If you are not willing to provide us with the details of why we all interrupted our days to assemble here—"

"You know, Cosgrove," Dr. Weekes said with a faint smile, "I recall you affecting a similar lack of details concerning one of your last experiments before the Electrical Society."

Cosgrove startled amid the nods surrounding him.

"That, Weekes, was no youthful flair for the dramatic but a well-reasoned attempt at keeping the minds of my respected colleagues open and receptive to something quite unexpected and remarkable." Cosgrove drew back his shoulders, half-closing his eyes. "I sincerely doubt this young nobody can produce anything today even half as impressive for us."

"I have no doubt, sir, that we will accomplish something far more unexpected and remarkable," Ib said, drawing back his own shoulders.

"Ho ho!" Professor Delby said, coming up from behind the circle of men. "I think we can all be assured of an entertaining and insightful afternoon. My lab assistant extraordinaire has a mind just made for science! I have had nothing but the deepest respect for his discoveries for months now!"

"Wherever did you find such a clever lad, Delby?" asked Dr. Weekes.

Ib felt the color drain from his face.

"We met—" Ib tried to explain.

"Simple enough!" Professor Delby said, said, placing a hand on Ib's shoulder. "I found this poor lad dead in my fireplace some time ago! Ever since then he's been an invaluable part of my work. I suggest when each of you returns home you check your own fireplaces!"

Ib slowly lowered the hand covering his eyes. He wondered if he might be able to hide in the confusion of the coal yard until the experiment was finished.

To his amazement, the men were smiling and laughing amongst themselves. Dr. Weekes even gave him a knowing wink. An older scientist leaned close to the person standing next to him and whispered something before motioning to Professor Delby rather than to Ib.

"Now then, Delby," Cosgrove said. "You asked us all to come out today, but you failed to explain exactly why. Your assistant has done nothing but avoid our questions. Tell me, what are you trying to accomplish with such a large electro-magnet, and here in a common coal yard of all places?"

There came a shout from the coal yard gates. Looking past the men around him Ib saw several coalmen pointing to the skies. Past the gates, Ib could also see the two Royal Guardsmen, looking to the sky as well.

"I do apologize, gentlemen," Professor Delby said, his eyes alight. "It seems the focal point of our experiment will be making his arrival in a few moments. In lieu of an explanation, I ask that you allow us to demonstrate instead. If you will all take your places, we shall begin."

"And where, exactly, would our places be, Delby?" someone asked.

"Ah, yes," Professor Delby said, looking about him as coalmen were scrambling to push wagons and horses along the walls of the coal yard. "Places," he repeated, tapping his chin. "There are usually places in such instances, aren't there?"

"Professor," Ib said, trying to sound calm. "There is a doorway with some windows next to it over there." He pointed to the opposite side of the coal yard and watched as a crowd of bewhiskered heads turned as one. "Would that do?"

"What did I tell you, gentlemen?" the Professor said as the scientists hurriedly departed. "A remarkable lad. See how well he plans out his first public experiment? He even has an observational area prepared for you all!"

Ib followed the Professor towards the iron platform. He stopped several feet away, not certain he wanted to go any closer.

He could see one of the men rapidly turning a handle that spun what looked to be a small glass cylinder. In front of the cylinder was a T-shaped bit of metal, lying on its flat side, attached to a raised stand.

The base of the T held a brass ball, slightly smaller than the ball that stuck out of the top of the Leyden jar only inches away.

He was a few feet from the men and the strange devices when he stopped in place. A thick, blue light flashed between the two brass orbs, accompanied by a powerful zapping sound.

Once the blue light faded, he could see the man's hair was standing straight on end.

Ib tried to swallow but found he couldn't.

"Nothing like the divine spark of electricity to awaken the senses and remind us we're alive, eh Ib?" Professor Delby said as he clapped Ib on the back, propelling him toward the iron bar.

Ib jerked his hands away as another blue flash ignited from a different part of the iron platform. He was certain he could feel the hairs on his neck rising.

"Although, a bracing cup of tea on a cold day and one of Mrs. Hudson's fine tarts will do just fine in a pinch, I suppose. Bentley! Are we ready?"

"Nearly, sir. If Sir and Master Ib would each take a static charger, I believe we shall have twenty Leyden jars fully charged in time for the imminent arrival of your wayward replica."

Bentley gestured to one of the unused hand-cranked devices.

"Simply turn the handle, Master Ib. The principles of science shall take care of the rest," Bentley said. Ib watched the Professor cranking a handle as the manservant gestured for several men carrying piles of coal in their leather aprons to come towards him.

"Place your coal on the platform, gentlemen, to the center of their coiled wire circles," Bentley instructed.

Ib watched a young gentleman work the mechanism in front of him. The strange device had a handle and a T-shaped piece of metal on top. The man cranking the shaft turned to him and gave an appreciative nod as a blue spark buzzed between the orb at the end of the T-shaped metal and the Leyden jar in front of him. Ib jerked back slightly as something stung his nose. A second blue burst came from the contraption, convincing Ib that the device must be even more dangerous than it looked.

He wondered if Mrs. Hudson's fear of "electrici-thingy" wasn't justified.

The other men were all turning similar crank handles with equal vigor. To a man, they were concentrating on their task, their expressions hardly changing when another blue spark shot out before them.

As he began turning his own crank, he tried to push aside the thought that perhaps it was electricity that made Professor Delby so odd.

"I saw you giving old Cosgrove what-for over there," the young man said. "Bully for you, that's what I say."

Ib nodded as he continued to turn the crank. A blue spark shot out in front of him, taking his breath along with it.

"I —," he said, pointing to the amazing thing that had just happened. He had seen the sparks before, but this one was different — he had created this one. He blinked. The blue spark had not hurt at all. If anything, Ib felt his skin tingle slightly with the knowledge that he had done something unbelievably amazing.

Moments later, a second blue spark jumped out in front of him. "Isn't science incredible?" he exclaimed.

"Exactly!" the man said, a blue spark of his own appearing before them.

Ib began cranking faster.

"Time, Bentley?" Professor Delby called out.

"Pterrence has begun his descent, sir. We must be clear of the area within two minutes."

"Are the discharging mechanisms all in place?" the Professor asked.

"Indeed, sir. The release wire has been attached and is extended to an area behind the coal wagons to your right."

"Our signals are clearly understood?" the Professor asked.

"Your raised hand, sir, lowered sharply," Bentley responded.

"Excellent!" Professor Delby said. "Then we shall have Pterrence back in no time!"

As the Professor spoke his creation's name, his expression fell. His eyes narrowing, Professor Delby shook his head and sighed.

"That Pterrible Pteranodon," he said.

"The Diabolically Dangerous Dinosaur," Bentley agreed.

"The Preadolescent, Prehistoric Provocateur."

"The Creaking Cretaceous Creation."

"The Fractious Facsimile Fossil," Professor Delby said.

"The Reprehensible, Repairable Reptile."

Professor Delby grew silent, looking off somewhere far beyond the walls of the coalyard.

The Professor shook his head with a start, asking, "Where was I?"

"Sir was about to conduct Master Ib's experiment in electo-magnetism which, if successful, shall recover your wayward Pteranodon."

"Ah, so I was! Brilliant plan as ever, Ib!"

Turning to the men still cranking sparks nearby, the Professor called out, "Gentlemen, I believe it is time for those of us on the front lines to take our places as well!"

Reluctantly, Ib carefully lifted his glass cylindrical mechanisms and carried them to a nearby wagon.

"What happens now, Professor?" he asked.

"Now, we wait and see if we have built and baited your trap correctly. If your hypothesis is correct and everything goes according to plan, Pterrence should be back in our control shortly. Then, tonight, we shall enjoy a leisurely celebration to the success of our experiment!"

Ib smiled. He liked the sound of that.

"But first, oh, lab assistant extraordinaire, you and I have one final piece to add to the trap!" Professor Delby gestured for Ib to follow him along the edge of the brick wall.

"Professor?" he hissed. "Where are you going?"

"It's where *we* are going, Ib. Follow along!"

Ib sighed and shook his head.

Overhead he heard a metallic shriek. The coal yard was now deserted; even most of the curious onlookers at the gates had left. He could make out the two Royal Guardsmen trying to make themselves look small by a gas lamp across the street.

Ib followed behind the Professor, staying close to the walls and the coal wagons. Incredibly, he saw Professor Delby was moving towards the electro-magnetic trap, not farther away from it.

They crept along until they reached a point behind the iron platform. Once there, the Professor motioned for him to assist in moving a large tarpaulin off to one side. Underneath, Ib saw what looked to be a large net with weights along the edges arranged neatly on the ground.

"Professor," he whispered, intimidated by the sudden empty quietness around them. "Why do you have a net?"

Professor Delby smiled and tapped his temple with his index finger.

"Your cunning trap will be enough to stun Pterrence, but only for a

moment," the Professor whispered in return. "Once Pterrence perches on our platform to eat, we shall rush forward, throwing this net over Pterrence's head!"

"Professor," he said, trying to keep his voice from rising. "Pterrence isn't going to sit there and let us throw a net over him!"

"Actually, Ib, he will," Professor Delby said as a wing-shaped shadow crossed over them. "Your ingenious electro-magnet shall take care of that!"

"He'll see us coming!" Ib protested.

"We shall sneak up behind him," the Professor said with certainty.

"We're too close to the building, Professor. Pterrence will land facing our direction and he'll see us!"

"But why on earth should he stay like that?" Professor Delby asked with a smile and a shake of his own head. "What is there to look at in this direction but a brick wall? Certainly, he will turn around on his perch to take in the view of the entire coal yard while he dines!"

"But he will see us when he lands!"

"Not at all! We shall be hiding. You under the tarpaulin and I under the very netting we shall use to capture him!"

"Under the netting?" he asked, already crawling under the tarpaulin. "Are you sure, Professor?"

"I can assure you, Ib, I am an old hand at such things," the Professor said covering himself. "This net shall only capture one creature today!"

A great dust cloud rose up from the ground as Pterrence landed. Ib could hear the wind growing stronger around him, almost as loud as his own heartbeat pounding in his ears. The wind settled and the silence was broken by a loud, "*Kawrr!*"

Ib lifted the tarpaulin enough to see Pterrence standing in front of him on the opposite side of the iron platform. The brass and gearwork Pteranodon clawed at the ground. He watched as the muted orange of Pterrence's eyes seemed to consider the display before him. He shut his eyelids, not wanting Pterrence to see his eyes.

There was an odd sound, something that combined a series of moving gears with metal scraping against metal. Ib peeked again from under his tarp. To his surprise, Pterrence had not only jumped onto on the iron

perch but, exactly as the Professor had suggested, had turned around to face the open coal yard.

"Ha ha!" Professor Delby whispered. He poked a triumphant finger through the netting. "Everything is proceeding exactly as planned! Ib, are you ready?"

Ib looked from the elated finger down into the netting, trying to see the Professor's face. Giving up, he whispered, "Yes, Professor."

"Excellent," Professor Delby grunted from under the net. "Just let me get out from under this and I shall give Bentley the signal to activate your electro-magnet!"

Slipping from under his tarp, he watched as various parts of the net rose and fell like bubbles boiling to the surface of a pot. "Professor," he hissed. "Do you need any help?"

"Heh, of course not!" the Professor grunted. "I'm only—*oof*—barely underneath this to begin with. Here, let me stand up and I shall—"

However, when Professor Delby attempted to stand, the netting caught about his feet and legs, sending him sprawling forward, one lurching stumble at a time.

One of the Professor's arms found its way clear of the netting and reached upward for freedom. Trying to catch his balance, Professor Delby brought that same arm down to his side. Unfortunately, as Ib remembered, this was also the signal the Professor had arranged with Bentley to pull on the string that would discharge all of the stored electricity in the Leyden jars and turn the iron platform into a giant electro-magnet.

A brilliant shower of blue sparks erupted from the base of the trap, followed by a molten orange glow. As the electricity flared, Pterrence dropped onto the platform. His wings lurched upward, then inward as he struggled against the electro-magnetic pull.

"Quickly Ib, throw the net!" Professor Delby called out from where he had fallen on the ground.

"I can't," Ib yelled. "You're wearing it, Professor!"

Professor Delby struggled for another moment. "Actually, I believe it is wearing me!"

Ib shook his head, trying to think what to do. Looking at the tarpaulin

at his feet he said, "I'll throw my tarpaulin over Pterrence's head, Professor. Maybe he'll be confused long enough for you to get out."

Ib grabbed at an edge of the tarpaulin and struggled to pull it behind him. In a few steps, the large cloth had opened up as he held it high.

The blue sparks and orange glow subsided, only to be replaced by an angry crackling and hissing coming from under the platform. Pterrence was striving to regain his footing when the Leyden jars became eerily silent. Gritting his teeth, Ib bounded on top of the iron platform close to Pterrence. In one sweeping motion, he leapt off the platform, throwing the tarpaulin over Pterrence's head.

All at once there was a blinding flash of light as the air around him filled with exploding bits of wooden jar lids, brass balls, rods, and chains.

Ib landed badly, rolling to a stop in the dirt of the coal yard. He covered his head as bits of glass and metal rained down on him. Peeking through his fingers, he saw a burst of flame erupt through the tarp, only a few feet over his head.

The mechanical Pteranodon shook his head forcefully, flinging the burning cloth off of him.

Ib tried to stay very still.

Pterrence spread out his brass-framed leathery wings and jumped on his perch. He let out another deafening shriek and opened the front plate to his chest. Scooping in the coal that had been set out as bait, Pterrence breathed out another long fiery breath.

Then he looked down.

Ib saw the pale orange eyes meet his own. He covered his eyes with his hands. *Maybe if Pterrence couldn't see his eyes . . .*

He heard the sound of Pterrence's front plate closing, then felt the impact of brass and gears landing on the ground.

Ib peeked between the fingers of his hand. Pterrence's foot was inches from his face.

"I say, Ib," Professor Delby called out from somewhere behind Pterrence. "I should be out of this two shakes of a lamb's tail!"

"What?" he asked, his voice rising.

"Two shakes — *ugh* — of a lamb's tail!" Professor Delby said. "Mind you, I have never actually shaken the tail of a lamb, if that's what you're surprisingly vague question was asking. It is merely — *argh* — an expression!"

Pterrence lowered his head at his neck. Ib looked into two large oval domes that glowed a light orange.

"Have you subdued our runaway replica yet?" the Professor called out, his voice bounding with optimism

"Not exactly, Professor."

Pterrence moved his head back, and then bent a wing behind Ib.

He felt himself being lifted up off the ground by the collar of his coat, Pterrence's body creaking with the effort to lift him.

"If he should give you any trouble, tell him, in no uncertain terms, exactly what is expected of him!"

Ib found himself being dangled inches away from Pterrence's eyes.

"*Kawrr?*" Pterrence said.

"That's the stuff, Ib!" Professor Delby called out. "Show him—*ugh*—who is in charge! I shall extricate myself from this—*gack*—infernal web momentarily!"

Pterrence placed Ib gently back on the ground. He then reached his wing back around and poked the boy in the stomach.

"Y-yes," Ib said, nodding his head. "It's me. Ib. You-you remember me, don't you, Pterrence?"

Pterrence tilted his head. Slowly, he reached out and poked Ib in the stomach again.

"Would you please come home with us, Pterrence?" he asked hopefully. "We miss you very much. We really would like you to come back with us."

Pterrence tilted his head to the other side, a thin but steady stream of steam appearing from his nostrils.

"*Kawrr?*" Pterrence murmured.

"Ta da!" Professor Delby cried, bouncing to his feet and flinging the weighted netting behind him. A moment later, the Professor's foot, which was still caught in an open section of the netting, was pulled out from under him. With a loud, "Whoop!" the Professor fell face-first back to the ground.

Pterrence screeched in response. He opened his wings wide, lumbering past Ib. Pterrence stepped forward, his legs awkwardly trying to match the languid beating of his wings. Finally, he took to the air, barely missing the top of the coal yard's outer wall.

Ib's knees gave way. Sitting on the ground with scraps of cloth and wood burning around him, he watched as Pterrence soared over the London rooftops and away from the Bransford Coal Yard. Something like admiration soon gave way to thoughts of the dark, cold cell that was waiting for him at the bottom of the Tower.

"Never fear," Professor Delby called out, lifting his coal dust and dirt-streaked face to Ib. "A Delby is here!"

Ib buried his face in his hands.

Well, that was it, wasn't it? he thought. *I'll die old in a dungeon in the Tower.* He hoped he could remember how comfortable his bed had been in the Delby Manor and how delicious Mrs. Hudson's food was after decades in prison.

The sounds of a great many leisurely men of science coming out from their safely concealed viewing station brought Ib back to the coal yard.

"Well," Ib said, trying very hard to find a bright side to the miserable situation. "At least we only have one Pteranodon to deal with."

Professor Delby sat upright, tossing the netting aside with a flourish. "What did you say?" he asked.

"Nothing," Ib said quickly.

"No, no," the Professor insisted. "You said something momentous, something bursting with scientific meaning!"

"No, I didn't," Ib insisted.

"Something about an army of Pteranodons," Professor Delby said, the top of his head popping out from under his hat.

"All I said was, 'At least there is only have one Pteranodon to deal with!' I didn't say anything about an army of Pteranodons!"

"Well, good thing!" Professor Delby said, tapping his chin. "We haven't the time to build an entire army of Pteranodons. However..."

Professor Delby continued tapping at his chin, his eyes darting from side to side.

"Professor?" Ib ventured.

The Professor continued tapping his chin, his eyebrows arching as his eyes moved back and forth, calculating something that Ib failed to see.

"Professor?" Ib asked again, the hope draining from his voice.

He watched as the smile on Professor Delby's face grew wider.

"The parts, the pieces, the plans," the Professor mumbled aloud as he nodded.

"Professor?" Ib asked.

"What a wonderful age we live in, Ib," Professor Delby said, far-off look to his eyes. "Can you possibly imagine a more exciting time to be alive?"

17

IN WHICH A GREAT MANY THINGS HAPPEN IN THE NAME OF TREACLE TARTS

"What an inspired brain-wave!" Professor Delby said, hanging his coat on a hook in the foyer. "Why, Mrs. Hudson, you should have seen it. One moment our own Ib successfully orchestrates his first public experiment in electro-magnetism—"

"Pterrence got away," Ib said.

"—and the next moment he formulates a second astounding plan for resolving our little problem!"

"Pterrence got away," Ib repeated.

"Mind you," the Professor chuckled, "I did have to step in and put a more realistic polish to his initial solution—one undoubtedly influenced by his youthful enthusiasm and imagination!"

"I never said anything about creating an army of Pterosaurs," the boy said, shaking his head.

"And he received a most impressive round of applause and hearty congratulations from his fellow scientists after the experiment was complete. They deemed it quite the success!"

"All of the static dischargers melted and all of the Leyden jars blew up!" he said. "And on top of that, Pterrence escaped."

"If I may, Master Ib, science has its own, unique standards by which experiments are judged," Bentley responded. "By successfully holding Pterrence to the platform you demonstrated a practical application of large-scale electro-magnetic properties. Therefore, it was deemed a success amongst your most prestigious peers."

Ib shook his head against the thought.

"And now we must make haste and put Ib's ingenious idea into action. To the laboratory, Ib, posthaste!"

Professor Delby dashed across the hallway and down the stairs to the laboratory.

Ib shrugged his coat off his shoulders, still shaking his head.

"I'll see that Bentley brings you both down some refreshments shortly," Mrs. Hudson said. "You'd best follow the Professor downstairs. It sounds as if you have a busy evening ahead of you."

He ambled down the stairs, afraid of what he might find behind the heavy wooden doors to the laboratory.

"Ah, Ib, excellent!" Professor Delby said when Ib entered. "I do hope you don't mind, but I've taken the liberty of drawing up some quick sketches to help us put your brilliant plan into action. I would hate to have you think that I was attempting to appropriate any of your well-deserved glory. I simply thought it best to put some ideas down on paper for us to start with."

"No, Professor," he said. "This is more your idea than you know."

"Both modest and generous! I say, Ib, you possess the true spirit of collaborative science!"

Ib looked at the drawing and saw what looked to be a sketch of Pterrence. Only this Pterrence had a number of arrows pointing to different sections, with notes scrawled along the sides of the paper.

"Well, I must admit, Ib, your initial idea was a bit too far-fetched, even for me," Professor Delby chuckled. "Imagine! How would we possibly build an entire army of Pteranodons in the short amount of time allotted to us? How could we control them? Oh, I am sure in your mind you saw yourself riding heroically on the back of the lead Pteranodon, bridle in one hand while waving a shining sword in the other! However, we must ground ourselves in reality."

"Professor, please don't tell me we're going to build another Pteranodon."

"Why wouldn't I tell you that, my lab assistant extraordinaire?" Professor Delby asked. "Unless, of course, you'd like to be the one to announce what we shall be doing? That is it, isn't it?"

"No, Professor! What is to stop a second Pteranodon from flying off just like Pterrence?"

"Oh, that," the Professor said with a wave of his hand. "This Pteranodon will be different in several essential ways, Ib. I can guarantee we won't be taking any such chances with this replica of our replica."

Ib stared at the Professor.

"Professor, do you give your word that this Pteranodon will be different?"

"Mind you, we will be starting with some of the early prototype parts and pieces for Pterrence, but I can assure you this Pteranodon shall be different."

Ib's expression did not change.

Professor Delby stood erect, raising a solemn hand in the air.

"I give my word as a Scientist, as an Inventor and as a Seeker of Knowledge."

Ib sighed. It was as good as he was likely to get.

"But, Professor, why a second Pteranodon?"

"Why, Ib!" the Professor laughed. "That was your idea! And, I believe you are correct: we need to fight fire with fire—or more specifically, in this case, fight Pteranodon with Pteranodon. Well, not 'fight' exactly, something more along the lines of holding a summit."

"What?" he asked, shaking his head.

"Exactly! Now, I'd like you to start construction of the new wings while I begin building the frame and shaping brass sections to form the body."

After a short while, Bentley appeared in the doorway with a silver platter with drinks and presented it to the Professor.

"Liquid refreshment, sir?"

"A splendid idea, Bentley!" Professor Delby replied.

"Lemonade or water, sir?"

"Lemonade, by all means!"

Bentley turned to Ib.

"Master Ib, water or lemonade?"

"Lemonade, Mister Bentley."

Ib took the remaining glass and was about to say 'thank you' when he looked closely at its contents. There was something that kept nagging at the back of his mind.

"Mister Bentley," he asked, turning the glass around in his hand, "what is this drink made from?"

"Ho ho!" Professor Delby exclaimed. "What an amazing scientist, eh, Bentley? Ib is not only working on the wing structure of our second

Pteranodon but he is also working on a formula for an improved lemonade!"

Ib smiled but continued looking to Bentley for an answer.

"I believe, Master Ib, Mrs. Hudson follows the traditional recipe of lemons and sugar for additives and water for the base."

Ib held up his glass and nodded.

"Water," he mused, thinking this must have been what Bentley meant the day before.

Bentley nodded.

"Not just any water," Professor Delby said as he struggled to fit the hammered brass sheet onto the Pteranodon's back beside Ib, "but Delby water! The same water that has provided generations of Delbys with aqueous hydration and sustenance!"

Ib sniffed at the pitcher of plain water Bentley had brought with him. There had to be something different about the water, but what?

"The best of waters carry no scent, Master Ib," Bentley stated.

Ib set the glass down on his workbench.

"Professor, what do you know about the Delby well water?" he asked.

Carrying the brass sheet back to the bench with his shaping tools, Professor Delby thought a moment.

"I can tell you this, Ib. In all of my world travels, I have never found any water that is more rejuvenating. It is as if we Delbys have been drinking from our well for so long that this water is as much a part of us as our love for science."

Professor Delby struggled as he attempted to set the brass sheet down against a worktable without dropping it.

Ib shot Bentley an uncertain look.

"The same water that was in the Leyden jars yesterday?" he asked.

Bentley nodded. "And the same water, Master Ib, that you have been drinking in your tea, the same water in which much of your food has been prepared and the same water in which you bathed after making your rather impressive entrance to the Professor's library."

The brass sheet clattered onto the floor as the Professor took up his glass of lemonade again.

"Cheers, Ib! To our success tomorrow and a long and adventuresome future!"

Ib picked up the glass and breathed out through his nose.

Raising it toward the Professor, he said, "Cheers, Professor."

Even trying to find something strange about the water, the lemonade still tasted quite good.

The Professor happily returned to shaping his brass sheet with the leather hammer.

"And, of course, the same water that Mrs. Hudson and I have been sharing with the Professor for much of our lives, Master Ib."

From Ib's workbench came a sputtering sound. Ib looked to see Sophie's head sticking out of the top of her brass egg. Several snapping spins later, the bird jumped up and down on the bench, one wing gesturing to her chest.

"My apologies," Bentley said with a nod. "And the same water Sophie has been drinking for the entirety of her time in the Delby Manor as well."

Ib thought he saw the corner of Bentley's mouth turn upward a fraction of an inch.

The manservant nodded and left the room, closing the large wooden laboratory door behind him.

He tried to work out how all of the things that he knew about the water fit together. He thought about Pterrence's glowing eyes. He thought about the Leyden jars exploding around him. Then he tasted the citrusy sweetness on his tongue.

He had to admit his baths had been rejuvenating. Almost too rejuvenating.

Taking another look at his half-filled glass of lemonade, he walked over to the pitchers Bentley had set on the table. He poured from the one that he thought was lemonade, but plain water filled his glass. The lemonade changed from a bright yellow to pale yellow and then almost clear liquid.

Ib took a sip of his very watered-down lemonade. He liked the way it helped him think more clearly. In fact, a rather strange thought was forming in his mind.

When they finally retired for bed, the new creature had already begun

taking shape. Professor Delby had a large amount of brass sheeting, bars, and cabling left over from his time making Pterrence. There was even a rough Pteranodon framework sitting to one side of the laboratory that the Professor had begun welding.

The next day Ib noticed something rather peculiar. He had been working with nothing but the sounds of tools being used for who knows how long when it occurred to him how quiet it was. He had known quiet before—after all, chimneys and houses with sleeping occupants are not the noisiest of environments. What was strange, however, was how silent Professor Delby had been all day.

Looking at Professor Delby, Ib saw he was engrossed in his work. Ib understood that this was the clever and fastidious mind at work that had created both Pterrence and Sophie.

As haphazard and muddled as he might appear, once in the laboratory the Professor became extremely focused on his work, putting his full concentration into deliberate and well-planned actions. It was almost, Ib thought, like seeing two different people.

Later in the morning, as he continued working on the wings, a knock came at the laboratory door.

"Good day, Professor," Mrs. Hudson called. "Oh, hello, Ib, dear. Hello, Sophie."

Ib smiled. "Hello, Mrs. Hudson."

Sophie twittered happily from where she was perched on his workbench.

"Good afternoon, Mrs. Hudson," Professor Delby said, hammering a brass sheet into a domed shape. "As you can see, we're in the midst of some very complicated work."

"Certainly, Professor," Mrs. Hudson responded. "I should think that would go without saying."

Ib looked up from the arm rods, gears, and cables he was sorting through. Mrs. Hudson returned his smile and gave him a wink.

Professor Delby hammered his brass sheet three more times before he stopped, the hammer still raised in his hand. The professor arched his

right eyebrow. It looked as if the professor was searching for something just above that eyebrow.

"Doesn't what go without saying, Mrs. Hudson?" he asked.

"Why, that you're working on something complicated, Professor," she replied. "If you're working on something here below my kitchens, it's always complicated! In fact, I'm surprised you mentioned it at all."

The Professor lowered his right eyebrow and arched his left, still searching the space above him.

"Mrs. Hudson," the Professor said, "remind me again why I called you down here?"

"You asked me to have Ib go to the grocers for us when my shopping list was complete, Professor." She winked again at Ib.

"I did?" the Professor asked, lowering his hammer to the workbench. "Why would I do that?"

"To give our Ib a bit time in the sunshine, Professor," she said. "You'll recall I'm making treacle tarts for dessert tonight, and Ib was going to bring back the ingredients I'm missing."

"Treacle t—" Professor Delby's face made the smooth transition from deep annoyance to contented bliss in seconds. "Treacle tarts, eh?" he asked, tapping his fingers on his chin and leaving greasy spots behind.

With a quick nod, he turned to Ib.

"Best run along, Ib."

"Professor?" Ib asked, his hands deep in a tangle of wing cables.

"Ib," the Professor said, an air of explaining the obvious in his voice. "You have had Mrs. Hudson's treacle tarts dozens of times over the years. You must remember how delicious they are. Not to mention how particularly fond of them I am."

"No, Professor," he replied slowly. "This is only my third day here."

"Third day?" the Professor asked, aghast. "Third day? Don't be silly, Ib. You've been with us for ages now." Professor Delby shook his head, chuckling to himself. He picked up his hammer and pointed it to Ib playfully. "You have quite the sense of humor for a lab assistant *extraordinaire!*"

"But Professor," Ib said, taking a quick look at the clock on the laboratory wall, "we only have twenty hours left!"

"You know what they say, Ib," the Professor said, aligning his brass

sheet over the curved mandrel, "when you're faced with the possibility of disaster, you should grab hold of all the treacle tarts you can and eat them with gusto!"

"They say that?" he asked, trying not to sound too doubtful.

"Well, I said it, and that's good enough for me!" the Professor said with a smile.

And with that, Professor Delby returned to his hammering.

"Sophie," he asked. "Would you like to come with me?"

The shiny bird jumped into Ib's open hand, then snapped and sputtered back into a brass egg. Ib shrugged to himself and then put the egg in a vest pocket.

As they walked up the stairs to the kitchen Mrs. Hudson said, "It's fine for the Professor to lock himself up in that laboratory of his, but a growing boy needs some fresh air and sunshine in his days."

"Thank you, Mrs. Hudson," he said before adding, "The Professor and I don't have much time left."

Mrs. Hudson clucked her tongue as they reached the kitchen.

"Ib, dear, I have lost count of the times Professor Delby has gone on about his deadlines, his emergencies, and all of the things that need to be done this time to save the world as we know it."

He swallowed. "Save the world?" he asked.

Mrs. Hudson crinkled her eyes and tousled Ib's hair.

"Don't you worry your head over any of it, dear," she said. "I'm certain with your help Professor Delby will find a way out of this latest problem."

Ib's cheeks were warm from having his hair mussed, but in a good way.

The housekeeper handed him a folded piece of paper.

"Here is the list you are to give one of the grocers," she explained. "They will charge it to our account and pack the order up for you to bring back. Just go out the gates, turn right, and the shop is at the end of the sixth street. Here, I've written the name of the store here so you can match the letters. And, here, take a few pence with you to buy yourself something special."

He looked at the money and the paper. Old memories came to his mind.

"Mrs. Hudson," he said, finally.

"Yes, dear?"

He took a deep breath. In a rush he said, "The grocers don't know me. They might think I stole this list and am using it to steal food."

"Oh, Ib," Mrs. Hudson said, placing her hand on his shoulder.

He looked up. She was smiling, but he could also see a touch of sadness in her eyes as well.

"I've already written a note at the bottom of the list introducing you to our grocer, Mrs. Wiseman."

She cupped his cheek with her hand. "I'll admit we're an odd household by most people's standards. But Ib, dear, you're one of us now. We all, somehow, belong to one other."

She looked up at a clock on the wall. "My word, look how late it's gotten! You'd best run along, Ib, if I'm going to have those treacle tarts ready for the Professor's dessert." She pulled a lace kerchief from her sleeve and dabbed at the corner of her eyes.

Walking down the long hallway to the foyer, he saw Bentley sorting through the afternoon mail. The manservant gave a slight nod.

He thought he saw Bentley's eyes settle on the money in his hand.

"It's for the grocers," he said, defensively. "Mrs. Hudson is making treacle tarts for dessert tonight."

Bentley's eyebrow arched a fraction of an inch.

"Of the many wonders of this world, Master Ib, Mrs. Hudson's tarts are amongst the finest. Prepare to be delighted, young lab assistant *extraordinaire*."

Ib shrugged to himself as he walked out of the foyer.

Closing the front door to the Manor behind him, Ib thought Mrs. Hudson was right. It was an odd household. However, just like his questions about the Professor's sanity, he realized it no longer mattered to him.

He had been wrong that first time he had been forced down a chimney. Life had gotten better. Much better. He was part of an unexpected and curious family now.

Gravel crunched under his shoes as he hurried down the path to the gates. He brushed against some of the flowers and smelled the wonderful fragrances that accompanied all of the colors around him. They were so different from the dirt and grays that had made up his life until now.

He brushed his hand over a cluster of small green leaves. His nose was rewarded with the scent of citrus. He continued toward the gate, the pleasant scent still on his fingers and in his nose.

Before he reached the gates, he stopped. He turned around again and saw the house through the trees and gardens. It was almost too good to be true.

Ib stepped through the gate and turned to close the latch. From the corner of his eye, he saw someone approaching. Thinking it was one of the Royal Guards watching Professor Delby, he clicked the latch shut and said, "I'm only going on an errand."

"GOTCHA!"

He felt a rough hand grab the back of his shirt and vest collar and rush him towards a familiar cart.

18

IN WHICH IB IS TAKEN FOR ANOTHER UNEXPECTED RIDE

"Ye don't looks so dead now, do ye?" the voice snarled in his ear. Off balance, Ib couldn't even fight when a burlap bag that smelled of stale ale and sweat covered his head and was pulled tight around his neck.

"That's right, ye miserable brat, just keep it quiet and ye won't get hurt," Mr. Bertram snarled. "Too much."

The man coughed and spat behind him. "And if ye don'ts, I might have to hand you back over to them coppers from yesterday. I can tells 'em you're the one what did all them robbery jobs, and that you dids them all yer own self. I knew nothin' about 'em." Ib felt rough rope being wrapped around his hands. "Besides, who're they gonna believe? A hard-workin' bloke like me or some thievin' chimney rat?"

The thief grabbed him by the rear of his pants and tossed him into the back of the open cart. He went sprawling blind into what he knew must be ladders and brooms before tripping over something sharp on the floor. His shoulder thudded into the back of the driver's bench.

"I don't likes it when my property starts thinking they's smarter than me," Mr. Bertram grumbled as he hoisted himself into the front of the cart.

Ib tried to think, but his shoulder and head hurt too much to allow him any peace. He was breathing hard, too hard. Each breath brought with it smells of the burlap sack, smells that reminded him of stealing and sleeping on cold floors.

Hot tears stung the corner of his eyes. Instead of wiping them away, though, he remembered having just seen tears. The ones on Mrs. Hudson's face minutes ago.

Now, all of that was gone.

"Ye put me in some nasty trouble with Brooker, ye did," Mr. Bertram said as the reins shook and the mule started pulling the card away. "I was wondering how ye was going to be able to pays me back fer all that. Lucky fer ye, I oughts to be able to get enough from selling off them fancy duds of yers to pay off what I owes him."

"These clothes aren't yours!" he shouted through the burlap bag.

"Oh, yes they are," Mr. Bertram sneered. "Yer my property, boy. I bought you simple as pie and don't ye ever ferget it. And that means anything ye might have is mine, including them fancy duds."

"I am not your property!"

"Ye are, too," the man said, sounding bored. "Now shut up ye miserable brat."

The front cartwheel hit a raised stone in the road, knocking his head against the raised edge of the cart.

He sniffled and tried to stay awake. In the darkness of the burlap sack, he saw lightheaded spots of twinkling lights that slowly faded into darkness.

He awoke sometime later to the Professor's voice echoing in his head. *"You're not a miserable brat. Why, you're a remarkable lad! An amazing apprentice."*

He wasn't a miserable brat, he remembered. Taking a deep breath, he told himself he was Ib, lab apprentice to Professor Humboldt Ignatz Delby, Scientist, Inventor, and Seeker of Knowledge.

He heard Bentley's voice correcting him:

"*Lab apprentice* extraordinaire."

As he let that thought steady him, his heart began buzzing. No, it was his stomach buzzing. With a start, he realized the vibrations were coming from his vest pocket.

Sophie!

He tried to reach his vest pocket but found his hands twisted together with rope. Working with his hands pressed together, Ib managed to get them close to his vest pocket. He couldn't reach into his pocket, but he could squeeze the egg out.

Soon Ib heard a dull *klunk* on floor of the cart beside him, followed by a sputtering and whirring sound.

"Sophie," Ib whispered, "can you help get me out of this?"

Ib felt the bird land on his wrists and begin poking at the ropes. He struggled to free his hands, but after Sophie poked him with her sharp beak several times, he decided to let her carry on without his help.

A few minutes later, he reached his freed hands behind his head and untied the clumsy knot that held the bag in place. Ib slipped it over his head, welcoming a deep breath of air that didn't stink of despair.

He found Sophie staring at him, then at the large man above them guiding the cart. Her eyes narrowed.

"Yes, I know," he whispered. "Don't do anything yet. Let me think for a minute."

He knew he could jump off the slow-moving cart, but there was nothing to stop Mr. Bertram from calling out to a well-meaning adult to help recapture a runaway boy. No, he had to do something more than running away.

Still lying on the flat bed of the cart, he looked at the thief. Mr. Bertram's head was leaning back, a hip flask at his mouth.

He looked around the cart. He didn't have much to work with: ladders, some brushes and brooms and the coils of rope he knew he had tripped over when he was thrown into the cart.

Rope.

One can do so many ingenious things with rope.

His face brightened. As a plan formed in his mind, the corners of his mouth turned upward.

Sophie's eyes opened wider.

"I'll need your help," Ib told her.

She nodded her head.

As silently as possible, he gathered a long length of rope, making loops about a broad shoulder's width apart. When he had enough loops in his hands, he looked up again at Mr. Bertram. The heavyset man was looking at the road in front of him, humming to himself in a way that he knew meant the thief was satisfied with himself. Even better, he saw that Mr. Bertram's arms were at his side, loosely holding the reins.

"Sophie, I need you to fly up over the cart."

Sophie tilted her head, staring at Ib.

"Then, when I nod my head, I need you to fly right into that fat man's belly. Can you spear him with your beak without getting hurt?"

Sophie's red eyes gleamed. She nodded, silently taking flight.

Years of traveling in this cart had taught him how to stand and keep his balance, even when they were riding over bumpy cobblestone streets

like the one they were on now. He stood slowly, careful to keep the loops of rope open in front of him.

He looked up. Sophie was flying in a slow circle overhead.

He nodded.

The brass bird flew out ahead of the cart and then turned. Flying fast and straight, Sophie flapped to build up speed and then tucked her small wings in.

He didn't see Sophie strike Mr. Bertram, but a sharp grunt from the thief told him that the mechanical bird's aim was spot on. Mr. Bertram leaned over with both hands protecting his large stomach.

With one easy motion, he lifted the coils of rope high and dropped them over Mr. Bertram's head, pushing them down to the large man's elbows.

Mr. Bertram yelled in surprise, but Ib already had his foot against the large man's back, pulling the ends of the rope towards him. The rope tightened around the man's arms and large stomach.

"You miserable brat!" Mr. Bertram roared.

Ib tied a quick double knot at the man's back. Taking the loose ends, he then wrapped the remaining rope around the bench board Mr. Bertram was sitting on. Picking up the burlap sack, he climbed onto the board next to his former boss.

"No," Ib said. "I am not a miserable brat. Not any longer."

"Ye are what I tell ye are," Mr. Bertram spat. He tried to stand and shake off the rope, but only succeeded in drawing the rope tighter around him. "And in a minute yer going to wish ye really had died in that fireplace!"

From the floorboards of the cart came a snapping, rustling sound. Sophie flew up to Mr. Bertram's face and began squawking and screeching at the red-faced man.

"You're wrong. I am a lab assistant," he paused a moment, deciding that the word *extraordinaire* would be lost on someone like Mr. Bertram. "I do not belong to you. I belong with Professor Delby and he belongs with me."

Sophie stopped her squawking and turned to him.

"And you, too, Sophie," he added.

Sophie nodded, then returned to her tirade against Mr. Bertram.

"You disgusting louse," Mr. Bertram glowered. "Ye belongs to me the same as them ladders and that mule. Now get me out of this. And shut that thing up!"

Ib looked at the red face that was full of hatred for him and realized that he felt a little sorry for the man who had caused him so much pain in the past.

"I am going back to my family," Ib said, surprised at how true the words felt. "Back to where I am wanted and where I want to be."

Mr. Bertram's eyes narrowed and grew dark.

"Ye just try running away again, you miserable brat," he hissed. "Go ahead. I bought you fair 'n square. Yer *my* property! I'll keeps coming back 'til I gets ye for good."

He dug into his pocket and pulled out the coins Mrs. Hudson had given him. He smiled at the thought of her telling him to buy something special for himself.

He threw the money into Mr. Bertram's face.

"There," he said. "We're even."

"Bah!" the man growled. "Yer mine and that's that. Shouldn't take much to convince that precious new family of yers that they'd be better off not harborin' a low-life thief like you. A couple o' rough visits from me an' me mates outta take care o' that."

He felt his face grow flush. His breathing quickened, but only for a moment.

As fear turned to anger, he narrowed his eyes, as Mr. Bertram had done to him for years, and leaned in towards the pudgy face before him.

"Have you heard about the dragon flying over London?" Ib spat back. "That's *our* dragon. If you come anywhere near us, I'll send that dragon out to eat you alive!"

Mr. Bertram reared his head back and spat out a loud, "**HA!**"

Ib glared at him. He didn't think he could talk Pterrence into doing anything of the sort but being laughed at only made Ib angrier.

"Oh, really?" he asked, grabbing Mr. Bertram's large nose between his thumb and forefinger and giving it a mighty twist.

Mr. Bertram opened his mouth wide to yowl in pain, but before he could cry out, Ib shoved the burlap sack deep into the oafish man's

mouth. Then, using the rope at the sack's opening, he tied a knot behind Mr. Bertram's head.

Sophie twittered with joy.

Through the muffled screams, Ib brushed the dust and soot from the wagon off of his new clothes. He looked at the bulging red face of his tormentor again and decided he was finished feeling sorry for him.

While considering what to do next, he absently rubbed his finger over his upper lip. His nose caught the citrus scent from the Professor's garden. He remembered the colors, the light, and the hope his new life held for him.

With a smile, he shoved Mr. Bertram's chest, pushing him backward. The big man, who was still tied to the bench board, slammed backwards onto the floor of the cart, his feet sticking straight up in the air.

Ib smiled as Sophie landed on his shoulder. She gave him a satisfied nod.

He got down from the cart and slapped the mule on its hindquarters.

"Go!" Ib shouted.

The mule took off at a quick trot, pulling a pair of legs kicking at the sky behind it.

He looked around. Two other carts were on the cobblestone road, but they were almost a block away. He and Sophie were alone and quite lost, somewhere in London.

Ib looked up and down the street, hoping to see something familiar, something to let him know where he was. The shops on either side of the street looked less fancy than those around the Delby Manor. He had a bad feeling he was far away from where he needed to be.

"Sophie, do you know where we are?"

The mechanical bird spun her head around without moving her body. When she faced Ib again, she shook her head.

Behind him he could still hear Mr. Bertram's muffled shouts and the rattling of the wagon. The street might be empty now, but it was only a matter of time before someone noticed the commotion and came to his rescue.

Thinking it better to be as far away as possible when that happened, Ib started down the street in the opposite direction. Not wanting to be noticed, he tried moving as quickly as he imagined a well-dressed boy on an important errand would, without actually running.

Sophie flapped alongside him for half a block before Ib patted his shoulder. She landed there, twittering in his ear.

"If I hadn't thrown all the money Mrs. Hudson gave me at Mr. Bertram, we might be able to hire a cab. Then again, we don't even know where the Professor lives."

Sophie chirped something that sounded helpful.

"The first thing we need to do is find out where in London we are."

At the next corner, he saw a woman in a maid's uniform carrying a sack in her arms. Ib scooped Sophie off of his shoulder and tapped her head. She sputtered and snapped her way back into an egg, which he then put into his jacket pocket. Walking toward the maid, he tried to smooth down his hair as he searched for a believable reason for being so lost.

"Excuse me, Miss," he said, deciding simple was best. "I beg your pardon, but could you please tell me how to get to Hyde Park? I'm afraid I've lost my way."

The maid looked at him and laughed a loud and friendly laugh. "I'll say you've lost your way, dearie. Why, you're more 'an five miles from Hyde Park! How'd a nice lad like you get yourself so lost then, eh?"

Five miles! It would take at least two hours to walk back that far. Ib felt the side of his head. Had he been unconscious in the back of Mr. Bertram's cart for that long?

Ib realized the maid was starting to look at him a bit suspiciously.

"Well," Ib started, trying to think of what to say. "It's a long story."

"Ah," the maid replied. "I knows all about long stories. Tell you what, young sir, why don't you come around to me master's house? I'll get you fixed up with a nice cuppa tea and you can tell me the whole story. My Alfie usually stops by it a little while from now, maybe he can help you."

"How could he help?"

"Why he's one of them constables, inn't he then?" she said with a smile. "He's out here keeping the streets safe for peoples like us."

"Thank you," Ib said, already backing away, "but I think I hear my uncle calling me. In fact, I'm sure of it. Goodbye!"

As he ran down the street, Sophie chirped and pecked at his ear.

He turned the corner of another short street and saw people walking on either side of a street that looked somewhat familiar. Sophie chirped again.

"No police!" Ib said quietly.

He looked around for a tall building. If he could get up high enough, he thought he could figure out where he was and, more importantly, which direction he needed to go to find the Delby Manor.

The street he was on was lined with tenement houses. He needed to get well above all of all of them to see all he needed to see.

In a few streets he saw what he was looking for: a church with a tall steeple. As he got closer, he recognized it as St. Paul's in Lorrimore Square. That meant Mr. Bertram had carried him all the way across the River Thames while he was unconscious—and that the maid's guess of five miles was probably not too far off.

Ib eyed the steeple. As he had hoped, there was an opening at the

top that displayed a large bell. That was certainly tall enough to give him the view of the city he needed. With nothing on the outside that would aid him in climbing up, he needed to find a way to do so from the inside.

The large wooden doors at the front of the church were unlocked. Reminding himself he looked like a respectable person who shouldn't attract much attention, he stepped into the building.

He found himself in an entryway. Through the opened doors in front of him, he saw rows of pews leading to the sanctuary. Colored lights illuminated the long wooden pillars arching up to the roof.

The door behind him swung shut, the sound echoing loudly throughout the church. Ib held his breath as he waited for the sound to stop reverberating.

He waited as the echoes faded into silence to see if anyone would come to investigate the sound. After a minute, he gave a sigh of relief and looked around him.

To his side, a narrow door stood slightly ajar. Peeking in, he saw a lone rope dangling a few feet from the ground. A dim shaft of light illuminated the rope from above. Stepping into the room, Ib followed the path the rope took upward and saw a narrow series of holes through the building that led to what must be the bell at the top of the steeple. He couldn't climb through the tiny holes, but at least he was on the right track.

He walked back into the entryway and into the main area of the church. The tall, narrow windows illuminated the church with brilliant jewel like reds, blues, yellows, and greens. Painted panels depicting scenes from stories were bordered by intricate patterns. If the Professor's laboratory had been a room of wonders, this was a room of grand and staggering beauty.

Ib shook his head, bringing himself back into the room. Looking along the walls he didn't see any staircases leading upward. He continued walking toward the front of the church, hoping to find a recessed doorway.

The ancient wood beneath his feet groaned all around him with every step.

A door at the front of the church creaked open. Ib's eyes widened before he thought to duck behind a pew to his right.

"Is anyone there?" called an elderly voice.

After a few moments, Ib peered over the top of the pew. A man wearing church vestments was facing away from him and appeared to be arranging some items on the altar. Ib crept to the far end of the pew, hoping the wall and the ends of the pews would make for a quieter exit than the center aisle.

Still crouching, he turned his back to the priest and stopped. There in front of him, in the front corner of the church, was a doorway. Carefully lifting his head he saw a second door in the opposite corner as well. Both were in line with the larger doors leading into the church. He shook his head. When he was busy being dazzled by the stained glass, he hadn't thought to look behind him.

Above the entryway was another, much smaller seating area. On either side were doors that he knew must match up with the doors below.

He took several cautious steps towards the stairs closest to him. Staying on the balls of his feet he found the floor was more forgiving—at least for the first few steps.

Then the floor groaned once again, sounding like a minor explosion.

"I say, who is there?" called the priest.

For a moment Ib considered trying to explain his situation to the clergyman. When he thought of the story he would have to tell, he wasn't sure if the priest would believe him or not. Or even take his side against Mr. Bertram. It was not a chance he wanted to take.

He ran for the stairs.

"The choir loft is closed except for church services!" Even in the small stairway the man's voice boomed. "You are welcome to use any pew in the Nave, but I must insist you come down this instant!"

The stairs ended at the choir loft. Looking around him quickly, he saw nothing but an empty passageway about the size of a closet. He shook his head and ran for the opposite doorway.

"Oh, I should have known! Yet another rascal. Young man, how many times must I tell you and your friends that this is a church not a playground!"

Ib looked down and saw the elderly priest moving with surprising speed to the back of the church.

Opening the door on the other side of the loft, he saw nothing but more steps leading down. Narrowing his eyes as he had done in countless chimneys, he looked harder into the darkness. There, to the side, was a wooden ladder braced to the wall. Following it with his eyes, he could just make out a hatch door in the ceiling.

He scurried up the ladder until he reached a large metal ring hanging down from the hatchway door. He pulled at the ring and then pushed against it. The door above him refused to budge.

Below him he could hear the clergyman muttering underneath his breath as he strained to climb the stairs.

Narrowing his eyes again, Ib sought out some reason why the hatch would not open. He traced the outline of the hatch with his fingers until he found it—a simple latch. Fumbling with handle, he slid it to the side as the priest mounted the last step.

The clergyman exhaled loudly as Ib pulled and pushed again. The doorway gave on the one side, but still refused to open.

"Now then," the priest intoned. "Will you come down or must I drag you down by your ear?"

Ib felt around on the opposite side of the hatch and discovered a second latch. Sliding it to the side, he gave a final push at the doorway above him.

It opened up easily, lighting up the darkened loft doorway.

He scrambled up the ladder, tugging the cuff of his pants leg from the priest's grip.

The hatch door dropped behind him with a thud.

Light from the steeple opening illuminated the bare wooden frame of the six-sided steeple. To his side he could see the bell rope disappearing into a small hole in the floor. Next to that was another ladder, one that led straight to the top of the bell tower.

He continued climbing until he reached the small platform at the top of the steeple. The belfry was narrow, circling the giant bell, but wide enough for him to walk around.

Before him, on all sides, was one of the grandest views of London he had ever seen.

From the tops of houses he had usually seen nothing on the horizon but more houses, more chimneys. However, from the height of the St. Paul's steeple, he had a sense of just how big London was. For a moment he thought about how easy it would be to disappear in such a vast metropolis. A few days ago, he might have been so tempted. Now, however, he had a family—a family that was depending on him to help the Professor stay out of the Tower.

He set about searching the horizon for landmarks.

The River Thames arched before him. Past that he could make out the Monument at St. Paul's Cathedral, the highest point in all of London. To his right he saw the flags atop the foreboding walls of The Tower. Not wanting to think about that building, he quickly scanned tops of the buildings in the distance to his left. There he saw the strange granite column being built for an admiral he couldn't name. Beside it sat The Fields Church.

Further to his left he could make out the top of Buckingham Palace, and past that, the angled Serpentine River in Hyde Park. Remembering his view of the side of the Palace from Hyde Park while they had been "Pterrence Watching", Ib felt confident he knew which direction he needed to head towards.

There were two bridges that crossed over the Thames from where he was into western London. The Westminster Bridge was further north, but closer to the palace. The Vauxhall Bridge was closer to where he was now, but the route to the palace was less direct. He rubbed his chin for a moment, trying to anticipate where Mr. Bertram might be watching for him.

Right past the Vauxhall Bridge lay the new Millbrook Prison, a strange shaped building that always made Mr. Bertram shiver whenever they rode past it. Hoping his former boss would want to avoid such an area, Ib decided to cross the river there.

Far below him, the hinges to the hatchway door squeaked open.

"I do not know who you are up there," panted the elderly voice, "but I am quite tired of you young ruffians making a sport of my church and this steeple! I have no idea what you hope to accomplish, but I shall be happy to give you plenty of time to think about it."

The hinges squealed again as the clergyman's voice grew more faint.

"I shall come back for you after supper, unless I should forget. At which point it will most likely be sometime tomorrow. Do enjoy the view."

The hatchway door closed and Ib heard the two latches slide into place.

He was trapped at the top of a steeple with no way down.

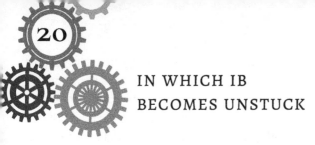

IN WHICH IB
BECOMES UNSTUCK

Ib climbed down the ladder and tested the hatchway door. It refused to budge, as he knew it would. He looked around him, hoping to find something that might help him pry the hatchway door open. There was nothing but the dust on the wooden steeple frame.

He had already been gone from the Delby Manor for far too long. Each additional minute away meant there was less chance of finishing their second Pteranodon in time. He had to escape, but how?

He made his way back up to the belfry where his thoughts didn't feel quite so closed in around him.

There was a slight ledge at the base of each of the six open sides. He sat down on the one that gave him the best view of the way back to the Manor. He followed the streets as best he could, planning his route to the Vauxhall Bridge and beyond.

Something in his pocket buzzed. He pulled out the brass egg that was already whizzing and popping. With a start, Sophie leapt from his palm and flew in a circle over his head. She landed on the ledge next to him and gave a low whistle.

"It is impressive, isn't it?" he asked. "They say this is greatest city in the world."

Sophie nodded.

"And, unfortunately, we're stuck. Well, I'm stuck. I suppose you could always fly down to the ground. I don't have wings and would just fall."

Sophie flew over to the bell and landed awkwardly on the bell rope, trying to look down.

"The priest locked the hatch behind me and won't be coming back for hours," he explained. Sophie looked at Ib and twittered.

As Sophie flew back and landed on his shoulder, he crossed his arms, contemplating the rope.

Mr. Bertram's rickety ladders were rarely strong enough to support his weight for long. Rungs often snapped in half on the way up, making the climb down treacherous. Once, so many of the rungs had broken that Mr. Bertram had forced Ib to climb down with the rope still tied around his chest. Ib had relied on the rope far more than what was left of the ladder to get back to the ground.

He wondered if he could do something similar now. If the bell rope reached almost to the floor of the church, he reasoned, it should almost reach the ground outside the church as well.

Looking over the edge of the belfry, he took in the sharp angle of the steeple. Sophie whistled in his ear. It was steep, almost vertical, in fact. He told himself if he was careful, he could make it.

For good measure, he repeated that idea aloud as he pulled the bell rope up through the church and into the belfry.

From his shoulder, Sophie chirped something. Ib chose to believe it was encouragement.

When the rope was all coiled at his feet, he took a moment to rub his arms. It was much heavier than he thought it would be. After a moment's hesitation, he picked up the end of the rope and dropped it over the belfry's ledge through an opening facing away from the road. He watched it slide down the side of the steeple.

The other end of the rope was firmly attached to one of the two pull wheels on either side of the wooden yoke supporting the bell. Holding on to the rope he pulled on it slowly, wanting to test its strength but not wanting to have the wheel spin so quickly to the side that the bell rang. He managed to ease the clapper onto the inside of the bell with only a slight sound.

So far, so good.

Sitting on the ledge, he swung his legs over the side. Shifting the rope around his waist and arms, he tried to find the best way to hold it securely while still being able to climb down. Finally, he settled for having it loop down one arm, not knowing what he would do if he really slipped at any point on his way down.

"Ready?" he asked Sophie.

Sophie blinked. Ib could have sworn she was shrugging her wings at him. Then she flew past him and hovered a few feet below him, chirping.

He leaned forward and slowly let the bell rope take on his weight. The bell wheel spun just enough to make him feel for an instant like he was falling.

After a few moments, he opened his eyes again.

Looking down, he quickly wished he hadn't. It would have been better if he were surrounded by darkness inside another chimney. Not knowing exactly how far down the bottom was in case he fell had been somewhat more comforting than he had ever realized.

He gave out a nervous laugh.

Sophie flew alongside his shoulder and twittered, her head cocked sideways.

"I was just thinking," he said. "So far being a lab assistant *extraordinaire* has been more dangerous than being a thief climbing down chimneys in the middle of the night."

He exhaled and tried to take his first step down.

The angle of the steeple made keeping his feet flat on the outside surface almost impossible. He tried shifting his weight as best he could while steadying himself on the rope, but he quickly learned the steeple, the rope, and the bell wheel all seemed to be working against him.

With his next attempted step, his feet slipped out from underneath him and he swung into the side of the steeple. He gripped the rope even tighter, only to find that the bell tolled softly and that the bell wheel was trying to lift him upwards.

Sophie began twittering and chirping loudly.

"Yes, thank you, Sophie," Ib said through clenched teeth. "I really am trying to be careful."

Pushing off with his feet, he moved sideways until he was facing one of the points where the sides of the steeple met. It wasn't much of an angle to work with, but he found that by keeping his right and left feet on different sides of the steeple he could keep himself better balanced.

Lowering himself in chimneys had taken his back and leg muscles to inch his way down. This was descending hand over hand holding using his arms and shoulders. It made for slow and painful going.

At last his feet felt something solid beneath him. Taking a quick peek downward, he saw he was standing on a small wooden ledge at the base of the steeple. It wasn't wide enough to stand on comfortably, but he took the opportunity to take some of the weight off of his arms.

A short step below him was the top of the vaulted church roof.

Sophie landed on his shoulder and chirped happily.

"Halfway, I think," Ib breathed. "The rest of the way down should be easier."

He stepped down and felt the bell wheel turn above him. He had forgotten to pull the rope taut again before putting his weight on it. The rope dipped lower, then rose up again a few inches.

As he clutched at the rope, the bell above him rang out once.

The angle of the roof wasn't nearly as sharp as the steeple. Balancing on the balls of his feet, he found he could better control his descent on the roof. Taking care to not ring the church bell again, he scuttled down the roof as quickly as he could.

In his rush, he didn't think about the edge of the roof until he felt his foot slide past it and into the air below him. He clung onto the rope as his other foot slipped off as well and his elbows crashed into the wooden roofing boards. His stomach took the brunt of the roof's edge as his legs swung forward.

It was hard to tell what was louder — Sophie twittering frantically at his ear or the bell above him.

Then the rope jerked upwards. With the edge of the roof digging into his stomach and his legs below him at an angle, Ib felt he was being pulled apart.

The weight of the bell pulled the rope through his hands. Gasping in pain, Ib released the rope only to feel himself falling all over again.

He grabbed at the wooden roofing board at the edge of the roof and closed his eyes. His hands ached, but he felt his legs swinging in place beneath him.

Above the sound of the bell pealing and Sophie's frantic chirping, Ib heard the roof board groaning from his weight.

He looked down. The ground was still a good fifteen feet below him. If he let go, he might land safely or he might break his ankle or his leg.

Straining to look behind him, he saw nothing but more dirt. In front of him, by the stonework wall of the church, were some scruffy bushes.

Deciding on the best of several bad options, he swung himself forward as best he could and let go.

Branches scraped and jabbed at him as he tumbled into the shrubbery. He only stopped when his back struck the stone wall. He collapsed face first, back into the bush, his hands fighting against branches and leaves to find the ground.

Gasping for breath he tried to regain his bearings. He looked up and saw Sophie fluttering in front of him. He couldn't understand why she looked so strange, jerking to the side every few seconds, then flapping her wings to right herself again. Ib shook his head, trying to catch his breath and clear his head.

Footsteps. He heard footsteps. Running his way. From the direction Sophie was motioning towards.

"This is most outrageous!" cried the priest running towards him. "I shall call a constable and have you taken away, you hooligan!"

Ib struggled to find his footing, trying to twist his way out of the bushes. Before he could, though, a hand grabbed at the collar of his jacket and jerked him forward, flinging him onto the ground.

"You wait right here until one arrives," the priest said. "I will not tolerate this foolishness any—"

From the ground, Ib could hear the priest struggling and waving his arms. Looking back, he saw Sophie diving at the old man.

Ib scrambled to his feet, staggering forward before he could catch his balance.

"Come on, Sophie! Let's get out of here," he called.

21

IN WHICH IB ATTEMPTS
TO BECOME UNLOST

After two blocks of running, Ib felt he had put enough distance between himself and the angry priest at St. Paul's. He slowed to a walk as he made his way onto one of the main thoroughfares.

That's also where he noticed the occasional person staring at him. Stopping in front of a large shop window on Kennington Road, he tried to make out his reflection in the glass. It wasn't very clear, but he could make out some leaves on his jacket shoulders. He gave himself a good brushing off and found a surprisingly large shrubbery branch tangled in his longish hair.

Making his way around the large oval-shaped Cricket Park he saw that the carts in the roadway to Vauxhall Bridge were stopped. The large intersection a block from the bridge, where five roads met, was clogged with carts, sheep, cows, and cabs. He tried walking around the confusion, but even crossing at a side street meant sidestepping carts driven by skittish horses and a large flock of geese that were not willing to be corralled easily.

Sophie landed on his shoulder, pecking at his ear. She fluttered down to his hand and snapped and spun herself back into a brass egg.

"I don't blame you," he said, sliding her into his pocket.

At least part of the traffic problem was due to a cart that was stopped near the approach to the bridge in front of him. Getting closer, Ib stopped in his tracks. A man behind him bumped into him, gruffly saying, "Mind your step!"

He recognized the cart. Scanning the scene, he found what he was looking for: Mr. Bertram was arguing with a constable. From the angry way the thief was gesturing, Ib could guess what he was describing.

Ib darted out into the crowd of people and livestock clogging the roadway. He needed to get as far away from Mr. Bertram as possible, starting with getting to the other side of the road.

Dodging between people and under carts, he made it partway across before being stopped by a small herd of cattle. Crawling under them wasn't safe, so he tried going around them. Following the edge of the cattle towards the bridge he discovered, too late, that they stood side-by-side with a team of two horses pulling an open carriage. Moving around the far side of the horses, he found himself at a seeming wall of sheep that were already nervous due to their confined space.

He pressed his way through the packed flock, or at least he tried to. The ewes began bleating, first one then another and then another until it sounded to Ib like the entire drove was turning against him.

Over the chorus of wavering cries around him, Ib heard a voice booming out:

"STOP THAT MISERABLE BRAT!"

He didn't need to look behind him to see whom the voice belonged to.

Using his hands to separate the tightly packed sheep in front of him, Ib wove his way through the herd and ducked under several carriages before finding himself on the other side of the street.

Behind him he could hear Mr. Bertram still ranting. Thankfully, no one seemed to be paying any attention to one more angry tradesman in a traffic jam.

He wound his way through the maze of livestock, carriages, and people to the far side of the road. Along the walkway, the going was much easier. With fewer animals in his way, Ib was able to rush to the Vauxhall Bridge and cross over the Thames at Lambeth Reach.

From the belfry he had seen that the road coming off of the bridge led in the direction of the Palace. He started to follow it on foot, but when traffic slowed, he jumped on the back of a cart. It was filled with tall clay pots that hid him from the driver. He allowed himself a slight smile, thankful for the chance to catch his breath and give his feet a rest.

"Hey, you!" shouted the cart driver. "No free rides!"

He turned to a red-eyed man glaring at him. The driver reached back, trying to smack him with the long pole he used to guide his mule.

Ib leapt off the cart, narrowly avoiding a carriage horse and two men crossing the street.

Looking above the buildings, he could see the flags of Buckingham Palace ahead and to his right. He crossed the street to his left, deciding it would be best to go a few blocks to his left, then a few blocks to his right to keep himself in the general direction of the Delby Manor.

It was also not a path that Mr. Bertram was likely to take, if the thief was even past the Vauxhall Bridge by now.

He walked through residential streets, most with shops on the bottom floor. He was glad that the people paid him no mind. Even to boys his own age he seemed invisible which, for the moment, was what he needed.

After half an hour of zigzagging through the streets, the road abruptly curved to his left. Suddenly he was in Sloan Square, one of the busier parts of Chelsea. Ib smiled, knowing he was on the right track home.

He pulled the egg from his pocket and whispered, "Sophie, we're getting closer."

The egg swirled and popped in his hand until Sophie was standing and nodding at him.

Then she started jabbing her break at his chest.

"What are you doing?" Ib asked, protecting his chest with his hand. When he felt something crinkle underneath his jacket, he raised an eyebrow to the bird. Reaching into his jacket pocket, he pulled out Mrs. Hudson's grocery list. At the top of the list was the name of the store, a store that was supposed to be a few blocks from the Manor.

Sophie gave him a contented blink of her eyes before snapping back into an egg.

"Yes, thank you," he said, sliding her back into his pocket.

He knew he would have to ask someone for help with reading it and with directions. As much as he wanted to avoid anything to do with the police, a constable seemed to be the best choice of someone to ask. They usually knew the city better than most.

After walking the nearby streets for what seemed to be ages, he finally spotted one. He was standing in a doorway, chatting with a young barmaid.

"Excuse me, sir," Ib said, trying to look more confused than scared. "Would you please tell me where I could find this shop?"

The constable smiled at the girl and touched the brim of his helmet. "Duty calls."

He took the note from Ib's hand and scanned it. His expression looked far from certain.

"Say, Maizy, isn't Wiseman's the grocers over on Cadogan Place?" he asked.

The barmaid shook her head. "No, love. The Wiseman shop is on Brompton Road. Wallis is the grocer on Cadogan." She looked past the constable to Ib. "A right nice lady, Mrs. Wiseman is. She'll get you taken care of."

The constable handed the note back with a shrug. "If Maizy says it, it has to be true, lad."

After explaining how he could get there, Ib carefully repeated the directions back to the barmaid. He thanked them both and went on his way.

He walked past more shops and houses, some he recognized by their locations and chimneys. When he finally turned onto Brompton Road, Ib felt his shoulders loosen. He even smiled as he looked for letters that matched those on Mrs. Hudson's note.

Across the street he saw a large shop window with canisters stacked in the shape of a tall triangle. He stopped, saw that the letters looked to be the same, and crossed the street in the middle of the block.

As he did so, a familiar cart came into sight. Ib ducked into the doorway, slowly turning to see if the heavy-set driver had seen him. Mr. Bertram was still in a fierce temper, driving his mule to pass a slower cart to his side.

Ib entered the grocers and waited his turn at the counter. When Mr. Bertram drove by, he was shaking his head and muttering to himself.

The woman behind the counter was as nice as the barmaid had promised. Ib introduced himself, explaining his new position within the Delby household. The grocer gave him a knowing smile and asked him if anything exciting had happened to him yet.

He opened his mouth to speak but suddenly realized he didn't know where to start. After a moment, he simply nodded. "Yes, ma'am."

Mrs. Wiseman laughed. "If half of what I hear from Mrs. Hudson is true, your employer is sure to keep you on your toes! Now be off with you. It's a bit busy at the moment. I'll have my delivery boy take this around to the Professor's Manor in a bit."

Back on the street, he kept a wary eye out for Mr. Bertram and his cart. However, he needn't have worried—he heard the oafish thief shouting at someone well before he saw the cart. After walking to the far side of two gentlemen to get closer to the cart, Ib hid behind a hedgerow to better hear what was going on.

Mr. Bertram was arguing with a costermonger about the right of way in the road. The other man's cart of tin scraps had bumped against Mr. Bertram's wagon one time too many, and now the two men appeared close to coming to blows with one another in the roadway.

Ib hurried across the street. If the argument continued, he should be able to get past them without being seen.

Less than halfway across, however, he heard Mr. Bertram roar, "YOU!!!"

From behind him, he could hear the rattling of the thief's cart along with a growling list of things that were going to happen to him once Mr. Bertram caught up with him.

Ib tried to hide himself amongst a small crowd of people. When a woman next to him opened the door to a shop, Ib followed her inside.

Finding himself in a dressmaker's shop, he sought out someone behind the counter.

"Do you have a back door?" Ib asked the shopkeeper.

She eyed Ib for a long moment.

"Please," he implored.

She gave a curt nod and pointed to the back of the store.

He made his way to a hallway where rolls of colored fabrics leaned against the walls. It opened into a room where seamstresses were busy sewing pieces of cloth.

"Back door?" he asked the one woman who looked up.

She motioned to the far corner of the room where he found a door to the back alley.

The alley continued several blocks before ending at a side street. Walking to the far corner, he peered around an overgrown corner hedge and looked down Brompton Road.

Mr. Bertram's cart was stopped half a block away from him. The thief was pulling at the mule's reigns, trying to get the cart turned around. The mule, for its part, was too distracted by the noise and commotion going on ahead of him to pay much attention to the string of oaths coming from the large man behind him.

Craning his head further away from the hedge, Ib tried to see what was causing the commotion. It wasn't until he stepped halfway out from behind the hedge that he could make sense of anything.

Through the growing crowd of onlookers, Ib could just make out at least four of the enclosed wooden wagons and too many men in black coats and bowler hats to count. His heart dropped as he saw the men herding something or someone out of the Delby Manor gates.

Ib's attention was stolen away as Mr. Bertram's swearing started anew. The large man climbed down out of the wagon and grabbed the leather straps along the mule's cheek, forcing the mule to turn away from the scene.

Ib moved back into the bushes.

"Don't want no part of that," the thief said to himself as he drove past the hedges. "Let them coppers take away that lunatic. I'll come back for that miserable brat tomorrow."

Emerging from the hedge, Ib tried hurrying down the street, but the crowd of onlookers blocked his path. He stayed to the side, trying to skirt along the edges, but even that proved to be difficult. People kept moving about, seeking a better view of the spectacle before them.

From over the crowd, Ib heard something that made him stop where he stood:

"I'm sure you chaps will find that my lab assistant *extraordinaire* and I still have a good many hours left on our agreed upon timetable before this need happen!"

Ib pushed his way through the throng and raced to the end of the block.

From the corner Ib watched as Professor Delby was shoved into the back of one of the enclosed wagons and was followed by six of the Royal Guardsmen. The door slammed shut behind them and a bolt was quickly locked into place.

Ib shook his head, trying to come up with a plan. If he ran alongside the far edge of the crowd he might be able to climb onto the back of one of the wagons. As long as he wasn't caught, he would be taken to Tower along with the Professor where he could then figure out a way to rescue him. It was going to be risky, but he had to do something.

As he was about to cross the street, he saw Mrs. Hudson waving at

him. From the concerned look in her eyes, Ib felt sure she knew what he was planning. She shook her head and motioned for him to follow her down the side street that ran between them, away from the confusion in front of the Manor.

Ib looked back at the wagons that were already starting to move down the street away from him. He took a deep breath and let it out slowly, trying to convince himself that trusting Mrs. Hudson and not running to the Professor's rescue was somehow the best thing to do.

22

IN WHICH IB TELLS ALL

Mrs. Hudson crossed the street and placed a hand on his shoulder.

"Oh, thank goodness you didn't do something foolish like trying to be a hero," she said. She led him away from the noise of the wagons being pulled down the street. "You would have just gotten yourself caught before you knew it. They were looking for you, too, you know. Are you alright, Ib?"

"Yes, I—," Ib shook his head, trying to shake away the afternoon. "Why is the Professor being taken away?" Ib asked.

"Apparently someone from the Electrical Society complained about the Professor's failure to capture his dinosaur earlier today. Someone named Cogswell or Cogs—"

"Cosgrove," Ib spat.

"Yes, that's the one," Mrs. Hudson agreed.

She turned abruptly to the right and opened a gateway door in the iron fencing that ran the periphery of the Delby Manor. Ib blinked. The gate was so well hidden he would have walked right past it if he had been on his own.

They walked along a path through the rear gardens. Ib breathed in the scents of the flowers and herbs, but the joy they had brought him just hours ago was gone.

"Then what happened?" he asked.

Mrs. Hudson walked down several steps at the rear of the Manor and opened a door that led directly into her kitchen. Ib followed behind her.

"Just what you saw when you arrived, dear," she said, shaking her head. "That Cosgrove person must have made quite the fuss to someone important because in marched an army of police and Royal Guardsmen without so much as a knock at the door!"

She put a kettle on the stove for some tea.

"I needn't tell you how irritated Bentley was by the intrusion," she added.

"But why?" Ib asked. "We still have plenty of time left!"

"Doctor Cosgrove is on close, personal terms with a great many influential people, Master Ib," came the even-toned response from behind him.

Ib jumped at the unexpected voice.

"The individual who forcefully escorted Professor Delby from the laboratory stated that Doctor Cosgrove had issued a formal complaint against both the Professor and yourself, Master Ib," Bentley continued as he walked to far side of the table across from Ib. "The complaint listed willfully endangering the lives of some of the most wealthy and preeminent thinkers on all of London as well as the gratuitous destruction of personal property."

"What?" Ib asked, rolling his eyes. "Nothing about Pterrence?"

"No, Master Ib. However, since the person who read out those charges to Professor Delby was your acquaintance, the Head of the Royal Guard himself, one can surmise that he, too, must believe the Professor has failed with ho further hope of recovering his wayward invention."

Mrs. Hudson set a pot of tea on the table along with some cups and saucers. She took a seat and began pouring.

"The Head of the Royal Guard was quite keen on discovering your whereabouts as well, Master Ib. We were, of course, unable to provide them with an explanation of your prolonged absence from the Manor."

"Bentley," Mrs. Hudson said softly. "We've been through enough today already."

She slid a full teacup towards the manservant with a knowing look.

"I must confess, Master Ib, that my own curiosity has been piqued. I cannot help but wonder if the pressures of your new position became too great and your desired to return to your previous illicit and felonious employment?"

Ib stared at his tea, clenching his fists.

"Mind you, Master Ib, with police presence outside the Manor at the moment, I doubt anyone could successfully carry out a larcenous attack upon our home without being immediately caught."

Ib drew a long breath.

"Mrs. Hudson," he said, still staring at the cup before him, "do you understand anything Mister Bentley just said? Because I don't. He keeps hiding behind all of those big words of his, but they sound as if he thinks I had something to do with this."

Ib turned in his chair and stared back at Bentley.

"Well now, isn't this just so helpful?" Mrs. Hudson said at last. "We've already had enough excitement in this house to last us a fortnight and here the two of you just want to carry on, making things worse."

Ib continued staring at the manservant, his face feeling flush.

"If the two of you don't stop this nonsense this instant," she continued, taking hold of the teapot, "I shall be forced to waste the remainder of this perfectly fine pot of tea by showering you both with it. This is my kitchen, and I will not put up with any more disturbances. We need to pull together, not tear at each other."

"Quite right, Mrs. Hudson," Bentley said, taking a seat in front of his cup of tea. "However, I do believe some lines of inquiry require forthright responses before we formulate any plans to aid the Professor."

Ib looked to Mrs. Hudson.

"He wants to ask you some questions, dear," she said.

"Specifically, Master Ib," Bentley said, adding some milk to his tea, "I wish to inquire as to your whereabouts during your prolonged absence this afternoon. The errand to the Wiseman Grocers should have only taken you ten minutes at best." Bentley stirred his milk and then set the spoon down on the saucer without making a sound. "Yet, you were gone for almost five hours. Where were you and why?"

Ib tried staring at Bentley again, but soon looked away. His mouth felt dry and the tea in front of him seemed to be mocking him.

"Ib, dear," Mrs. Hudson said, "It was an awfully long time to be gone. What happened?"

"Perhaps, Master Ib, you decided to return to your previous career and gained illegal entry into a few of the nearby houses to see what you could steal from them?"

"No!" Ib shouted.

"Surely, Master Ib, you do not deny your role in the recent nighttime robberies in this area, do you?"

Ib looked up from the table and met Bentley's eyes.

"No," he said simply. "And I'll bet if Mr. Bertram had beaten you as much as he beat me, you would have done it, too."

Ib saw Bentley's eyebrow raise a fraction of an inch.

He looked back at his teacup. Mrs. Hudson poured some milk into it for him. Ib watched as what looked like clouds swirl around in the cup.

"I suppose you should just send for the police now," he said.

"Why don't you just start from the beginning, Ib?" Mrs. Hudson suggested instead.

"What difference will it make?" Ib said, shaking his head.

"Just tell us, dear," Mrs. Hudson said, adding, "please?"

Ib sighed and looked at the wood grain pattern in the table.

He told them about growing up in the orphanage and being sold off to Mr. Bertram. He told them about being forced down that first chimney, about his boss' gambling, and decision to start stealing through chimneys instead of cleaning them. He told them how he said no to the idea and then being beaten and starved until he finally agreed. He told them about the places he had stolen from, the things he had taken, and the places where Mr. Bertram had sold them all.

And then he told them how Mr. Bertram had lost a lot of money the other night and forced him to do a daytime job the next day. And how he had found the strangest metallic bird in the chimney that day.

Ib felt a buzzing in his vest pocket. With a sad smile, he paused his story to take the Sophie egg out and set it on the table.

Sophie sputtered and popped along the table until she stood up, shaking out her wings. She chirped at Ib while gesturing towards Bentley.

"I believe, Master Ib, that Sophie agrees with my earlier observation that she was the one who found you."

Sophie chirped with a definitive nod of her head.

Ib gave a short, humorless laugh.

He continued, telling them about leaving the Manor earlier in the day and Mr. Bertram grabbing him outside the gates. He told them about escaping from the thief, getting caught in the steeple, and making his way across town, all the while trying to avoid Mr. Bertram. He told them about arriving at the grocers and having to make his way out the back of the dressmaker's shop when Mr. Bertram had spotted him in the street.

"When I was looking out from the steeple at St. Paul's I could see all of London. Still, this was the only place I wanted to be." He stopped and took a drink of his cold tea.

"What happens now?" he asked.

"Well, I don't think we'll be contacting the police," Mrs. Hudson said. "Will we, Bentley?"

"Not at this time, Mrs. Hudson. No."

Ib looked at Mrs. Hudson. "I don't understand."

"You have done the Professor a world of good, Ib. I haven't seen him this engaged in the world outside of the Manor in years. Don't you agree, Bentley?"

Bentley lowered his gaze at Ib, saying nothing.

"I also don't believe the two of you being locked up will do any of us any good," she added.

"Indeed, Mrs. Hudson," Bentley said eventually, as if coming to a decision. "I do not believe it will."

"Does this mean I can stay?" Ib asked, still confused.

"Until such time as the Royal Guard returns to collect you, Master Ib, yes," Bentley said.

"But what can we do?"

"About what, dear?" Mrs. Hudson said, returning to the table.

"About the Professor!" Ib exclaimed.

"That rather depends, Master Ib," Bentley said after a moment. "The original problem of how to recover Pterrence has been compounded by the need to also recover Professor Delby. Were the Professor here he would, undoubtedly, arrive at a most unique and creative answer. However, since he is not, the solution to that problem now resides with one person and one person only."

"And who is that?" Ib asked, not sure he wanted to hear the answer.

"Why, the Professor's trusted laboratory assistant *extraordinaire*, Master Ib."

Ib closed his eyes in disbelief.

"He's quite right, dear," Mrs. Hudson said. "You're the only scientist in the family now."

"But I'm not—"

"Dear," Mrs. Hudson patted his hand. "Stop trying to say what you aren't and start believing in what you are."

Ib looked back at the table.

"Perhaps, Master Ib, you should walk about the laboratory. The Professor has always found it to be a great source of comfort and inspiration whenever his is perplexed by a difficult problem."

Ib fought back the urge to say, 'But I'm not the Professor!' Instead, he got up from the table and nodded.

With Sophie chirping advice from his shoulder, Ib walked down the stairs to the laboratory.

23

IN WHICH IB COMES UP
WITH A PLAN

Twenty minutes later, Ib found Bentley polishing silverware in the dining room.

"I have an idea," he said, "but I'm going to need your help, Bentley."

Bentley set aside a soupspoon and his polishing cloth. He motioned for Ib to continue.

Ib stepped into the room and stood beside the manservant.

"We know Pterrence isn't going to come back on his own," he started. "And even if we could help the Professor escape tonight, the Royal Guard would only come back here and wait for him—for us."

"That is correct, Master Ib."

"However, if we manage to capture Pterrence before time runs out tomorrow, the Royal Guard should let the Professor go."

Bentley considered this. "Perhaps, Master Ib," he allowed.

"The only way I can think to get Pterrence back is to finish the second Pteranodon and have it bring Pterrence home."

"Why should this mechanical replica act differently from the first, Master Ib? Don't you risk having two escaped Pteranodons to contend with instead of just the one?"

"I thought of that," Ib said. "I think the Professor did, too." He pulled a piece of sketch paper from his pocket and laid it on the table facing Bentley.

"I found this in the laboratory. It's the Professor's plans for the second Pteranodon." Pointing to a roughly drawn cylinder on the page he continued, "In the main part of the body there is nothing that shows the Professor was going to use another stove and boiler. Instead, he left this Pteranodon's body empty—and I think he made it longer."

"You believe he did so for a reason, Master Ib?"

Ib faced Bentley and nodded.

"I think the Professor meant for me to fly it."

Bentley's eyebrow arched for a fraction of a second. He picked the paper up and studied the drawing.

"I do not think you can accurately discern the Professor's thoughts from these drawings, Master Ib. Without detailed, written notes we have no idea what his true intentions were."

"There is no drawing of a boiler or a stove, though," Ib said. "I think he was trying to avoid using steam with this Pteranodon. Don't you?"

Bentley considered this. "Perhaps, Master Ib."

"Did you see where the wings meet the body?" Ib took the sketched plan from Bentley and laid it on the table where they could both see it.. "These look like cables attached to a pair of handles to me," he said, pointing to a part of the drawn Pteranodon's shoulders. "Why would he put handles inside the body unless someone was supposed to use those handles?"

"Use them to what end, Master Ib?"

"To flap the wings and make the Pteranodon fly."

Bentley regarded the plans again.

"That," Bentley said at last, "would be sheer madness, Master Ib."

Ib nodded in agreement. "And it sounds just like the Professor, doesn't it?"

He thought he saw the corner of Bentley's mouth twitch for an instant.

"Indeed, Master Ib. However, I fear the folly of your decision to fly this creature will only end in great calamity."

"What?" Ib asked.

"Put another way, Master Ib," Bentley said slowly, "should you follow through with this, there is every possibility you may injure yourself or possibly even die."

"Mrs. Hudson said things have a way of working out for the Professor," Ib replied.

Bentley nodded. "However, Master Ib, you are not the Professor."

Ib took a deep breath.

"Please, Bentley. I don't know if it will work or not, but it's the only thing I can think of to try. The problem is, I can't build all of it tonight by myself. I need your help."

Bentley regarded the sketches again for several long minutes before turning to the boy.

"Master Ib, are you proposing that I become a laboratory assistant *extraordinaire* laboratory assistant?"

"Just for the night. You can even be a laboratory assistant *extraordinaire*'s laboratory assistant *extraordinaire* if you'll say yes."

"This goes against all of my better judgment, Master Ib. However, I will do so under two conditions."

Ib nodded.

"Firstly, Master Ib, you will give me a full accounting of the houses you and your former associate robbed, and all the items taken from those dwellings. Secondly, you will provide me with the names of all the businesses your former associate sold those items to."

"Agreed," Ib said, feeling his shoulders loosen. "Should we start with the houses or the businesses?"

"Given the impending deadline, Master Ib, I feel we should start with the second Pteranodon."

"Then we have a deal, Bentley?" Ib asked, extending his hand.

Bentley nodded and shook Ib's hand.

"We have a deal, Master Ib."

24

IN WHICH WE MEET PTERRY

Back in the laboratory, Ib and Bentley reviewed the remaining sketches and papers Professor Delby had made regarding the second Pteranodon.

"The Professor's handwriting can be somewhat challenging to decipher under the best of conditions, Master Ib. I fear I cannot make out anything useful from these notes."

Ib looked at the tables of unfinished work around them and began rubbing his chin with his thumb and forefinger.

"The Professor was working on the body," he said, pointing to the incomplete brass frame and jumble of partially formed brass sheets at the Professor's workbench. "And I was working on the wings," he gestured to the rods, cables and bolts of material on his own workbench.

"I was hoping you knew how to use the soldering torch," Ib said, looking at his own lab assistant *extraordinaire*. I saw the Professor working with it but I was too busy with the wings to see how it worked."

Bentley nodded. "I am familiar with its operation, Master Ib."

"Good. If you'll pick up where the Professor left off and finish the frame and body I can continue with the wings. Once I'm done, we can work together on the head and feet."

"A well-reasoned plan of attack, Master Ib."

"There are some changes that need to be made, though," Ib said. He pointed to the base of the Pteranodon's body. "I'll need some sort of platform to stand on before liftoff. It doesn't need to be anything fancy, since I'll be lying down while I'm flying. However, that also means I'm going to need something to lie on instead of the brass chest." He pointed to what would be the chest of the finished Pteranodon.

"Which brings me to another thought: can you add some sort of window here? I'll need to be able to see where I am when I'm inside this thing and flying about."

Bentley paused, then nodded. "I congratulate you on your detailed perceptions of this Pteranodon's design deficits, Master Ib, especially given the short period of time in which you have had to make such considerations."

Ib shrugged. "I think that means I did something good."

Bentley bowed, slightly. "Problems well spotted, Master Ib."

"I think Mrs. Hudson's tea helped," Ib said.

"If I might follow your last recommendation with one of my own, Master Ib, we should alter the head in some fashion so you might see ahead of you as well as below you."

Ib smiled and returned the bow. He hadn't considered that at all—and, once in the sky, he knew it would be essential.

"I can see why the Professor says you're an indispensable part of the household."

"I try my best, Master Ib."

Bentley donned a thick leather apron and covered his face with an odd mask with dark glass eye slits. He adjusted a knob, picked up a long nozzle attached to a thin hose, and with a **POP** he was controlling a spout of orange and blue flame.

Ib smiled to himself. Bentley certainly did know what he was doing in the laboratory.

Assessing his own workbench, Ib took a long look at his wings. Knowing that he now had to attach cables to both the wing arms and a new set of handles inside the frame, made him reconsider all of his work to that point. He spent some time testing different configurations and eventually settled on one that he felt would both work and could be completed in the least amount of time.

After constructing several sets of new pieces that would allow the cables to run through adjoining pulleys, Ib set about screwing them into place. Keeping his eyes on the precariously balanced coupling and screw, Ib reached down for a screwdriver. His hands felt over a number of different tools, his fingers now recognizing the shapes and sizes of their tips. Feeling a screwdriver, he felt along the tool to the tip and immediately sensed it was too big. Three screwdrivers later, his fingers found the one he needed.

Putting the screwdriver's slotted head into the back of the screw, he grinned. A few days ago he would have never been able to do something like this. Even better, he felt he was good at this work.

Later, when the wings were ready to be attached to the body, Ib went to help Bentley.

Extinguishing the shooting flame with a twist of a knob, Bentley lifted his metallic mask.

"I am pleased to report that the frame and front torso are almost complete, Master Ib. If you would take charge of joining the brass pieces for the back and sides it would be of considerable help."

Ib looked at the collection of cut brass sections that were laid out on the next table and nodded.

"However, since we only have the one soldering torch, might I suggest you take a different approach to joining the brass pieces for the back and sides? You should find a selection of rivets on the workbench behind you, along with appropriately sized drill bits."

"Rivets?" Ib asked.

Bentley set the torch handle down and removed his face shield.

"Unlike the process of joining metals through heat, rivets may be used as a cold processed manner in which metals can be held together, Master Ib." Bentley explained. He lined up two loose brass panels and tapped a mark into them with a sharp-pointed tool and hammer. Then he drilled matching holes.

"Would you please select a rivet from the container, Master Ib?"

Ib picked up what looked like a smooth screw with a domed head and went to hand it to Bentley.

Instead, Bentley handed him a hammer.

"Simply insert the rivet in to the two holes, setting the flat end downward and onto this block of metal, Master Ib." As Ib did so, Bentley lifted the face shield back onto his head.

"Now strike the domed head of the rivet with the hammer until the bottom compresses and secures the two pieces together, Master Ib. I suggest you drill holes and use at least ten rivets per section to reliably hold each pair together."

Ib hit the rivet several times, but the shape remained unchanged.

"Strike the hammer with enthusiasm, Master Ib. I can assure you, this process has been in use for thousands of years."

Ib swung the hammer down hard on the domed top again and again. Soon, the bottom had flattened and the brass pieces held together.

Drilling holes and pounding rivets flush appealed to him. It was uncomplicated but effective work.

It was some time later, when Ib and Bentley were working to piece together the head of their creature, that Mrs. Hudson stepped into the laboratory. She cleared a space on a workbench and set down a platter with tea and small sandwiches.

"If the two of you aren't sleeping, then I shan't be sleeping either," she announced. "But I do suppose we can all sit for a moment and have a cup of tea and a bite to eat."

Ib welcomed the break. He pulled three stools over to the table by Mrs. Hudson and gratefully accepted a hot cup of tea from the cook.

"What do you think?" Ib asked, motioning his teacup towards their Pteranodon. He took a sip of the hot liquid and felt it gently waking his tired mind.

"Well," Mrs. Hudson said, handing Bentley his cup and saucer, "it looks every bit as disturbing as the Professor's first one, if I'm being honest. I hope you're doing something different with this one, though."

"Yes," Ib said, not wanting to say much more.

"Would any of those changes give me cause to worry?" she asked.

Ib took another long sip of tea.

"Master Ib has given the safety aspects of his creature considerable thought, Mrs. Hudson. However, I believe we can both attest to their always being the possibility of risk when working with a scientist, inventor, and seeker of knowledge."

Mrs. Hudson glanced at Bentley, then took a bite of her sandwich.

She regarded the mechanical brass creature on the workbench for a few moments before saying, "This might sound silly, but from this angle it sort of reminds me of my sister Mary's son."

"It does?" Ib asked.

"Yes. It's the nose. Our side of the family all has fine wee noses. Poor Terry inherited his from the Romans on his father's side."

She went back to her sandwich.

"Master Ib," Bentley said, setting down his teacup, "I should mention that tradition in the Delby Manor dictates that you should provide your creature with a name. As you have yet to do so, perhaps Mrs. Hudson's observation might serve as a fine suggestion."

"You wouldn't mind, Mrs. Hudson, would you?" Ib asked.

"Oh, dearie, no," she laughed, setting her sandwich down. "My nephew might, but I wouldn't mind it a bit."

"Then Terry is it," Bentley said.

"Don't forget the silent 'P'," Ib added.

Bentley nodded. "I stand corrected, Master Ib. Pterry it is."

Ib rubbed his eyes.

He was trying to think of a way that Pterry's mouth could open. It was the only way he could think to provide a forward-flying view. The problem was, though, that this meant a variety of moving parts at the beak all attached to a handle that Ib needed to be able to reach from a prone position while flying.

He understood the idea of how it should work, but he could not see how to make it work. It had been a very long day.

Ib climbed into Pterry's framework and tried to picture the completed machine around him.

"The wing handles will be here," he said, holding his fists in front of his chest, "and the glass plate will be a bit higher, in front of my face. Pterry's head will be above my head so the gears that open and close the mouth should be mounted on his neck."

He reached up and pushed against an imaginary lever with both hands.

Ib looked out at Bentley. "Or should it be on one side instead of the middle?"

"I had thought, Master Ib, of placing another glass window in the front. That might prove more stable in flight."

"No," Ib insisted. "Pterry needs to look as much like Pterrence as possible."

"In that case, Master Ib, given the hour might I suggest attaching it

to one side. I believe that we shall require fewer parts and, therefore, less time."

Ib agreed, stifling a yawn.

"Might I recommend you take a short rest, Master Ib. You do have a rather strenuous morning planned. I assure you, I can assemble the head and jaw mechanism myself."

"No," Ib said, trying to shake himself awake. "I'll see what I can find for gears that might work for Pterry's jaw."

After carrying several heavy trays of gears and shafts to his workbench, he began sorting through them, looking for sets that made sense to him.

Instead, all he saw was a swirl of gear shaft teeth and then darkness.

Ib awoke with a start. He pushed a blanket away from him and sat up on the edge of a folding cot.

Daylight illuminated the laboratory through the high windows by the ceiling. He stood up, looking around him. The worktables were all but empty. There was no sign of their Pteranodon anywhere.

"Bentley!" he called out. "Bentley!"

The door to the laboratory opened.

"Ah, good morning, Master Ib. I trust you slept well."

"Where's Pterry?" he asked.

"Calm yourself, Master Ib. You fell so soundly asleep at your workbench that I thought you would be better served by rest than with constructing the jaw. I do hope you don't mind that I moved you to the cot Professor Delby uses on occasion."

Ib shook his head, trying to clear his mind.

"Where is Pterry, Bentley?"

"Currently atop the Manor on a platform the Professor designed for several astronomical experiments many years ago. I thought it best that you start your flight from on high rather than here in the basement as Pterrence did."

"He's upstairs?" Ib said, still trying to make sense of it all.

"Yes, Master Ib, upstairs. Where he currently resides in a great many separate pieces all needing our facilities to assemble them into a proper Pteranodon."

Ib nodded, still taking this all in.

"I can assure you, Master Ib, that deconstructed, Pterry was surprisingly lightweight and quite easy to carry."

"Bentley," Ib said seriously, "I think I need some tea."

"I have taken the liberty of securing us a pot of Mrs. Hudson's most bracing morning tea, Master Ib. It, along with scones and a selection of jams, is awaiting our arrival at the former stargazing platform."

Bentley motioned to one of two wooden boxes with handles on a workbench. "As your own laboratory assistant *extraordinaire*, I do not wish to overstep my bounds, Master Ib. However, I would be most grateful for your assistance in carrying one of the collections of tools we will need to complete the assembly."

Ib shook his head, trying to wake himself. He walked over and picked up a box of tools.

"Lead on, my laboratory assistant, *extraordinaire*."

From inside Pterry, Ib pushed against the wooden handles in front of him. He felt the brass frame around him rock with the movement of the wings.

"I must say, Master Ib, that is quite impressive. I know Professor Delby would take great pride in this moment."

Standing inside the sealed Pteranodon body, Ib wished his stomach would stop rumbling.

Pterry stood more than twice Ib's height, with a long-beaked head extending well above Ib's own head. As Ib had specified, he now stood on a bar across the top of the Pteranodon's legs. A padded board was bolted in front of him, extending the length of his chest. When he was flying, Ib would be lying face down on the board, parallel to the ground.

"Now then, Master Ib," Bentley said, checking his pocket watch. "You have just over an hour to find and retrieve Pterrence before the original deadline ends. I dare say you should be able to hear any number of bells tolling the hour and quarter hour from your vantage point in the air. Meanwhile, we shall put our faith in your success and the Royal Guard keeping their initial word."

Ib nodded, wondering why this ever seemed like a good idea.

"From my limited knowledge of aerodynamics, Master Ib, I state that darker areas on the ground will result in warmer air. Warm air will cause you to rise. Seek out darker areas when you wish to gain altitude and avoid them when you wish to descend."

"What?" Ib asked, not understanding.

"Dark patches of ground will lift you up, Master Ib."

"Oh," he said, wondering why that mattered. "Okay."

"I do believe it is time to don your flight goggles, Master Ib."

Ib pulled the glass eye coverings over his head and adjusted them. If anything, they only seemed to limit his view even further.

"Are these really necessary?" Ib asked.

"Safety first and last, Master Ib."

"Bentley," Ib asked, his stomach feeling very uncertain, "is this really going to work?"

"I have found, Master Ib, that courage is only necessary for the first few seconds of any endeavor. After that, things rather take care of themselves. Are you ready?"

"No," Ib answered honestly.

"If it is any consolation, Master Ib, if I were in your place, I would not be ready either."

Bentley turned his head suddenly and raised a finger. "One moment, Master Ib."

Through the glass window in Pterry's chest, Ib saw Bentley move to the edge of the platform and look down. He cupped a hand behind one ear.

Standing once again before Ib, Bentley nodded.

"Who is it?" Ib asked. "The Professor? The Royal Guard?"

"No, Master Ib. It is your former employer."

"Mr. Bertram?!"

"Indeed, Master Ib. He has returned asserting his claim over you and insists that you present yourself or he shall contact the police concerning his stolen property."

Pterry's frame suddenly seemed very tight around him.

"What should we do?"

Bentley glanced over the edge of the platform once again.

"If I am not mistaken, Master Ib, your trajectory from our current location should put you directly in the path of that lowlife ruffian."

"What does that mean, Bentley?" Ib said a bit louder than necessary.

"My apologies, Master Ib." Bentley eased Ib and his Pteranodon to the edge of the platform.

"As you leave the platform, Mr. Bertram will be directly before you, Master Ib. If he wishes to see you, perhaps you should present himself to him."

"But I'm in Pterry!"

"Precisely, Master Ib. I dare say you and Pterry might change his mind."

And with that, Bentley tipped Pterry from behind.

"Godspeed, Master Ib."

Ib felt the Pterry's brass frame lurch forward. He leaned onto the padded board in front of him as he fell. He tried using his arms to steady himself, but they only banged into the brass sides of the Pteranodon's body.

Through the glass, Ib saw his world tipping downward. Tree limbs and trunks, garden terraces and the curved walkway to the manor gates scrolled up into view.

"AHHHHHHHHH!"

Mr. Bertram came into view, standing at the edge of the Delby Manor garden.

For an instant he was looking right into Mr. Bertram's eyes. Only Mr. Bertram's eyes were bigger than Ib had ever seen them before, and the man was screaming.

Ib felt his own surge of fear, one he realized had less to do with Mr. Bertram than the sight of the ground coming towards him surprisingly quickly.

Frantically, Ib pumped the handles in front of him. Through pure adrenalin, he beat the huge wings with all his might at the same time his breath was being squeezed out of him as his chest pressed into the board at his chest.

When Ib's mind cleared enough to realize he had missed the ground, he looked through the glass window. Below him he could see the small figure of Mr. Bertram trying to leap over the spiked fence at the manor gates. The heavyset man only succeeded in getting the seat of his overalls caught in one of the tall spikes on the fence, leaving him hanging upside down. Inside Pterry, Ib was glad he could not hear what Mr. Bertram was saying.

Past the dangling Mr. Bertram, Ib saw the two not-so-secretive Royal Guardsmen running down the street, looking nervously to the sky as Ib flew past them.

Still pumping at his Pteranodon's wings, Ib soon became aware that the ground was remarkably far away. He was used to seeing the city from the rooftops before being shoved down chimneys, but this

was something different. Whole neighborhoods were nothing but tiny clusters of rectangles with thin, cobblestone lines running between them.

For Ib had been too distracted by Mr. Bertram to notice something very important.

He was flying.

"AHHHHHHHHH!"

Ib pumped the handles even harder. His breathing was shallow and quick; in moments, Ib became lightheaded. Lying face down in the enclosed Pteranodon body meant that Ib had to lift the weight of his chest with each new breath. This, combined with the pumping action necessary to make the wings flap, made breathing that much harder. Ib felt a wave of dizziness overtake him that wasn't helped by the view through the glass window.

All of that pumping had taken Ib even higher in the air. Now he could make out entire sections of the city, not just rooftops. The lines between the rows of houses were a crisscrossed maze far, far below him.

Over the sound of his heart beating in loudly in his ears, Ib heard a clock tower chime out the time. He now had less than one hour to find Pterrence and figure out a way to convince him to come back to the laboratory.

"Okay," he said aloud. "Okay. I can do this. I wasn't sure it would be possible, but I am doing this so I can do this. Right? Sure. Sure, I can do this."

Ib bit his lower lip to keep it from trembling.

Steering. He needed to remember how to steer. He knew he and Bentley had talked about steering earlier that morning over tea. However, talking about it was so completely different from flying high in the sky in a brass Pteranodon that it was as good as never knowing about steering in the first place.

Without thinking too much about it, Ib leaned his body to the right. As he did so, he pushed forward on the right handle. Pterry turned easily to the right.

Ib tried leaning to his left. As he pushed forward on the left handle, he tried pulling back slightly on the right. He found this made him fly

in a tighter circle. He discovered he could make Pterry turn wider or tighter, depending on how much he worked one or both of the wings.

Ib began laughing. He was flying his own giant Pteranodon! It was the most impossible, the most absurd thing he had ever done in his life.

A rush of wind above him brought him back into the moment. He looked through the small window below him but saw nothing but clouds and the city far below.

He lifted the wing handles and pushed them into their locked position. Reaching forward to Pterry's neck, he found the handle he needed. With several awkward cranking movements, he managed to open Pterry's beak slightly.

As he did, air came rushing at his face, filling his ears and blowing his hair about. He tried angling his head back to keep his hair out of his face, but nothing worked. Pushing his hair away with his hand only helped as long as he held a hand up to his head.

Ib realized the goggles might not be such a bad idea after all. The hair beating at his face was annoying, but the goggles were protecting his eyes.

Pterry lurched to the side. Ib bit at his lip again, steadying himself by putting his hands against the inner sides of the brass body. Trying to look through the slightly opened beak, he saw that the top of the head was shuddering. After a moment it snapped to the left, causing his Pteranodon to lurch once more.

Ib suspected Bentley's idea of a second window in the front of Pterry was the better choice. Pterry did not fly as well with its beak open.

He was trying to decide which was more important, seeing what was in front of him or stability, when he felt Pterry jolt with a loud *clang!* He looked from side to side and back again, desperate to see what was happening.

From the glass window he saw the edge of a leathery wing swooping up and off to his right.

He looked back up, desperately trying to see something through the gap in the beak and his own dark hair blustering about his face.

For a long minute, there was nothing.

Then a second, louder *clang* came from above his head. Over a

thousand feet above London, Ib felt Pterry's body stagger. Ib's stomach lurched as he was pushed downward.

When the downward pressure stopped, he frantically tried to see what was happening. Soon a third *clang* was followed by another downward thrust.

A sour taste filled his mouth and he fought back the urge to be sick.

Pterrence was attacking him from above.

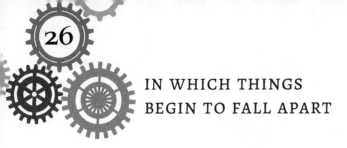

26

IN WHICH THINGS
BEGIN TO FALL APART

The clock tower bells rang once, telling Ib fifteen minutes had already gone by. He wished he could spend time being impressed by how well sound traveled this high in the air.

Through the small glass window, he saw Pterrence's yellow eyes roll wide to the left below him. As Pterrence spun out of sight, he leaned Pterry into a tight right turn. The ground twisted below him until he thought he was flying in the opposite direction. He wanted to put as much distance between himself and his mechanical assailant.

Ib looked up through the thin opening in the beak again. There was nothing to be seen there but a sliver of blue sky and the occasional slice of white cloud. He closed his eyes for a moment and exhaled. How could he possibly convince the Pterrence to come back to the Delby Manor if the Pteranodon was intent on attacking him?

When he opened them again, he could see a long streak of brass in the nearby distance. As it got closer, he made another tight turn away from the oncoming Pterrence.

He tried spinning downward, hoping to make himself a harder target to hit. His circles in the air grew tighter and tighter as he slowly lost altitude. He opened his mouth and breathed through his teeth to keep from being sick.

Just as his stomach was about to allow him to revisit his breakfast, he straightened Pterry's wings and leveled himself. He was still frighteningly far from the ground, but seeing that the buildings were at least a tiny bit larger than before helped to settle his stomach. Or at least that's what he told himself.

Then a streak of orange flame zoomed down past him.

Ib locked the wings in place and wrestled again with the jaw hinge. If he was going to avoid being burned out of the sky, he needed to see more of what was in front of him.

He worked the ratchet again, cranking the top of Pterry's head open several additional inches.

Pterry's body lurched again. Ib grabbed onto the inside edge of Pterry's neck. Looking up, he saw the top of the head had twisted to the side even more.

He had more than doubled the gap in the beak, but he still only saw sky and a bit of the clouds. Then he saw another stream of fire streaking past him, and he wished all he was seeing were sky and clouds.

As Pterrence came level with him, he saw Pterrence look towards the earth. Folding his wings back slightly, Pterrence flew downward, disappearing from view. Ib tried following him through the glass window in Pterry's chest, but Pterrence was not to be seen.

Ib pumped the metal handles in front of him and Pterry's wings began to beat. He wasn't sure how he could fold his wings back like Pterrence had, but he knew he would have to do something similar if he were going to get closer to the ground before Pterrence smashed him to bits.

Then he saw something that made no sense at all. Pterrence flew in front of him and started rocking sideways in the air.

Ib did not think this was how one animal attacked another animal, no matter how confident it was of its victory.

He clenched his jaw for a moment. Shaking his head, he reached up and gave the ratchet several more clicks upward. The beak opened wider still. He needed a better view of what Pterrence was doing, regardless of how Pterry had been designed.

Looking through the beak again, he saw Pterrence still swooping slowly from side to side. After watching this for almost a full minute, Ib had two thoughts. First, Pterrence seemed to be having trouble controlling the way he flew. It was as if his joints were stiff or he was tired. Second, and most peculiarly, after each sideways roll Pterrence always returned to fly straight in the direction his own Pteranodon was flying in. It was as if Pterrence was trying to lead the way.

At the same time, he was getting a sense for Pterrence's sideways rocking rhythms. Uncertain of what else to do, Ib decided to follow along. When Pterrence banked to the right, he moved his wings and flew to the right as well. When Pterrence banked back to the left, he followed him again.

Pterrence gave a loud mechanical *"Kawrr!"* that Ib could just hear over the rushing wind in his ear.

The boy shook his head in disbelief. Pterrence wasn't attacking him. Pterrence was trying to get Ib to *play* with him.

Pterrence folded his wings back slightly and tipped his nose downward, vanishing from sight again.

Trying to not think too hard about how to pilot his Pteranodon again, Ib twisted the metal handles inward and leaned his body forward. His Pteranodon slowly cooperated, tilting slightly downward. He looked out of the open beak and was grateful to see the horizon line again.

As he picked up speed through his descent, the top of his Pteranodon's head began rattling back and forth. The entire brass body shuddered. Then came a long, low creaking sound behind him.

There was a loud CRACK as the top half of Pterry's head snapped backward, flipping over onto its back.

Involuntarily, Ib ducked his head below the padded board he was resting on. Pterry staggered. Ib grabbed at the handles, trying to regain control of the wings. He gulped air, trying to stabilize his Pteranodon. It didn't help that over the sound of the wind rushing past his ears, he could hear the top half of Pterry's head banging against its brass back—and feel it bashing the metal right above his head.

Ib locked the wings in place, hoping to steady his flying machine. He lifted himself on his elbows and realized that a bolt on one side was the only thing connecting the top half of the head to the jaws.

Pterry's head continued pounding its brass back. Ib jerked his head around as far as he could to look behind him. As the curved brass sheets bashed into his shoulders as he could see a small ragged crack of blue sky winking through the back brass casing.

His grip on the handles was so tight his knuckles had gone pale. If his Pteranodon's back split all the way, it would tear apart. He knew once that happened his wings would collapse, and he would fall from the sky like a rock.

A sound that seemed to come from everywhere around him filled his ears. Two chimes from the clock tower to mark the half-hour.

"I still have plenty of time," he said aloud, hoping by hearing the words they would be more encouraging. Then he remembered the frightened expressions on the faces of the two Royal Guardsmen as they ran down the street. He hoped their superiors might be on their way to get Professor Delby.

Maybe he didn't have plenty of time after all. In fact, he had already used half of his time. After all, Pterrence was playing with his new friend, high in the skies. What could possibly make him want to land?

Then he remembered Pterrence's expression in the coal yard the day before when he had spoken to Pterrence. But how could he possibly talk to Pterrence this high in the air?

Ib unlocked the wings and twisted his wrists inward, leaning forward again. His dive was more controlled this time, but it also caused a new round of shaking all around him. He opened his Pteranodon's wings, slowing his descent. As he slowed, he felt another loud creak.

He looked up just in time to see the bottom half of Pterry's head tearing free from the bolts that held it to the inside of the body. As it spun sideways and tore loose, the lower jaw hinge took a section of the upper body with it. Shaking, he looked out at the sky in front of him and saw another sharp, jagged edge of brass. Only this one was mere inches from the side of his head.

Ib flinched at the sound of another booming crash from above. He looked up and saw Pterrence's outstretched claws coming at his head. When the two Pteranodons had flown within a few feet of each other, Pterrence folded his wings in slightly. With his curled and pointed claws, he grabbed onto the flapping top of Pterry's head.

Pterry jerked downward again. Pterrence was trying to push off of Pterry's back. To Ib's disbelief, Pterrence began twisting from side to side, trying to take the top of Pterry's head with him. Ib was knocked from side to side, all the while straining to keep his wings in their locked position.

The bolted jaw hinges strained with each sideways shift. When the first hinge broke free, the force twisted the head to the side. Pterrence, still clawing into the head, twisted as well. The second hinge ripped off the metal jaw, exposing another jagged edge of brass.

Ib tried to see how close the edge was, but his vision was too murky to see anything. The left lens of his goggles was smeared with something that his hair was sticking to. From the way the wind blew at it, smearing

it a bit, Ib knew it had to be something wet, but it was too red to be any of the mechanic's grease they had used on Pterry's joints.

With Pterrence off of his back and head, he ventured a hand to the goggles and then to his head. He winced as his fingers found the gash at his hairline.

He wiped the blood from the goggle lens as best he could, but there were still reddish, filmy streaks over it. At least he could still see well enough through his right lens.

He shifted his weight to his right elbow and turned sideways on the board. With his left hand, he pushed the serrated brass edge in front of him forward. He managed to move it out a few inches, far enough to keep him from cutting the side of his head against it any further.

Pterrence flew in a wide arc, his wings having a harder time beating. He glided alongside Pterry. Ib hoped Pterrence might be curious to see what was inside the headless Pteranodon. He locked his wing handles in place and tried to shift himself onto his side again and then waved at Pterrence through the opening where the head used to be.

He cupped both hands on either side of his mouth and shouted, "PTERRENCE!"

The brass and gearwork Pteranodon flying beside him tilted its head toward Ib. Ib waved, trying to catch Pterrence's pale yellow eyes.

Ib tried yelling again. "PTERRENCE, IT'S ME!"

Pterrence lifted a wing slightly, drawing even closer to Ib's Pteranodon.

"PTERRENCE," Ib shouted. "HOME! LET'S GO HOME!"

Ib swore Pterrence nodded his head.

"KAWRR!" Pterrence cried and dove off to the side.

Ib twisted himself so he was lying on his stomach again. He had done it! He had talked Pterrence into going back to the Professor's Manor. Pterrence would land and the Royal Guard would be satisfied. He and Professor Delby wouldn't be locked away in the Tower, and he would be able to keep his new family and his new position.

He felt so relieved he laughed again.

Through the glass window, Ib caught sight of Pterrence flying beneath him.

"HOME!" Ib cried out.

Ib wiped more blood from his forehead. He scanned through the glass window, trying to make out where the Delby Manor was in the maze of streets below.

Then he saw Pterrence strain to beat his wings and fly past him. Pterrence raised his head. From his mouth he blew a long burst of flame into the air, right into Ib's path.

Ib ducked his head again, his chest pushing against the padded platform.

"*Kawrr!*" Pterrence called out again as he swept past Ib's Pteranodon.

Pterrence swooped close in front of him. Ib jerked back, gasping. His hands disengaged the handle locking mechanism and both wings lifted upward. Ib's stomach pitched again as Pterry dipped downward. More anguished creaking came from the brass body around him.

Pterrence flew back in sight and breathed a blast of fire into the air as he circled Ib's Pteranodon.

Ib realized all Pterrence wanted to do was play with him. In the air. Not on the ground. And certainly not back at the Delby Manor.

A buzzing began to tingle his feet. He tried looking down through the Pteranodon body, but he could see nothing past his knees. Looking back in front of him, he felt the buzzing slowly growing in intensity. His feet were soon shaking, causing his legs to shake as well. He heard a dull popping sound that was soon followed by a second.

The rivets, he thought as several of the pressed metal pins shook loose from the back of his Pteranodon. He clenched his hands around the wing handles again.

In moments, enough of the rivets had pulled loose that a brass panel tore away at his feet.

There was a moment of silence, then a single, resonant chime.

Ib pushed the thought of only having fifteen minutes left from his mind.

Pterry was rapidly falling apart around him and he couldn't escape even if he wanted to.

IN WHICH THAT WHICH REMAINS ALSO FALLS APART

Pterry's brass frame groaned as Ib banked to the right and descended. Pterrence plunged down, snorting a thick trail of steam in his face as he did. When Ib came through the haze, he banked to the left, continuing his descent.

Playing Follow the Leader was better than risking Pterrence bouncing on Pterry's back again. He wasn't sure the rupture in his Pteranodon's frame could withstand another of Pterrence's encouragements to play.

With a long creak, Pterry shot upward. Looking down through the glass window, he checked to see if he had really left his stomach down below him. Instead, he saw a large, dark section of ground beneath him. Then he remembered Bentley having said something about dark areas lifting him upwards.

He didn't want to be lifted. Just the opposite, in fact. He needed to get back to the ground before Pterry fell apart around him.

Pterrence appeared to be thrilled by his friend's unexpected rise in altitude. He let out another loud, *"Kawrr."* As he flew past, Ib took a long look at the faint yellow hue of Pterrence's eyes.

With a ferocious beating of his wings, Pterrence spewed a long flame into the air.

Ib smelled something. This, itself, was odd, because there wasn't much to smell miles up in the sky. He looked around his limited space to see what it might be. Seeing nothing, he tried pulling himself forward to look outside of his Pteranodon for something wrong, but his trouser leg was held firm by the spear.

Looking through the glass plate in Pterry's chest, Ib pumped the wing handles. On the downbeat he saw a series of glowing orange spots flickering along the bottom edge of the right wing that were slowly inching their way up the wing.

"FIRE!" Ib yelled.

He locked the wing handles in place and reached out to the wings with his hands, as if he could somehow beat the flames out. Instead, he only knocked his hands against Pterry's brass inner shell. Ib cried out in pain. Twisting, he leaned forward to protect his hands. His Pteranodon responded by pitching downward, with a mournful grating sound that threatened to widen the crack running down its brass back.

Ib realized he could yell it as loudly as he could, but he was too far above London for anyone to hear, let alone help him. His heartbeat only slowed slightly when he looked out again and saw that the downward speed had already reduced the flames to thin orange lines that flared and vanished along the edge of the wings.

Gritting his teeth so hard his jaw hurt, Ib forced himself to breathe through his nose. He took the wing handles in his hands again and looked through the window in Pterry's chest. Pterrence was nowhere to be seen.

Ib leaned forward and to his right, making Pterry dive into a wide spiral. Pterrence couldn't have gone far.

The tail end of an orange flame caught his eye from the corner of the window. Leaning towards the flame, a second blaze came into view. Ib exhaled at the sight of Pterrence flying below him.

Pterrence breathed another long flame from his mouth. As he sped by Ib, the flame unexpectedly stopped. Ib watched as Pterrence continued past him, expecting to see the flame reignite.

But no flame appeared.

He saw Pterrence look downward, moving his head from side to side. Then, with a creaking sound even Ib could hear, Pterrence folded his wings back and started to dive.

Leaning further forward as well, Ib attempted to give chase. At once, Pterry's brass platework started to shake. Settling back just enough to keep the frame from complaining, Ib tried to keep Pterrence in sight.

He nodded, knowing where Pterrence was heading. All of the playful bursts of steam and flames had used up most of Pterrence's coal and water reserves. As it was, Pterrence had been due for another coal and water refueling soon. All of his aerial exuberance must have caused Pterrence to run low that much faster.

Ib only had two chances to keep Pterrence on the ground, providing

Pterry didn't fold up around him and crash to the ground first. It was up to Pterrence to see if the first chance would be at the coal yard or the river.

Buildings started to take on greater dimension as he came closer to the ground. Through the glass window, he was starting to see the shapes of hansom cabs and their horses. He coughed as he flew through the acrid smoke rising from a factory chimney.

His view of the street below was partly blocked by the trailing edge of a leathery wing that began to snake beneath him before steadying. Ib saw they were flying in line with a road now. He looked ahead for the coal yard, knowing it must be close by.

The day before, when the coal yard was full of workers and wagons and scientists, it had seemed so large. Now, looking at it as a landing spot, he could see that the grounds weren't as big as he had thought. A small walled-in coal yard was not the best place to learn how to land. If he tried and failed, he was certain he would not survive a crash into a brick wall.

A sudden thought startled him: he had no idea how to land Pterry. He had put all of his efforts into making Pterry fly and hadn't given a single thought to landing.

His mouth was still too dry to swallow. Shaking his head, Ib pushed the thought out of his mind.

He pushed on the metal handles in front of him, wanting to be above the rooflines of the buildings and factories around him.

The brass section above him groaned. He rushed to lock the wings back in place again. The back plate between the wings was not going to last much longer

Below him he could just make out men and women shouting. Looking through the glass plate, he saw some people pointing ahead of him and others pointing up at him. He moved his head away from the glass window, not wanting to be seen.

Several blocks away he could see that Pterrence had landed. He watched as the Pteranodon once again used a claw at the end of one wing to open the furnace door in his body. With the other winged claw, Pterrence rapidly scooped coal into his torso.

He lifted one metal handle and leaned to his side. He made a slow circle in the air, hoping to see Hyde Park. Having failed to stop Pterrence from getting coal, he knew he had to keep the Pteranodon from getting water.

But how?

The back plate began creaking again, sending shudders all along the brass framework. This time both the sound and the shaking lasted for several long seconds. As he set the handles back into their locked position, Ib noticed his arms were shaking, too.

With another rush of fire streaking along his side, he saw that Pterrence had finished his meal of Bransford coal. Pterrence darted from side to side, then looped back to Pterry.

He pushed a metal handle out of its locked position. As he did, the low creaking started again, louder this time. When he scrambled to replace the handle Pterry's entire body shuddered.

Pterrence looped around him two times, then three, creating a long spiral of flame around Pterry. With a final loop, Pterrence flapped his wings to gain altitude and veered off to his left, towards a thin, crooked body of water.

Ib had no choice but to risk moving the left handle and dipping to the right to follow. The creaking began as soon as he moved the handle, growing louder and louder until—

SNAP.

Squeezing his eyes shut, he held his breath. He imagined he was already plummeting down to the street or the rooftops below.

Somehow, though, he remained in the air.

There came a second snap, then a third. Looking all about him, he tried to see what was breaking loose. Nothing around him looked different.

When the fourth—and loudest—snap came, Ib tried wiping away the smears on his goggles to have a better idea of what was happening.

Pterrence was making a wide, descending arc over the park. Ib knew he had less than a minute before Pterrence scooped up another beakful of water and flew off again.

His heart beating fast, Ib leaned forward. Pterry responded by pointing downward, but not far enough. If he kept going like this, he would fly past Hyde Park entirely, crashing somewhere in the Kensington Gardens.

Ib shimmied down the padded board and then pushed himself

forward as far as he could. Pterry pitched forward sharply with another loud *SNAP*. Now Pterry was diving sharply—and gaining speed.

He looked over the top of the jagged neck and saw that he was going to crash into the ground at least a hundred feet past the pond. Knowing he was going too fast to survive a crash, he saw Pterrence swooping down underneath him. His only chance was to land on top of Pterrence and hope the Pteranodon would be able to stop for both of them.

The sound of creaking brass filled his ears as he moved his Pteranodon's wings, jarring his Pteranodon's body onto Pterrence.

That was when the back panel finally tore apart.

On a down stroke, he felt the body fold up around the wings at the shoulders. Ripped in half along the back, Pterry's body snapped shut around him, trapping him tightly inside the remains of the brass torso.

There was a horrible crashing all around him. Ib's head was jarred, first into the brass torso, then into the folded back plating, and then in front of him again. A monstrous hissing erupted, followed by thick gray smoke.

Ib gasped for air, thrashing his arms about him to escape.

Then his world went dark.

After the blackness came the water. Ib's heart beat in his throat as the river poured in all around him.

The cold jolted him into action. He wrenched his hands in front of him and strained to pull himself free from the metal prison.

A rush of water hit his face, filling in the rest of the Pteranodon's wrecked body. Ib barely had enough time to gasp a lungful of air before his head submerged. He pulled again, trying to wrestle himself free, but his body was still stuck.

He fought back the urge to scream.

Bracing his right leg against the platform once more, he pushed with more strength than he knew he possessed. His trouser leg tore to the rolled and hemmed cuff, where it stubbornly refused to give any further. Kicking and thrashing his left leg, he strained again with his right leg until he felt it rip.

Ib broke through the surface of the water, gasping greedily at the air. He pushed at the wet darkness over his head and struggled to find a foothold beneath him.

In the distance, he heard a clock tower strike ten o'clock.

28

IN WHICH A MESS
IS CLEANED UP

He stood in water up to his chest. Holding a strange wet curtain over his head, he saw a flash of light coming from his left. Trailing the curtain behind him, Ib walked towards the light reflecting on the surface of the water.

Stepping into the sunlight, he let the back edge of a leather wing fall back onto the water behind him.

Dense fog rolled past him. Turning back, he saw it wasn't fog but steam from the twisted wreckage of Pterrence's furnace.

He climbed onto the grassy shore, his clothes soaking wet, badly torn and more than a little bloody here and there. He sat down, trying to catch his breath, close to the water's edge and shivered.

The world around him was shattered.

He managed to think about this for a moment, then removed his goggles.

It wasn't the world that was shattered, only the goggle lenses.

"I need to make a better pair of these," he said aloud over the quieting sound of his own heartbeat.

Ib stared at the tangled wreckage of brass and leather beneath the billowing steam that, only moments ago, had been Pterrence and his own Pterry. He knew he should feel happy that he was still alive, but he also felt sad about Pterrence. Pterrence had only wanted to play. It was all very confusing.

A tiny fluttering of wings came from above him. He watched as Sophie lowered her feet and lifted her wings. Instead of beating downward, she pushed the lower part of her wings slightly in front of her and flapped them quickly.

"So that's how you do it," he said as Sophie landed on his hand.

Sophie gave Ib a long wink. The sunlight sparkled in her deep red eye.

"Are you quite pleased with yourself?" Ib asked the bird.

Sophie twittered happily.

To his side, he heard footsteps approaching. He turned and looked up, shielding his eyes against the sun.

"Might I inquire as to your state of health, Master Ib?" Bentley asked. There was genuine concern in the manservant's voice.

Ib flexed his arms, legs and hands, as he had when he fell into Professor Delby's library days earlier.

"I ask, Master Ib, because you have just been involved in a rather impressive collision. Pterrence had lowered his jaw and was about to take in water when Pterry's flight took a rather sharp downward turn. Your wings appeared to crumple behind you, and you fell directly on top of your escaped escort."

"I think I'm alright, Bentley," he said, nodding.

Ib looked at the tangled mess of leather and brass still hissing in the river in front of him.

Bentley gave a satisfied nodded, then brushed at the grass, and sat next to Ib.

"Bentley, have you heard anything about the Professor?"

"Indeed, Master Ib. The Royal Guard was in a state of extreme agitation when a second Pteranodon was sighted in the skies. We received them as graciously as possible at the Manor and informed them with utmost earnestness that Professor Delby was the only man in all of London who could possibly contain such an outbreak of horrifying creatures."

"And they believed that?" Ib asked.

"My informants assure me the Professor should be arriving here in a few short minutes, Master Ib."

The boy's smile faded as he looked back at the steaming wreckage in the Serpentine River.

"I know Pterry was nothing more than brass and gears and wings," he said. "And I thought Pterrence was, too, but Pterrence just spent the last hour trying to get me to play with him in the sky."

Bentley's eyebrow arched slightly more than a fraction of an inch.

"Play with you, Master Ib?"

"Yes, Bentley. Pterrence wanted me to play with him," Ib said with certainty.

"How unexpected, Master Ib," Bentley said at last. "And curious."

A thought struck Ib.

"Bentley, did I kill Pterrence?"

"That would be a somewhat complex question, Master Ib. However, as I believe only our creator has the power to truly create life, I do not believe that to be the case."

"But..." Ib said, remembering too much of the past days to think otherwise.

"Yesterday, at the coal yard, he recognized me," Ib said, shaking his head. "I asked him to come home with us and I think he wanted to. Then the Professor tripped on his net and Pterrence got frightened and flew away."

"Indeed, Master Ib?"

"And today, just a little while ago, I asked him the same thing again. Bentley, I think he wanted to come back to the laboratory."

"Most unexpected and curious, Master Ib."

"He was having some trouble flying today. I think I might know what was happening to him. But that doesn't explain why he wanted to play with me."

Bentley nodded. "And your hypothesis, Master Ib?"

Ib glared at the manservant.

"Ah, yes. My apologies, Master Ib. What do you believe was taking place within Pterrence?"

Ib wrung some water from his hair to stop it from dripping onto his face.

"When Pterrence first came to life in the laboratory, his eyes were deep red. Do you remember?"

"I do indeed, Master Ib."

"The next day, at the Bransford Coal Yard, he and I were as close as you and I are now. His eyes weren't red anymore. They were orange."

Bentley nodded.

"Then, today, when he flew next to me, I could see that his eyes were pale yellow."

"And you believe this to mean what, Master Ib?"

"When we were flying, his eyes reminded me of the color of my lemonade from the other night when I accidentally filled my glass

with water instead of more lemonade. It turned from bright yellow to a very light yellow."

Bentley was silent.

"I think Pterrence's eyes were bright red because his furnace was full of Delby well water and whatever strange things it contains. Since he escaped, he's been drinking regular water from the Serpentine River." He pointed to the body of water before them. "The more regular water he drank, the less special the water in his furnace became. That's why his eyes started growing more pale."

Sophie fluttered onto Ib's hand, blinking.

"And Sophie's eyes have remained dark red because she only drinks water from the Professor's well."

Sophie twittered happily.

"A dilution of those powers beyond their steam, Master Ib," Bentley said finally. "Well reasoned. As such, to revisit your earlier question, I would consider Pterrence not to have died, but, rather, to have gone dormant."

"Dormant?"

"From the French *dormir*, Master Ib, meaning to sleep. I am told large mammals do so all winter long in the colder climes. In this case, I should postulate that were Professor Delby to refill Pterrence's boiler with water from the Delby well ignite the furnace, the creature would pick up his escapades where he left off."

Ib took another long look around him. Aside from being soaking wet, bruised, and a bit bloody, Ib realized what a beautiful, sunny day it was.

"Bentley—I was flying," he said.

"It would appear so, Master Ib,"

"And even though I didn't mean to force Pterrence into the water, I did sort of capture him."

"Agreed, Master Ib. An effort worthy of the title lab assistant *extra-ordinaire*."

Ib smiled.

"You will, I trust, be pleased to know that Father Pottermore of St. Paul's Lorrimore Square sends his kind regards. Publicly he will only acknowledge his annoyance with the hooligan who caused such a commotion yesterday; privately, however, he was quite impressed with the skill and daring employed by said hooligan to escape from the church tower."

Ib laughed, shaking his head.

"And Miss Slattery at the dressmaker's shop down the road has invited to you to tea. She claims she is owed a fine story in exchange for pointing the way to the rear exit."

"Professor Delby speaks highly of your sources of information," Ib said, water again dripping from his nose.

"There is, I'm sure you'll agree wisdom to be found in the old Slavic adage, 'Trust, but verify,' Master Ib. And although I am certain the police are most eager for an anonymously presented inventory of items, places, and recipients of many recently stolen goods, I recommend we wait until tomorrow before beginning such a list."

"What do we tell the Professor?" Ib asked.

"This is not up to me, Master Ib. However, I believe you have proved yourself worthy of the Professor's trust. You have certainly earned mine."

Within ten minutes Hyde Park was filled with officials, all of whom wore dark coats and bowler hats. They had not only emptied the park of any onlookers, save for Ib and Bentley, but they had also started clearing the pond of all the debris. Ib had tried to question some of the men, but they would not even acknowledge his presence.

A team of four horses came down the path, pulling a long wagon with tall wooden sides and a tarpaulin covering the top. At the back of the wagon sat Professor Delby and two men Ib recognized as the Head of the Royal Guard and the Commissioner of the Metropolitan Police.

"I say, Ib!" the Professor called out as he hopped off the wagon. "I hear the show you put on was stupendous, splendiferous, sensational, septenarius, and . . . *whatnot!*"

The Head of the Royal Guard set about directing the men pulling wreckage from the river, leaving the Commissioner with Professor Delby.

"I suppose so, Professor," he said. "I'm afraid I was a little distracted and didn't get to see much of it myself."

"Bentley?" Professor Delby asked.

"Master Ib performed most admirably, sir," Bentley responded. "With

his Pteranodon crumbling about him, your lab assistant *extraordinaire* managed to subdue his quarry and escape only slightly worse for the wear."

The Professor watched as several men used long hooked poles to pull the remains of the two brass Pteranodons and their soggy, leather wings from the water. As they loaded the pieces onto the back of the horse-drawn wagon, Ib looked back at the Professor.

"Where are they taking them?" he asked.

"I'm not quite sure," Professor Delby replied. "Perhaps our friend the Commissioner can enlighten us?"

The two turned and looked at the Commissioner who only glared back at them.

"I don't know what you're talking about," the Commissioner said blandly.

"Where are those men taking our Pteranodons?" Ib asked.

"Pteranodons?" the Commissioner asked, somewhat surprised. "Young man, Pteranodons have been extinct for millions of years. Isn't that right, Delby?"

"Even longer than that, Commissioner! Perhaps fifty to eighty million years might be a closer estimate."

Nodding his head, the Commissioner looked around him as if seeing nothing, including his men pulling metal and soggy leather from the pond and handing it up to the nearby wagon.

"No. No Pteranodons here, lad. Those silly stories of flying dinosaurs and dragons were nothing more than tales created by overactive imaginations and spread by rumormongers."

"I mean the Professor's inventions—our inventions!" Ib insisted.

"No inventions, either," he said, apparently satisfied that there was nothing amiss. "My men did report finding two rather large kites, however. They both had very elaborate paintings of some sort of dragon or dinosaur on them. Some poor children must have let go of them. My men had reports of kites flying madly about. Perhaps that is what you're referring to?"

"Oh!" Professor Delby exclaimed. "I'm sure they must have come from that chap Bernstein in the northwest part of town. He sells the most impressive kites, Bernstein does."

The Commissioner motioned to one of his deputies, saying, "Make a note of that."

Ib shut his eyes tightly. Standing there, dripping wet, bleeding, his clothes torn and wearing only one shoe, he balled his hands into fists.

"They weren't kites, and they didn't come from anyone named Bernstein. The first was built by Professor Delby—"

"With your invaluable assistance!" Professor Delby quickly added.

"—and the second was built by Bentley and me. And I flew the second one!"

"I say, Bentley. However did Ib convince you to return to the laboratory?"

"Master Ib and I came to a most agreeable understanding, Professor."

"I almost drowned and now I'm standing here bleeding!" Ib shouted.

"Hmmm," said the Commissioner, glancing at Ib's torn and red stained trouser leg. "Looks nasty. You'll want to have someone take a look at that for you."

"What I want," Ib said through clenched teeth, "is to know what those men are doing with those." He turned and pointed to the cart, still being filled with soggy items carried to it by other members of the police force.

"That? Why, young man, that is a fine bit of parkland beautification as requested by Her Majesty, Queen Victoria," the Commissioner said, "and carried out in a joint effort by the Royal Guard and the London Police."

"Parkland beautification?" Ib said angrily. "Parkland beautification? Don't you understand what happened here today? We did the impossible—I did the impossible! I flew in a brass Pteranodon all over London. I crashed it right here in this pond on top of another brass Pteranodon and I nearly drowned! And now you're trying to pretend none of that happened?"

The Commissioner looked Ib in the eyes.

"Lad, do you know how hard we have had to work to keep this out of the newspapers? Prince Albert himself has had to get involved—in fact, it was his decision to keep all of this quiet out of admiration for your employer. The last thing the public needs to believe is that Britain is capable of producing an army of flying, fire-breathing dragons—"

"That was Ib's very idea!" Professor Delby said enthusiastically.

The commissioner slowly shifted his glare to the Professor. "Much less that a flying monster actually existed, even if it is just one of your Professor's runaway inventions. Buckingham Palace fears other nations might see these dragons as weapons of war and join forces against the Crown. As a result, *nothing* is exactly what happened here today."

Ib looked around to Professor Delby and Bentley, his hands shaking.

"But that's not fair!" he said.

The Commissioner sighed.

"Young man, if it's any consolation, my job is even less rewarding at times."

29

IN WHICH SCIENCE IS FUN

Ib sat in the hansom, his wet arms crossed over his wet chest. His harsh glare was aimed at the empty space in the seat across from him.

He was intentionally not looking at Professor Delby or Bentley.

After many deep scowls and heavy sighs, he was no closer to getting Professor Delby's attention than when they had first gotten into the cab.

Instead, after tapping at his chin for several moments, the Professor said:

"I have been considering our options for a celebration in line with our success today and of your remarkable achievement. Do you have any suggestions, Ib?"

Ib started to give the Professor an angry look, but the smile on the Professor's face stopped him. Instead, Ib sighed and shook his head to himself.

"Professor," he finally said. "Don't you see? I flew today."

"I did see!" Professor Delby said. "Well, only for a few moments. It was the most extraordinary thing, though, wasn't it?"

"As far as I know, I'm the only person alive who has ever flown in a brass Pteranodon."

"Ah, I understand your anxiety, Ib," the Professor said, brightly. "I shall begin making inquiries this very afternoon to verify your claim."

"But that's just it, Professor. You can't. The metropolitan police have taken away all of the evidence and are saying it never happened!"

"Oh, that," Professor Delby said, dismissively.

"Professor, aren't you angry that they've taken away Pterrence? Bentley, what about Pterry?" Ib asked.

Professor Delby looked confused.

"Pterry?" he asked.

"Master Ib's Pteranodon, Professor. Named by Mrs. Hudson herself."

"Ho, ho! Well done, Ib!"

"Professor, doesn't it bother you that they've taken it all away?"

"Why should it?" he asked.

"They have all of the evidence that two flying gearwork Pteranodons ever existed. All of your hard work—"

"*Our* hard work," Professor Delby interjected. "And your work with Bentley!"

"Fine, Professor. All of *our* hard work, from all of us, is gone!"

Professor Delby shook his head.

"Not at all, Ib," he said with a smile. "Those police chaps were actually extremely helpful today. They simply carted away the remains of two prototypes, two early versions of the experiment. If they had not been there to carry it all away, I would have undoubtedly had to pay some scrap metal person to haul it all off for us!"

Ib sighed again, looking out the window.

"They took it all," Ib said.

Professor Delby looked upward and jerked his head about. "No, they didn't," he responded, confused. "It's all still right here." He pointed to the side of his head. "The police simply collected all of the broken parts and pieces. They could never cart away the knowledge behind it! All the science and all the plans are still with us."

"But, Professor," Ib said, searching for the words. "It's as if it never happened."

"Nonsense!" Professor Delby said. "Bentley, you saw it, didn't you?"

"Indeed, sir."

"And I saw it," the Professor added. "I suppose the only one here who didn't see it is you, Ib. But that's only because you were so busy doing it that you couldn't stop to watch yourself do it."

The Professor tapped his chin, adding, "Perhaps we could install a small mirror on the inside of the next model. That way you could see yourself doing it as you did so."

"That's not necessary, Professor," Ib said, shaking his head again.

After a moment, he added, "Professor, shouldn't we be the ones to decide what happens with an invention?"

"But we are!" the Professor insisted. "We imagine them, we build them, we test and fine tune them, and then we put them into practice."

"And then the London police takes them all away and claims they never existed."

"Ib," Professor Delby said, "did you choose to be a chimney sweep's apprentice?"

"No," Ib admitted.

"And did you choose to fall to your death in my fireplace and become my assistant?"

"I didn't —" Ib started.

"I know you didn't choose that fate, either," the Professor said, holding up a hand. "And, yet, they both occurred. Why? Who knows? Some things we get to choose, and some things are chosen for us."

"And that's just the way things are?" Ib asked.

"That's about right," Professor Delby said, nodding. "Wouldn't you agree, Bentley?"

"I would, indeed, sir."

"And that is life," the Professor said, adding, "and life isn't necessarily fun. But science, well, science is always fun!"

Ib rolled his eyes but still had to smile at the Professor's exuberance.

"Now then," Professor Delby said. "When the Royal Guard described your take off this morning, it occurred to me that what we needed was a better launching system. Something of a long, sloping ramp, or tracks, perhaps. You could ride down it on a wheeled platform that would allow you to sail off into the air with sufficient height and speed to make the start of your flights that much easier."

Ib imagined what the Professor was describing. He saw himself rushing down a slope from the top of the Delby house, about to be launched into the sky again. Despite wanting to remain in a bad mood, Ib raised one corner of his mouth while shaking his head. He started to speak, then simply sighed.

"You were about to say, Master Ib?" Bentley asked.

Ib paused. "I was about to say I think I really like this job."

Sophie jumped up and down on Ib's shoulder and twittered into his ear.

"Well, I should hope so," Professor Delby replied. "It's a rather

important qualification for a lab assistant *extraordinaire*, don't you agree, Bentley?"

"Undoubtedly, sir."

Ib grinned. Not only did he like it, he thought he was good at it, too.

BUT WAIT! THERE'S MORE DARING EXPLOITS WITH IB, PROFESSOR DELBY, AND BENTLEY TO COME!

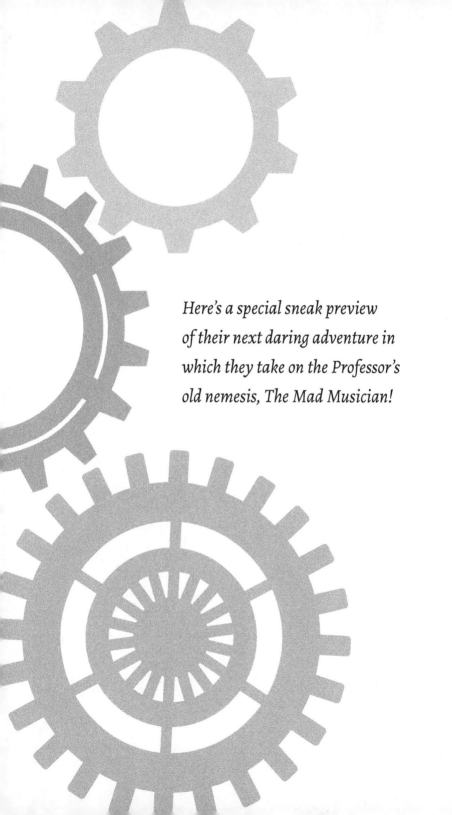

Here's a special sneak preview of their next daring adventure in which they take on the Professor's old nemesis, The Mad Musician!

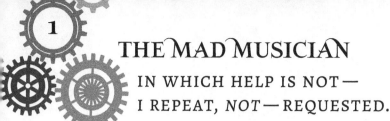

THE MAD MUSICIAN

IN WHICH HELP IS NOT —
I REPEAT, NOT — REQUESTED.

"Scotland Yard? Here?" Professor Delby asked.

The Professor dropped the curved brass plate in his hand, scattering springs, flywheels and gears across his already crowded worktable. "Did they say why?"

"Alas, sir. Not the entirety of Scotland Yard," Bentley responded from the laboratory doorway. "Merely a single representative of that fine public trust."

"And?" the Professor asked, nodding his head expectantly at the manservant.

Ib looked up from the array of carefully assembled gears and rods on his workbench to see a blur of indistinct shapes. Reaching his fingers to his temples, Ib flipped the 4x magnifying lenses of his EyeWerks goggles up, away from his eyes. The ground glass lenses joined the others resting above forehead like a strange series of antennae.

Professor Delby and Bentley came into focus just in time for Ib to see Bentley pause and look thoughtful.

"Forgive me, sir. I sense you are on the verge of another major scientific breakthrough. As you know, I would rather sacrifice one of my own limbs than cause even a momentary delay to your next invaluable contribution to the betterment of mankind."

"Yes, yes," the Professor waved his hand as if to sweep the words away. "All very much appreciated, Bentley. But why is The Yard here?"

Ib smiled as Bentley's eyebrow arched a fraction of an inch as the manservant regarded their employer's hand.

"Indeed, sir," the manservant replied. "The gentleman requests your opinion on what I presume is a rather confounding piece of evidence."

"Aha!" the Professor exclaimed. Jumping to his feet, he ran a hand through his unruly white hair. "Duty calls, Ib. It's time, once again, to find practical applications for our scientific imaginings!"

In two strides Professor Delby stood before Ib's workbench. Gripping the sides of the table he leaned towards Ib, knocking over a tool rack that held many of the boy's more finely calibrated instruments.

"Ib! Are you ready to venture forth into our fair city to assist The Yard?" the Professor asked with a broad smile.

Sophie snapped and spluttered out of her egg-shell into her small yet regal bird form. She began chirping excitedly.

"And, of course you as well, Sophie!" the Professor said.

Since he had begun working for Professor Delby, Ib's days had been filled with learning about scientific theories, understanding how the ordinary and the extraordinary worked, helping with the daily running of the laboratory, and assisting the Professor with more projects than Ib would have thought possible. Most of that work, however, had kept him indoors. After spending so many years on the streets and rooftops of London, Ib had discovered a certain comfort in staying inside the Delby Manor. With the possibility of doing work with a purpose—and knowing Mr. Bertram was locked up in Margate Prison—he felt he was ready to venture back out into the world.

Ib was about to say so when Professor Delby pushed himself away from the workbench, causing a container of half-domed brass casings to spill across the table, covering much of what Ib had spent the last several days working on.

From under the pile of casings came several shaking motions. Sophie's head popped up, followed by her wings as she pushed herself free. She leapt up, fluttering around Ib's head, finally landing on his shoulder.

"But, of course you are!" The Professor jabbed a fervent finger in Ib's direction. "Why, Ib, your mind works at such a fevered pitch that you have likely been anticipating this moment for days now!"

Professor Delby drew in a very satisfied breath, shaking his head in wonder. "Such an incredible boy!"

The Professor began pacing in front of Ib's workbench, the fingers of one hand tapping his chin. Ib recognized the far-off look coming over Professor Delby's eyes.

Ib had learned when the Professor started looking at something in the distance that only the Professor could see that it was pointless to interrupt his employer. Cautiously, Ib set down the tiny clockwork

gears he had been aligning against a brass honeycomb frame and began picking the tiny half-domes from his partially assembled gears. He hoped he might salvage something of his work before the Professor returned, enthusiasm fully intact.

"Still, Ib, we know our obligation to our beloved Queen Victoria and all her subjects," the Professor nodded solemnly moments later. "For when the police are confounded, confused, conflicted, conjugated, consomméd and…" He waved his hand dismissively in front of his face, "…whatnot…"

He stopped and turned to Ib.

"They come to us, Ib. And what do they come to us for?"

Ib opened his mouth to reply.

"That's right! They come to us for the answers only science can provide!"

Raising a wagging finger into the air the Professor exclaimed, "Answers through science!"

Ib closed his mouth and gave what he hoped looked like an emphatic nod of agreement.

From his shoulder, he could feel Sophie nodding as well.

"Oh, bravo, sir," Bentley said, removing an errant speck of dust from his formal jacket sleeve. "I can sense fear rising in the hearts of evildoers everywhere."

The Professor held up a hand towards Bentley.

"No, no, Bentley," he said, shaking his head. "While true, we mustn't get too ahead of ourselves just yet. The evildoers behind whatever dastardly deed we are being called in to investigate shall, indeed, fall under the mighty hand of justice. Still, we must take first things first."

"You are correct, as always, sir," Bentley said. "Shall I show the Inspector down to the laboratory before ordering the celebratory crackers and party favors?"

Professor Delby beamed. "An excellent suggestion, Bentley!"

"Very good, sir."

Bentley returned with a short man in a gray, all-weather coat and black bowler hat. His mustache was as thin and dark as his eyebrows. His face was contorted into a well-creased frown.

Ib still believed the laboratory to be one of the most wonderful places imaginable. The first time he had seen the lab, the sense of possibilities all about him had left Ib speechless. From the spreading look of annoyance on the newcomer's face, however, Ib could tell their guest did not share his views.

Ib followed their visitor's eyes as he regarded the glass piping that stretched and curled over and around large beakers spread over several tables. Upon seeing the metal works area, with its compact boilers and steam valves leading out to several adjacent workbenches, Ib noticed the man's upper lip curl. One project Ib and the Professor had been working on recently caught the Inspector's eye — a tall, thin frame that reached to the ceiling of the basement laboratory where it supported a circle of angled blades that looked like it had been pierced from behind by a large arrow. From their experimental windmill, their guest followed the path of the rafters to the upside-down bicycle-like contraptions with their paddle wheels that served as the laboratory's ventilation system.

The man from Scotland Yard closed his eyes and slowly shook his head. Looking about him again, their visitor took a cursory sniff about him before spotting the Professor seated at his desk. Ib wasn't sure if it was the mix of grease, gaslight, and coal fire or the excited look on the Professor's face that made their visitor's expression deeper into a scowl.

"May I present Inspector Lestrade, sir," Bentley said.

"Lestrade! Why, Bentley, why didn't you say so in the first place?" the Professor said, rushing across the room to take the Inspector's unoffered hand. Shaking it energetically he continued, "The Inspector and I are old friends!"

Inspector Lestrade cleared his throat vigorously while extracting himself from the Professor. "Now then, Delby," he grumbled as he stepped away. "Let me make two things immediately clear. Number One: I am only here at the insistence of my superiors. They are suffering under the misguided notion that you might be able to shed some light on an odd bit of evidence."

The Inspector continued stepping away from Professor Delby. Ib was about to warn the Inspector when the police officer did a quick double-take inches away from a pair of badly damaged human-sized wings hanging beside him. Inspector Lestrade shuddered, then closed his eyes and took a deep breath. Stepping away from the wings he

continued, "Were it up to me I would have been perfectly happy to live out the rest of my days holding true to my word at the end of that McCormick mess you involved yourself in last year."

"Ah, yes," Delby said wistfully, smiling towards Ib. "The McCormicks. Fine people, Ib. Fine people. They were most grateful for my assistance in the recovery of several invaluable artifacts."

"If by grateful you mean they agreed not to press charges against you for the 'excavations' under their home that caused the collapse of their entire east wing, then perhaps they were," Inspector Lestrade said. "I rather think of it as cutting their losses to be rid of you."

"Oh, Inspector," Delby chuckled. "Come now. I made certain you and your fellow officers received full credit for your part in solving the case."

"Yes," said the Inspector, all expression leaving his face. "That is exactly why I never wished to see or speak to you again. Unless, of course, it was to wish you a long and unhealthy stay in Murdock Prison."

The Inspector gave a low growl. "Still, orders are orders."

"Apology accepted!" Delby exclaimed, moving forward and giving Lestrade a congenial slap on the shoulder. "Spoken like a true gentleman, Lestrade. We shall simply let bygones be bygones and speak no more about it!"

"Um, what," the Inspector asked a bit uncertainly.

"So, Lestrade," Professor Delby said, rubbing his hands together. "What shall we be working on together this time?"

"Wait right there!" Lestrade snapped with a quick shake of his head. "Number Two: You are being asked only for your opinion on a single piece of evidence. Your opinion, Delby, nothing more."

Inspector Lestrade pulled out a long, narrow object wrapped in sackcloth from his pocket. He thrust it like a dagger at the Professor.

"You are not—I repeat, NOT—to take this as a request for any further involvement. You are NOT being asked to become part of any investigation. You are NOT to concern yourself with this after I leave. Do I make myself clear?"

Professor Delby nodded with a wide grin. Leaning forward and to the side, he gave a broad wink to the Inspector.

"Why, of course, Inspector! I wouldn't think of joining the hunt for any dangerous criminals!"

The Professor leaned to Ib.

"You see, Ib," he said, whispering loudly. "This is obviously a very treacherous case, one fraught with perils aplenty. Our fine guest, the Inspector, cannot, in good conscious, ask us to risk our own lives in pursuit of whatever roguish rascal he is up against."

Professor Delby gave Inspector Lestrade another knowing wink. Ib watched the Inspector's cheeks puff out and his face turn a darker shade of red.

"Oh!" the Professor suddenly exclaimed. "Where are my manners? Inspector, allow me to introduce you to Ib, my lab assistant *extraordinaire*! Young though he may be, Ib is a most ingenious boy. A brain just teeming with science!"

Ib smiled at the Inspector, waiting for what he knew would be the next words the Professor would say.

"I found him dead in our fireplace years ago. Fascinating story."

A month before, Ib had been a chimney sweep's apprentice, doing all the dirtiest and most hazardous work of the trade. While it was true he had fallen from the chimney into the Professor's fireplace, Ib had very much lived through the experience. He had been alive enough, in fact, for Professor Delby to offer him a position as the Professor's first lab assistant. When Mr Bertram, the chimney sweep had come to collect his apprentice, Professor Delby had insisted Ib pretend to be dead in the fireplace. In the following weeks Ib had come to respect the Professor's knowledge of science, of mechanics and his sense of invention. For the life of him, though, Ib could not figure out why Professor Delby insisted on believing some of the oddest things. Things like Ib having died in the fireplace. Years ago.

Worse, was the Professor's insistence on repeating this version of how he found Ib at every opportunity. Scientists, shopkeepers, hansom cab drivers, bank guards, everyone the Professor knew or did business with had come to know Ib as the poor, dead boy from the Professor's fireplace.

Equally confusing to Ib was how no one had ever bothered to question the Professor, or himself, for that matter, about the story. To a person, they had each continued smiling at the Professor and Ib in the same manner as they had before hearing the story.

Sophie twittered loudly from Ib's shoulder.

"Well, yes. I suppose that's true," Professor Delby acknowledged. "However, Sophie, you found him moments before he breathed his last."

Sophie cocked her head to the side, considering this. She gave a nod of approval.

Lestrade's eyes narrowed. He glanced around the Professor to get a better look at the boy and the bird seated at the workbench.

Ib raised his brass EyeWorks goggles onto his forehead, making it look as if he had two extra sets of eyes above his own gray eyes along with the strange set of antennae coming from the top of his head. Ib smiled self-consciously, hoping he looked very much alive.

Leaning back to Ib, Professor Delby continued. "It's something of a game of polite society, Ib. The Inspector says, 'Don't help us, it's too dangerous' and we say, 'Of course not, Inspector.' All the while we both know that what our friend here is really saying is, 'I desperately need your help.' And he knows we are really saying, 'We shall do everything in our power to assist you!'"

"**NO!**" thundered the Inspector. "That is absolutely **NOT** what I am saying!"

Professor Delby nodded slowly and leaned closer to Ib's ear. "Obviously," he said, "We are up against an incredibly fiendish mastermind!"

9 781952 834011